STAR TREK

WHO

KILLED

CAPTAIN

KIRK?

Peter David
WRITER

Tom Sutton & Gordon Purcell
PENCILLERS

Ricardo Villagran
INKER

Tim Harkins & Helen Vesik
LETTERERS

Michele Wolfman
COLORIST

Based on STAR TREK
created by Gene Roddenberry

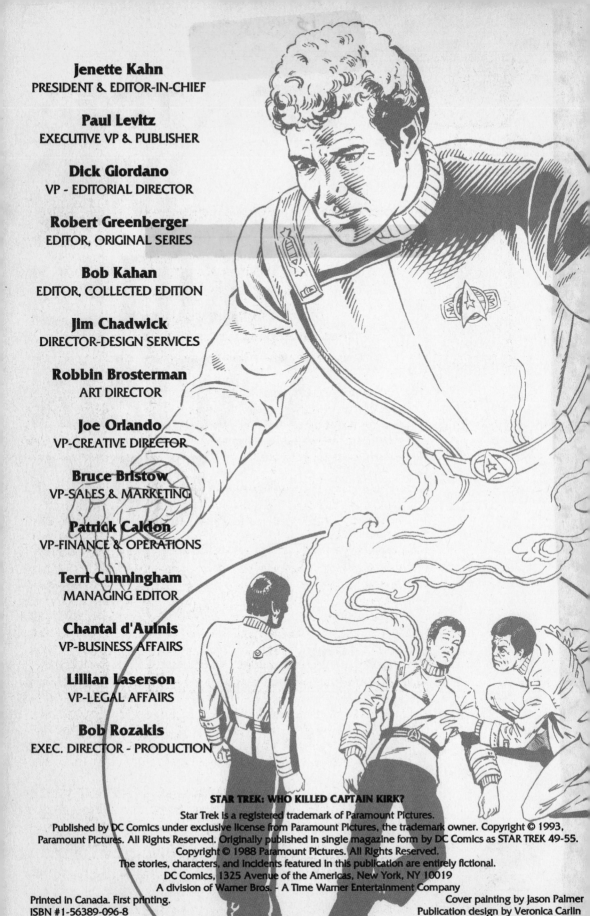

Jenette Kahn
PRESIDENT & EDITOR-IN-CHIEF

Paul Levitz
EXECUTIVE VP & PUBLISHER

Dick Giordano
VP - EDITORIAL DIRECTOR

Robert Greenberger
EDITOR, ORIGINAL SERIES

Bob Kahan
EDITOR, COLLECTED EDITION

Jim Chadwick
DIRECTOR-DESIGN SERVICES

Robbin Brosterman
ART DIRECTOR

Joe Orlando
VP-CREATIVE DIRECTOR

Bruce Bristow
VP-SALES & MARKETING

Patrick Caldon
VP-FINANCE & OPERATIONS

Terri Cunningham
MANAGING EDITOR

Chantal d'Aulnis
VP-BUSINESS AFFAIRS

Lillian Laserson
VP-LEGAL AFFAIRS

Bob Rozakis
EXEC. DIRECTOR - PRODUCTION

INTRODUCTION

BY
GEORGE
TAKEI

"These are the voyages of the Starship Enterprise.

Its five - year mission:

To explore strange new worlds,

To seek out new life and new civilizations,

To boldly go where no man has gone before."™

These gleaming words that set spirits soaring when first heard almost three decades ago, words that over the years have become almost emblematic and with changing consciousness have been revised to "where no one has gone before," still seem to have the power to engage the imagination. Incredibly, they still produce the unimagined.

Back in our struggling television years in the sixties, even the most ardent of fans could not have conceived of a series of enormously successful *Star Trek* feature motion pictures, much less two very popular spinoff television series, an animated series and a multibillion dollar merchandising industry. Even on that crisp, brilliant September morning in 1976, when we – Gene Roddenberry and the members of the cast – attended as guests of the National Aeronautics and Space Administration the "roll out" ceremony of the first space shuttle, christened "Enterprise" after our fictional ship, could we have imagined that *Star Trek* would one day be a major exhibit at the National Air and Space Museum of the Smithsonian in Washington, D.C. Indeed, that installation became the single most popular attraction in the history of the Museum and its run had to be extended to accommodate the record-smashing attendance. And even in the eighties, when *Star Trek* had become an established phenomenon, could I have imagined myself writing the introduction to a collection of *Star Trek* comic books. Absolutely unimagined! But this too, I now realize, is part of the voyage. So boldly I shall go.

I grew up on comic books. As a boy growing up in East Los Angeles I used to devour comics. Superman – and woman. Wonder Woman. Captain Marvel. Phantom. Tarzan. Mandrake the Magician. Batman and Robin. They were heroic figures. The stories were fantastic – on the level of wondrous, escapist fantasy. So I suppose it never really bothered me that I never saw anyone who looked like me in the world of comics. Nobody looked like Superman. No one I ever knew went running around dressed like the Phantom or even Mandrake. Then I discovered  the comic-book versions of classic literature. Daniel DeFoe's *Robinson Crusoe*, Robert Lewis Stevenson's *Treasure Island*. Charles Dickens's *A Tale of Two Cities*. They were wonderful stories. They were real stories—history, in fact. And they were based on great books. And yet, I still didn't see anyone who looked like me in these comics. I knew we had a history. My grandparents came to America from Japan. I was told fascinating stories about the colorful reign of the Shogun and about the exciting adventures of the samurai. How come these stories weren't told in comics, I started to wonder. And how come any comic-book characters who looked like my friend, Willy Johnson, were only servants or savages like Robinson Crusoe's Friday? Willy's father wore a suit and tie and worked in a big office building downtown. No one in comic books looked like him or Willy. I used to wonder about such things as a boy who loved comic books.

But I grew up and grew away from comics. It was a whole lifetime before I peeked into the pages of another comic book. It was prompted by my curiosity over a whole new manifestation of the *Star Trek* phenomenon—the *Star Trek* comics. And when I did, an unimagined universe opened up for me. First of all, the shock of recognition—of seeing not only another Asian face on those pages but of seeing someone who literally looked like *me!* A strong-jawed, thick-haired, heroically-built me! Well, perhaps a tad idealized but nevertheless a more than reasonable facsimile of me.

Then the shock of content. The *Star Trek* comics, like the *Star Trek* film and television series, were science fiction with subtext that addressed contemporary ideas, issues and dilemmas. These were comic books that engaged the mind, stimulated thought and challenged the imagination. The comic books I remembered were total fantasies on good versus evil—with good always winning out.

The third shock was the shock of actual participation. Never in my wildest childhood dreams did I ever imagine myself actually writing a comic book. Never! But one morning in 1990, Bob Greenberger, then DC Comics *Star Trek* editor, called me to ask if I would be interested in writing a *Star Trek* story for his comic-book series. "You've written science fiction before, George. I read *Mirror Friend, Mirror Foe*, and I really liked it." "Yes, but that was narrative storytelling," I demurred. "I don't know how to tell stories in comic-strip pictures."  He assured me that that would not be a problem. He would assign someone, Peter David maybe, to work with me on the structural aspects of comic-strip storytelling. I remember first meeting Peter at a long-ago *Star Trek* convention in some long-ago city in the Midwest. He is a man you do not forget easily. A bespectacled nose poised on the precipice of a mustachioed face precariously balanced on a body that seems at the point of bursting with pent-up energy. And that energy escapes through his mouth in rapid-fire, staccato bursts of the most amazing display of ideas, opinions, wisdom, trivia and sometimes outright nonsense. You can't help loving the guy. It was too delicious an opportunity to let slip by. "I'll do it,

Bob," I assented. "But only on the condition that I work with Peter David." "You got it," he said. And thus began the comic-book part of my life trek.

I feel I have been lucky in life and this was one of those strokes of luck. What an opportunity. What an absolutely unimagined turn of events! During our television series days, one of my frustrations was with the extent of Sulu's participation in the action. Sitting at the helm console informing Captain Kirk that the ship was at warp three and holding steady was all well and good but hardly the most active involvement in the drama. So I used to bombard Gene Roddenberry and any other powers-that-be with story and character ideas to enhance Sulu's role. Mostly, these efforts went for naught. The few that were used often ended up embellishing the other characters. What Sulu got from my relentless lobbying campaign was perhaps a syllable here, an additional gesture there. Frustrating, but all a part of the career struggle in Hollywood.

What Bob had offered me was a fourfold opportunity: The challenge to come up with a fast-paced, pictorial story that would hold an action-oriented audience. The opportunity to shape and mold the content and perspective of the narrative. The chance to work with an energized original, truly a one-of-a-kind guy, Peter David. And finally, that long-sought, often-frustrated opportunity to reveal a bit more of that dashing, romantic and ever-engaging character called Hikaru Sulu. It was another of life's quirky, unsought, unanticipated and quite unearned blessings. Me — writing a comic book!

But this was to be a *Star Trek* comic book, not a stock super-hero fantasy, a simple good-versus-evil conflict. What made the successful *Star Trek* stories so uniquely gripping was the imaginative science-fiction interpretation of some burning contemporary issue. And that was what personally engages me. Here was the chance to deal with concerns of our world incorporating my own passion, build a strong, visual science-fiction narrative from them and hopefully stimulate some thought in the reader. Peter and I discussed many issues. We decided on two global horrors of our time that seem almost science-fiction dreads just as they are – the human animal's stupidity in bespoiling its own habitat – the water that we drink, the air that we breathe, the very earth that feeds us – to the point of virtual suicide; and a disease that kills through the act of love, AIDS.

Drama requires conflict. We needed an antagonist to these issues. It was very clear what that was: the blind denial of the reality before us and the destructively single-minded imposition of reactionary dogmas – an attitude most personified by Sen. Jesse Helms of North Carolina. His stern, owlish visage I thought would be great fun to play with as the villain. His round rimmed glasses were the ideal form to depict a look of perpetual, mindless outrage. His sharp beak of a nose like the vicious weapon of a killer owl. His rotund body the very epitome of massive greed. This was too delicious a prospect. It was irresistible. Alas, it was too good to prove true. The legal counsel at DC Comics got uncomfortable, and ultimately the evil Shelm (get it?) looked quite unlike the dinosaur of the U.S. Senate. He was drawn as a gaunt, darkly malevolent oppressor. Another of life's little frustrations.

But there are the great compensating rewards as well. And that for me was working with Peter. The human dynamo I had met at that midwestern convention, I discovered, was only the bare outline of a wonderfully multifarious man. Certainly, he is a highly charged, opinionated and voluble force. He has a mind like a floppy disk that retains every scintilla of information that ever engaged him and with the ability to retrieve that very quintessential byte of whatever it might be to support whatever point he wants to make. But the much more fascinating quality of that mind is its openly imaginative aspect. The ability to freely wander uncharted terrain, to peer through those quizzical spectacles of his at the unknown and wonder, "What's next?" And when he is on those mind forays he is a changed person. There is, believe it or not, a stillness about him – a quiet, keenly focused intensity. And when he comes back, he returns with wondrous ideas. You also get the familiar Peter back as well, except now white-hot with passion. Imagine your video on fast forward and you get the picture.

This tome is a collection of the bounty Peter David has brought back from many such forays. It is a rip-snorting good sci-fi adventure. There are familiar characters from *Star Trek* history like Finnegan and from classic myths like Medusa interwoven into a rich narrative. Our heroes are placed in fantasmagorical jeopardy and there are galactically muscular life struggles. But we find in this story that the greatest adventures and most daunting challenges are found not in sweat and sinews, but in that vast, complex realm of our psyche. Love and hate, heroism and cowardice all spring from the same place– the mind. Galactic romance, which in *Star Trek's* time might involve interspecies miscegenation, an issue with all its resonances for our times, is explored. A human crew member is deeply in love with a Klingon, a member of a race of beings who were, only a generation ago, mortal enemies. What might the offspring of such a union be like? How might society react to them? The fear of the unknown pitted against deep, intimate love. It is classic, wrenching drama. Spock observes in this story, "Marriage...to anyone is a series of unknowns. And if you are daunted by the unknown, you may be pursuing the wrong vocation."

His words ring true for all of us who have been involved with *Star Trek* in one capacity or another. For our vocation has really become a marriage to this phenomenon as well. Whether actor, producer, distributor, and most certainly, audience – for all of us, it has been a 28-year romance through thick and thin, from one precarious rescue to the next peril, from one unimagined godsend to the next boon – ours has been a journey into the unknown. Spock, with his gentle wisdom to the confused young crewwoman in love with a Klingon is essentially saying to her, "Boldly go where no one has gone before."

Why don't you do that with this story. You'll enjoy it. And besides, you'll discover the dashing, romantic side of an old friend.

CAPTAIN'S LOG, STARDATE: 8987.T. WE ARE PROCEEDING AT WARP SIX TO THE PLANET MIRALUD UPON BEING ADVISED OF AN INEXPLICABLE ATTACK...

...AN ATTACK UPON A PEACEFUL SCIENTIFIC KLINGON OUTPOST— APPARENTLY BY A RELIANT CLASS FEDERATION STARSHIP.

WORD HAS REACHED US AT APPROXIMATELY THE SAME TIME IT REACHED THE KLINGON EMPIRE. OUR HOPE NOW IS TO REACH THE PLANET BEFORE THE KLINGONS...

TO TRY AND FIND SOME EVIDENCE, SOME ANSWERS, BEFORE THE KLINGONS CAN COVER IT UP. THEY ARE...NOTORIOUSLY SECRETIVE.

BUT THERE ARE SOME MATTERS THAT THE KLINGONS ARE BEING OUTSPOKEN ON. THERE WERE 17 KLINGONS ON THAT SCIENCE BASE. MEN, WOMEN...

...CHILDREN...

...AND THE KLINGONS, TO PUT IT MILDLY, ARE NOT HAPPY.

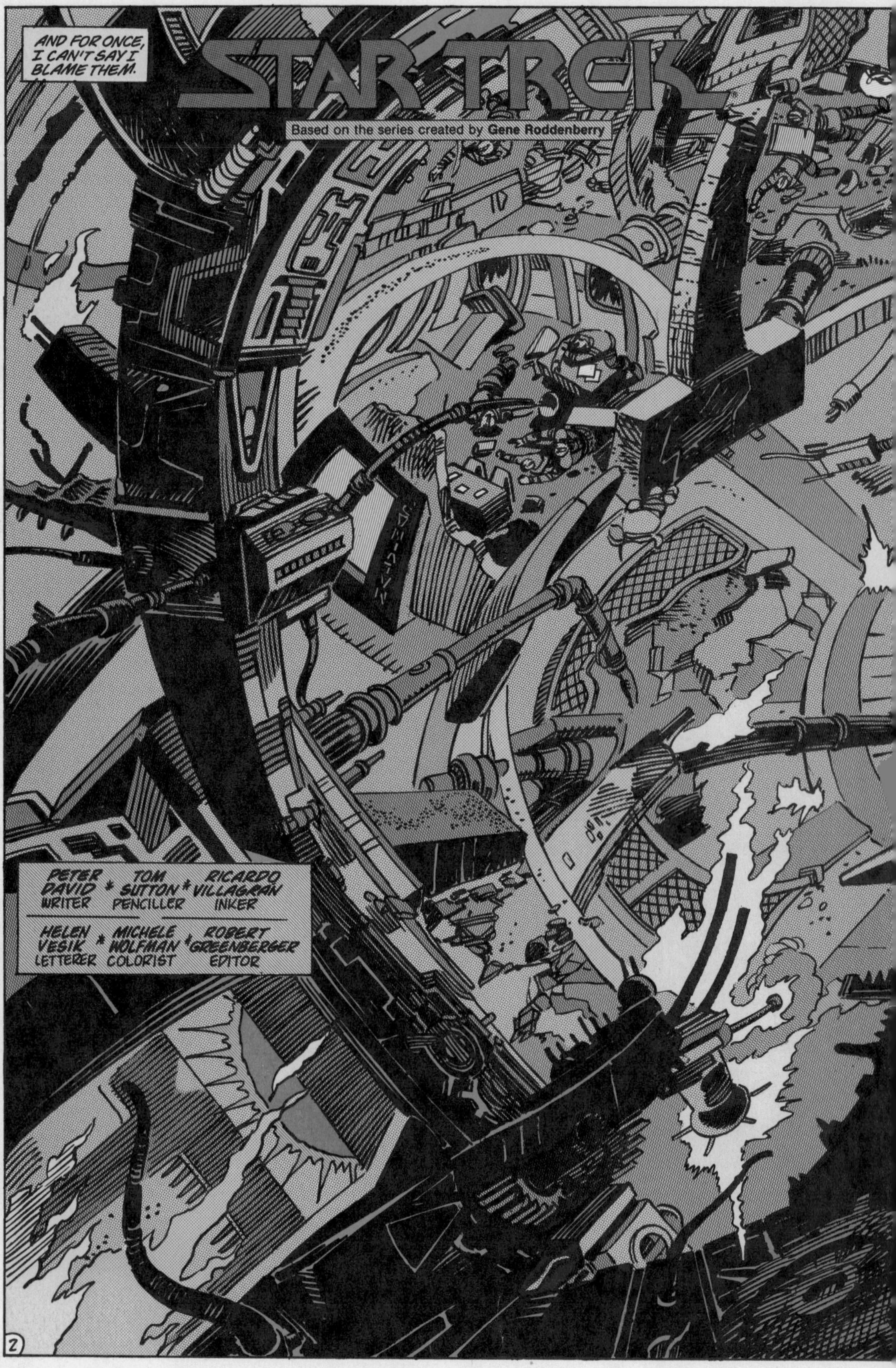
AND FOR ONCE, I CAN'T SAY I BLAME THEM.
STAR TREK
Based on the series created by Gene Roddenberry
PETER DAVID WRITER
TOM SUTTON PENCILLER
RICARDO VILLAGRAN INKER
HELEN VESIK LETTERER
MICHELE WOLFMAN COLORIST
ROBERT GREENBERGER EDITOR
2

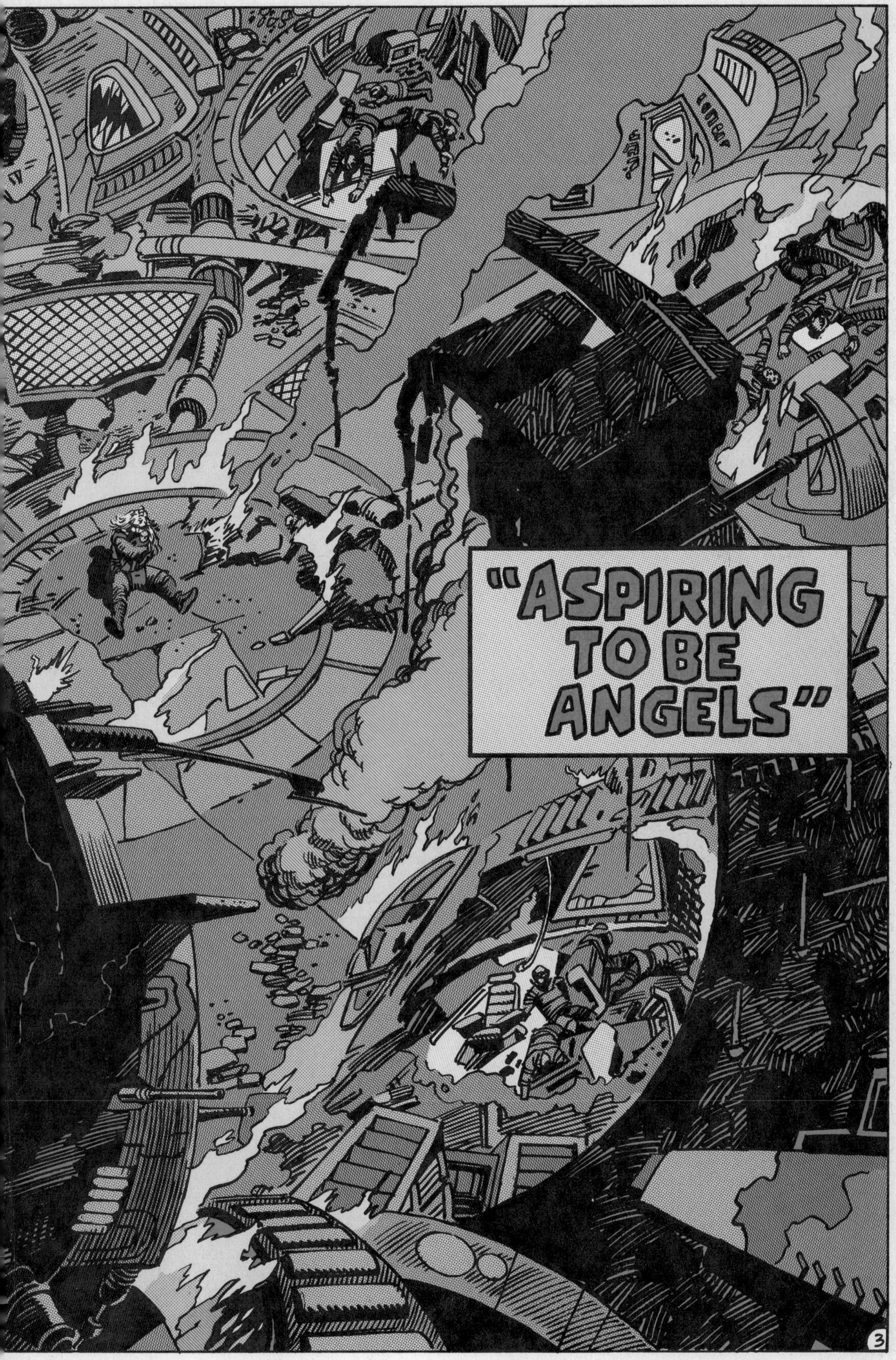
"ASPIRING TO BE ANGELS"
3

ARE YOU QUITE *SURE*, MISTER KONOM?

AS SURE AS ONE *CAN* BE WHEN DEALING WITH THE KLINGON EMPIRE, CAPTAIN.

THE PLANET'S ENVIRONMENT WAS VERY SUITABLE TO EXPERIMENTS IN FARMING DEVELOPMENT. PLUS THERE WAS SOME MEDICAL RESEARCH.

IT WAS ALL UTTERLY HARMLESS. NO MAJOR WEAPONS OR THE LIKE. I'M PRETTY SURE OF THAT.

I WOULD TEND TO AGREE WITH MISTER KONOM. MOST SERIOUS KLINGON WEAPONS RESEARCH IS DONE DEEP IN *ROMULAN* TERRITORY.

WHERE THE FEDERATION WOULD NEVER *DARE* GO.

WITH ALL DUE RESPECT, SIR... I SEEM TO RECALL AN INCIDENT SOME YEARS BACK REGARDING THE ROMULAN CLOAKING DEVICE. KLINGONS AREN'T BIG ON TAKING THE FEDERATION'S WORD FOR *ANYTHING*, SIR.

POINT *TAKEN*, MISTER KONOM. ALL RIGHT, GENTLEMEN, DISMISSED.

SCOTTY, BONES, CHEKOV... A MOMENT OF YOUR *TIME*, PLEASE.

4.

SO *TELL* ME, GENTLEMEN... HOW WOULD YOU RATE MR. KONOM'S BACHELOR PARTY WHICH YOU ORGANIZED?

IT... HAD ITS MOMENTS.

VERY...UH, *EXCITING*.

I...DON'T RECALL.

THAT'S HOW *YOU* FOUND IT TO BE?

AYE, SIR.

WOULD YOU LIKE TO KNOW WHAT *I* FOUND?

I DON'T TEENK SO.

I HAD THE *PUNCH* ANALYZED. THE PUNCH EVERYONE WAS DRINKING *BEFORE* THE DRUNKEN BRAWL BROKE OUT.

STANDARD WATER AND DISTILLED FRUIT CONTENTS...PLUS SOME *EXTRAS*.

LIKE *SCOTCH*...

...*ROMULAN ALE*...

...AND *"WODKA"*.

I CAN FIGURE OUT WHAT HAPPENED. YOU EACH THOUGHT THE PUNCH NEEDED SOME MORE *KICK* TO IT AND THOUGHT YOU'D HELP IT.

I APPRECIATE YOUR "NOBLE" MOTIVES. BUT THAT FIGHT RESULTED IN SOME INJURIES, INCLUDING YOUR *BELOVED* COMMANDING OFFICER.

AS A RESULT I'M AFRAID I HAVE TO TAKE...*STERN* MEASURES.

⑤

YOU'RE ALL *DRY* FOR THE NEXT MONTH. TURN IN ALL ALCOHOL IN YOUR QUARTERS TO THE EXECUTIVE OFFICER, SULU.

ANY *PROBLEMS* WITH THAT?

NO SIR!

NO.

NO, KEPTIN.

GOOD. DISMISSED. MR. CHEKOV, PLEASE INFORM MR. BEARCLAW THAT I'D LIKE TO SEE HIM IN MY QUARTERS.

YES, KEPTIN. WHEN DO YOU WANT TO SEE HEEM?

YESTERDAY.

FEELING BETTER SINCE *YESTERDAY,* LOVE?

OH YES. I GET DRUNK VERY EASILY, BUT I *NEVER* HAVE A HANGOVER.

LUCKY YOU. HOW'D THE BRIEFING GO?

I COULDN'T OFFER ANY REASONS AS TO WHY SOMEONE WOULD ATTACK THAT OUT-POST. IT DOESN'T MAKE ANY *SENSE.*

BUT THAT'S NOT THE MAJOR PROBLEM. I COULD SEE IT IN THE CAPTAIN'S FACE.

HIS MAJOR CONCERN IS THAT A FEDERATION STARSHIP HAS BEEN IMPLICATED. TO KLINGONS, THE REASONS ARE *IRRELEVANT.* ONLY THE *ACTIONS* MATTER.

6

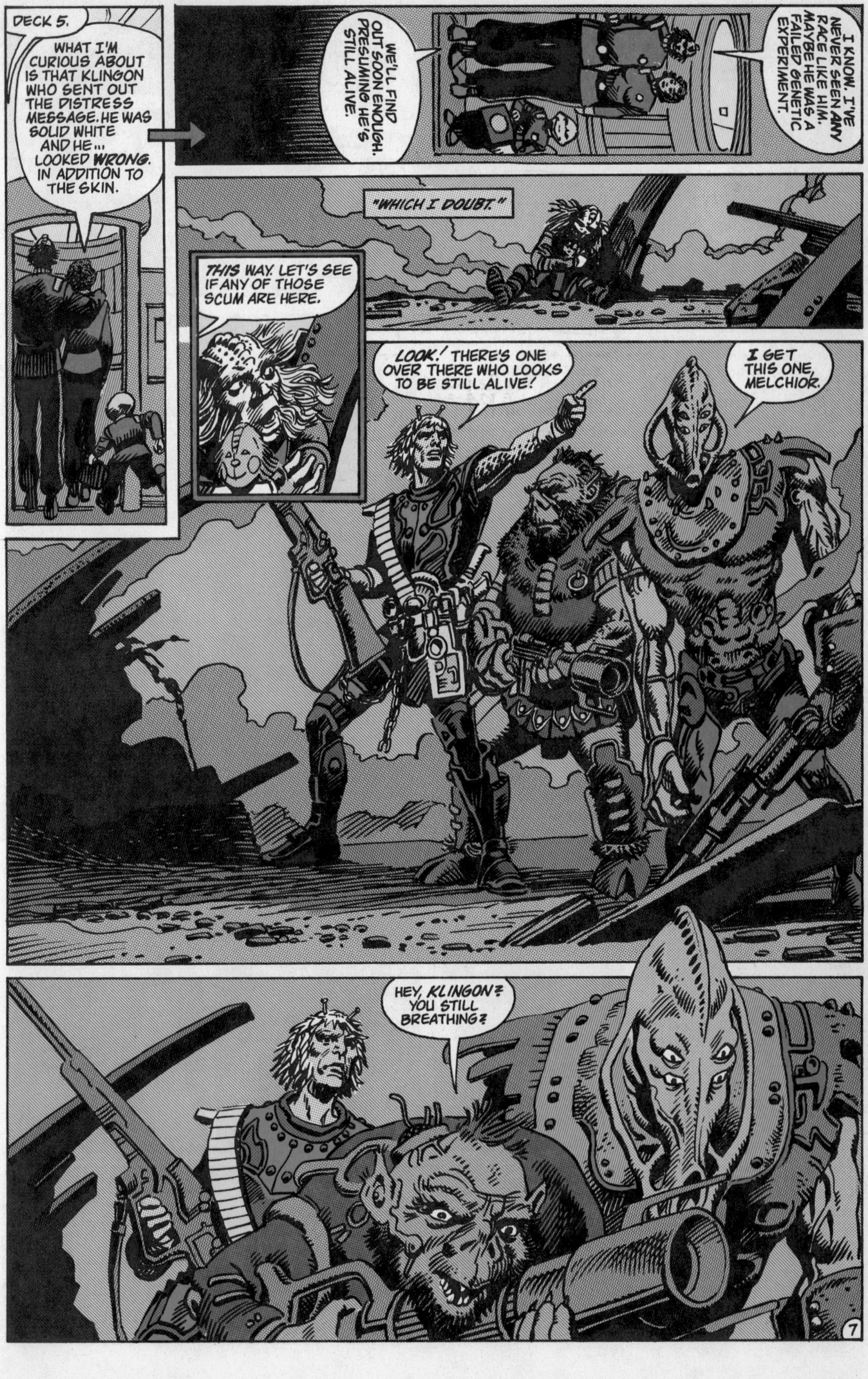

DECK 5.
WHAT I'M CURIOUS ABOUT IS THAT KLINGON WHO SENT OUT THE DISTRESS MESSAGE. HE WAS SOLID WHITE AND HE... LOOKED WRONG. IN ADDITION TO THE SKIN.
I KNOW. I'VE NEVER SEEN ANY RACE LIKE HIM. MAYBE HE WAS A FAILED GENETIC EXPERIMENT.
WE'LL FIND OUT SOON ENOUGH. PRESUMING HE'S STILL ALIVE.
"WHICH I DOUBT."
THIS WAY. LET'S SEE IF ANY OF THOSE SCUM ARE HERE.
LOOK! THERE'S ONE OVER THERE WHO LOOKS TO BE STILL ALIVE!
I GET THIS ONE, MELCHIOR.
HEY, KLINGON? YOU STILL BREATHING?
7

GO TO HELL.

BENDAR, GRUNT... I THINK HE'S HURT. IF HE BEGS US FOR HELP MAYBE WE CAN DO HIM SOME *GOOD*.

OH, BRAVO! *BRAVO!* GRUNT, LET OUR POOR, INJURED FELLOW OUT. *THAT'S IT.*

WHEN YOU'RE A MEMBER OF THE GLORIOUS KLINGON EMPIRE, THE *SKY'S* THE LIMIT, ISN'T IT?

GRUNT, SHOW HIM THE LIMIT.

YAAARRRRRRR!

TARGET PRACTICE AND... *GO!*

ZZZZZZZ ZZAAAT

ARYYYA*

14

I GOT HIM.

WHAT DO YOU MEAN, *YOU* GOT HIM? I GOT HIM!

YOU! YOU'RE JOKING. YOU'RE NO MARKSMAN.

OH YEAH! THE CAPTAIN SAID THAT I CAN DESTROY *ENDICOR.* WHAT DO *YOU* THINK OF THAT?

ENDICOR? I THINK THE CAPTAIN'S *CRAZY.*

I'LL TELL HIM YOU *SAID* SO.

YOU DO AND IT'S THE LAST THING YOU *EVER* DO.

NOW C'MON. LET'S SEE IF ANYBODY ELSE IS AROUND TO HAVE *FUN* WITH.

KIRK TO BRIDGE. TIME UNTIL *ARRIVAL?*

FIFTEEN MINUTES, CAPTAIN.

THANK YOU, MR. SULU--I'LL BE UP.

BREEP

COME IN.

BEARCLAW REPORTING, SIR.

YOU WANTED TO *SEE* ME?

9

NO, MR. BEARCLAW, I DIDN'T *WANT* TO BUT IT IS... NECESSARY.

SIR... I'D LIKE TO APOLOGIZE AGAIN FOR THE INJURY YOU SUSTAINED THROUGH MY CARELESSNESS. I TAKE *FULL* RESPONSIBILITY.

THANK YOU, BEARCLAW. YOU'LL BE HAPPY TO KNOW I WON'T BE PURSUING CHARGES OF ASSAULTING AN OFFICER. NOR WILL MR. KONOM, WHOM YOU ALSO ATTACKED...

THANK *YOU,* SIR.

I WISH TO LEAVE ALL THAT BEHIND. IN FACT...

I WISH TO LEAVE *YOU* BEHIND.

SIR, WITH ALL DUE RESPECT, THAT'S NOT *FAIR!* I WAS DRUNK, AND--

I THOUGHT YOU WERE TAKING FULL RESPONSIBILITY.

THAT WAS *BEFORE!*

BEFORE YOU REALIZED THE FULL CONSEQUENCES. FOR THE *RECORD,* MR. BEARCLAW, YOUR *ASSAULT* ON ME, YOUR... CONDITION... ARE ONLY *SECONDARY.*

10

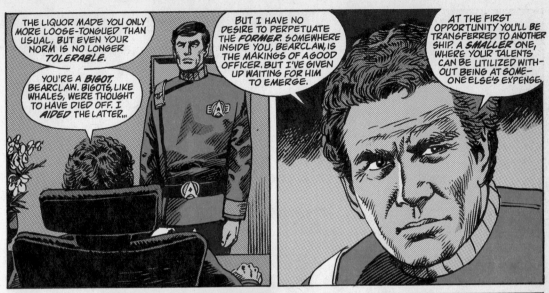

THE LIQUOR MADE YOU ONLY MORE LOOSE-TONGUED THAN USUAL, BUT EVEN YOUR NORM IS NO LONGER *TOLERABLE.*

YOU'RE A *BIGOT,* BEARCLAW. BIGOTS, LIKE WHALES, WERE THOUGHT TO HAVE DIED OFF. I *AIDED* THE LATTER...

BUT I HAVE NO DESIRE TO PERPETUATE THE *FORMER.* SOMEWHERE INSIDE YOU, BEARCLAW, IS THE MAKINGS OF A GOOD OFFICER, BUT I'VE GIVEN UP WAITING FOR HIM TO EMERGE.

AT THE FIRST OPPORTUNITY YOU'LL BE TRANSFERRED TO ANOTHER SHIP. A *SMALLER* ONE, WHERE YOUR TALENTS CAN BE UTILIZED WITHOUT BEING AT SOMEONE ELSE'S EXPENSE.

SIR, YOU *CAN'T!*

I CAN AND *WILL,* MISTER.

BUT...BUT I WANTED TO *PROVE* SOMETHING TO YOU, PROVE THAT YOU HAD *MISJUDGED* ME.

THEN YOU'VE *FAILED.*

THERE'S NO LAW AGAINST IT. *EVERYONE* FAILS SOMETIMES. THE IMPORTANT THING IS TO LEARN FROM YOUR FAILURES... AND *GROW* FROM THEM.

IF YOU'RE THE MAN I THINK YOU CAN BE YOU'LL GROW. YOU JUST *WON'T* BE DOING IT ON *THIS* SHIP.

DISMISSED.

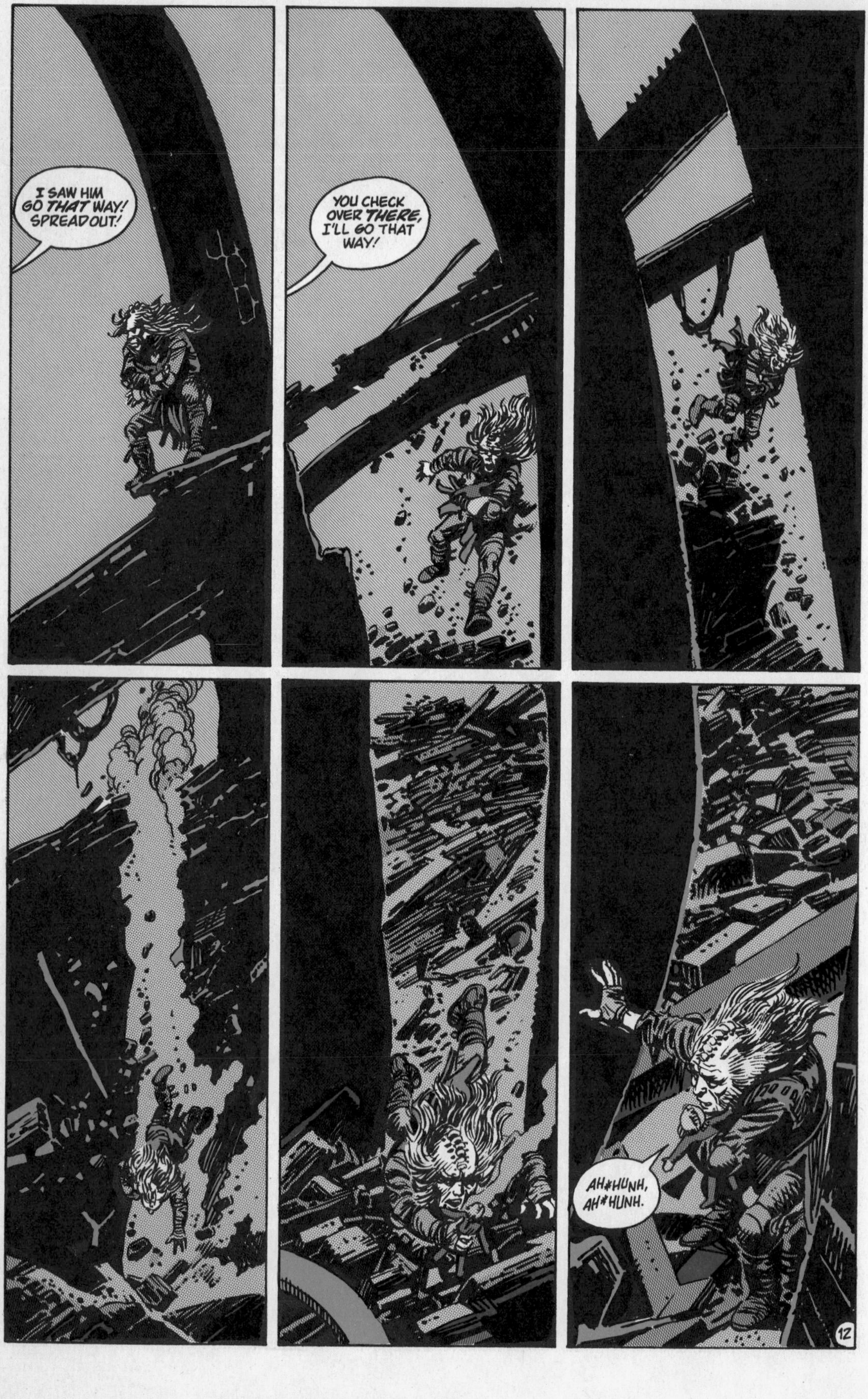
I SAW HIM GO THAT WAY! SPREAD OUT!
YOU CHECK OVER THERE, I'LL GO THAT WAY!
AH*HUNH, AH*HUNH.
12

WELL, WELL, WELL...

LOOK WHAT WE HAVE HERE.

NO! NO THROW ME! NO THROW ME!

OH, SO YOU SAW WHAT WE DID TO YOUR *BUDDY.* AND YOU DON'T WANT US TO DO IT TO YOU.

YOU'RE A DISGUSTING-LOOKING ONE. WHAT'S YOUR *NAME,* FREAK?

MUH... MORON.

MORON! OH, THAT'S BEAUTIFUL!

I'M GOING TO ENJOY THIS ONE, GRUNT--GIVE HIM THE HEAVE-HO. BUT LET HIM KEEP HIS DOLL.

NOOO! NO HEAVE-HO! NO!

13

PUT HIM DOWN. SLOWLY.

I SAID SLOWLY.

NO HURT ME! NO--

IDENTIFY YOURSELVES.

WE CAN DO BETTER THAN THAT. WE CAN IDENTIFY YOU.

YOU'RE WALKING DEAD MEN.

ARE YOU RESPONSIBLE FOR THE SLAUGHTER OF MY PEOPLE?

KONOM--

ANSWER ME!

14

YEAH. YEAH, WE'RE RESPONSIBLE. US AND THE REST OF THE CREW... AND CAPTAIN ZAIR!

WE'RE THE CREW OF THE GOOD SHIP RENEGADE...

AND WE'RE GOING TO SET THE FEDERATION AND THE KLINGONS AT EACH OTHER'S THROATS.

IN THE NAME OF KAHLESS, WHY?

YOU CAN ASK CAPTAIN ZAIR HIMSELF... AS SOON AS HE'S FINISHED DESTROYING WHATEVER SHIP YOU CAME FROM.

KIRK TO ENTERPRISE. SPOCK... CHECK YOUR SENSORS. YOU MAY NOT BE ALONE UP THERE.

MR. SULU?

SENSORS SHOW NEGATIVE, MR. SPOCK.

YOU'RE SO SEXY WHEN YOU'RE BEING EFFICIENT.

OH BOY.

15

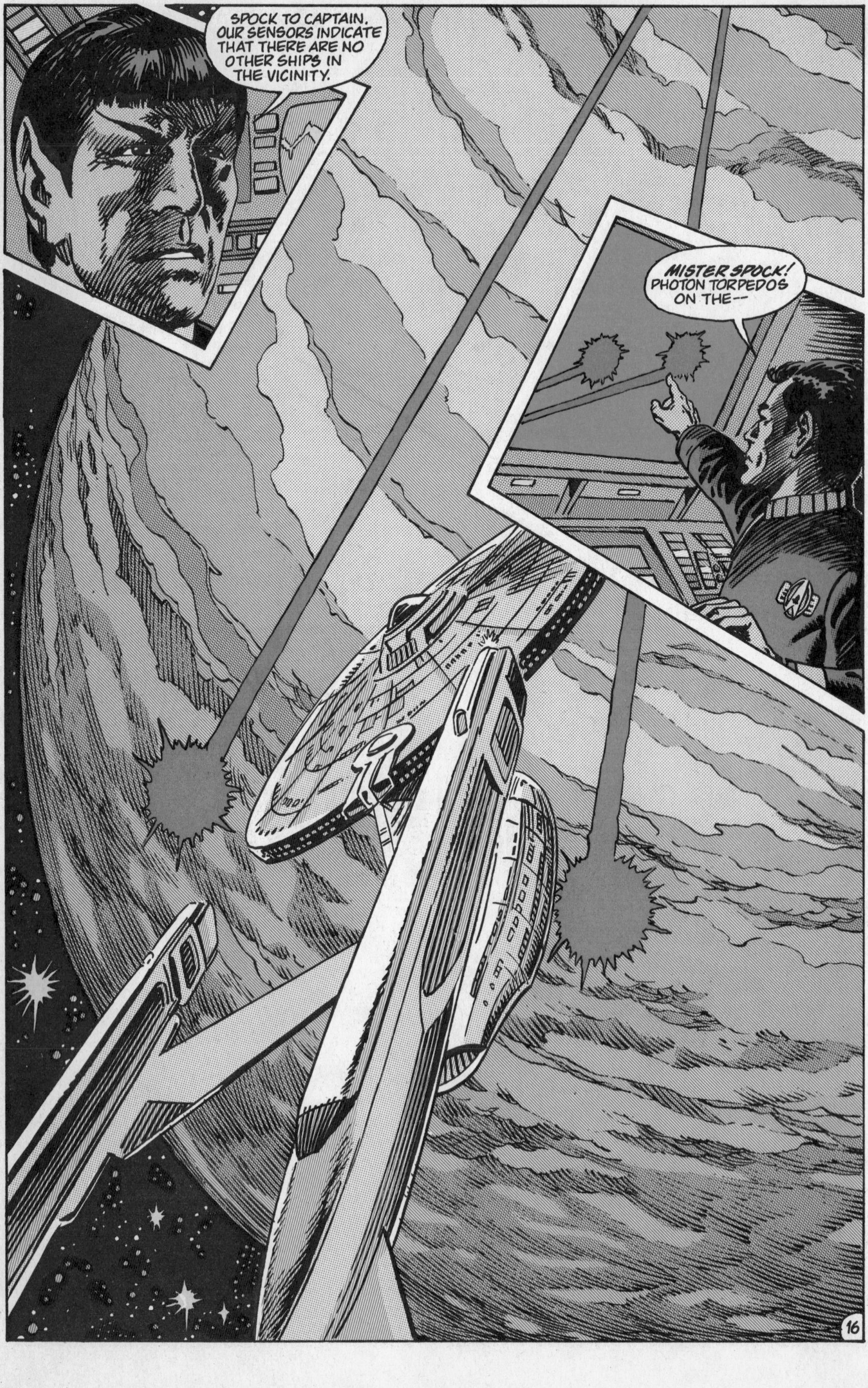
SPOCK TO CAPTAIN. OUR SENSORS INDICATE THAT THERE ARE NO OTHER SHIPS IN THE VICINITY.
MISTER SPOCK! PHOTON TORPEDOS ON THE--
16

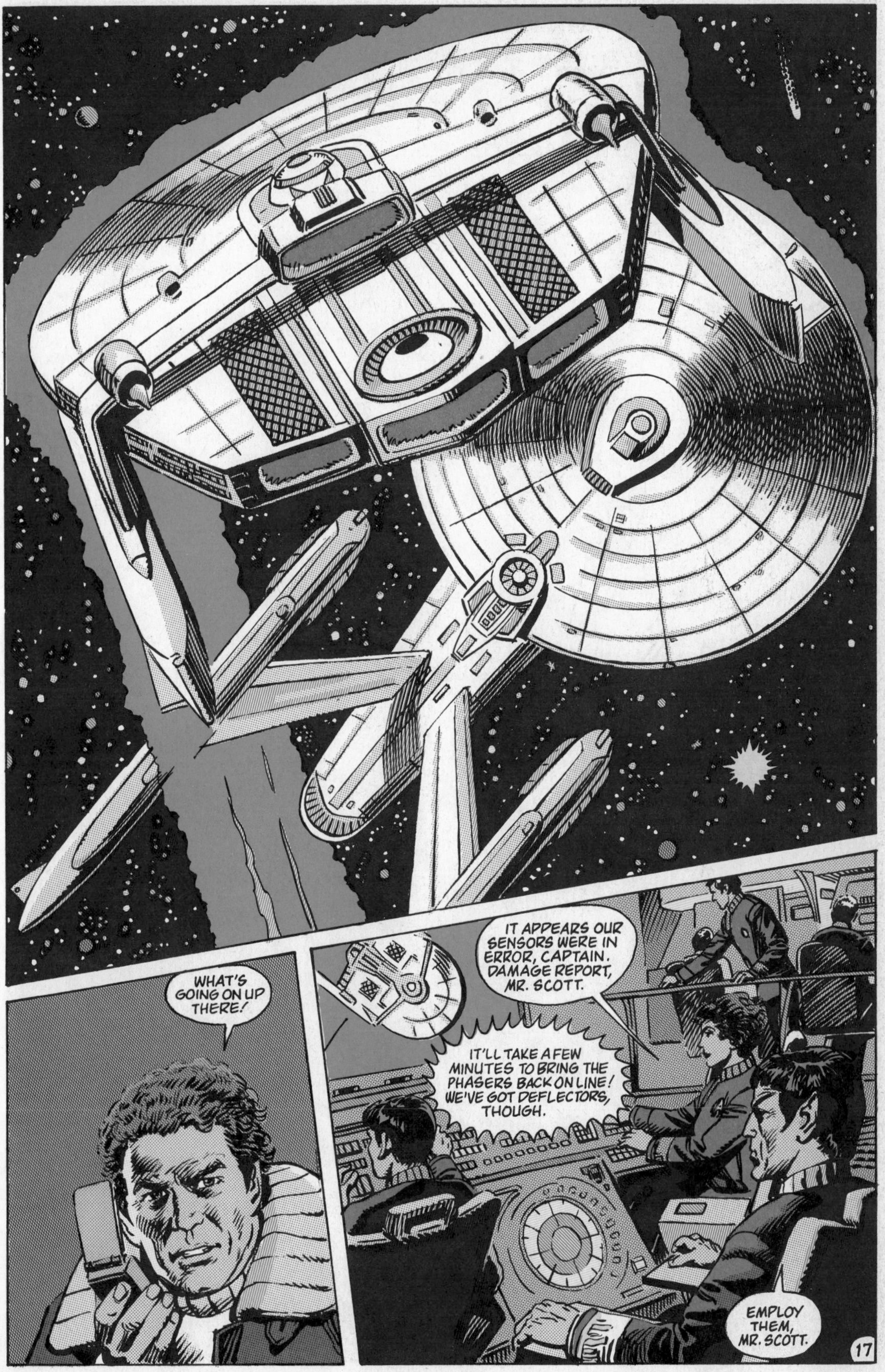
WHAT'S GOING ON UP THERE!
IT APPEARS OUR SENSORS WERE IN ERROR, CAPTAIN. DAMAGE REPORT, MR. SCOTT.
IT'LL TAKE A FEW MINUTES TO BRING THE PHASERS BACK ON LINE! WE'VE GOT DEFLECTORS, THOUGH.
EMPLOY THEM, MR. SCOTT.
17

They appear to have a cloaking device, captain. More sophisticated than--

Transporter room to Captain Zair! We've picked up some passengers in addition to our own people!

We're on the other ship! The Renegade!

Got them, Mr. Spock! They dropped their shields for some reason.

Let us hope that they do not have someone of Mr. Scott's calibre to effect weapons repair.

18

CAPTAIN! WE HAVE PRISONERS FOR YOU, SIR!

WHAT?

GET THEM IN ENVIRONMENT SUITS. QUICKLY!

PHIL? PHIL BURROUGHS? WHAT'S GOING ON?

HURRY, DAMN YOU...

...BEFORE I REGRET MORE THAN I ALREADY DO RISKING THIS SHIP TO SAVE YOUR WORTHLESS HIDES.

THEY'RE DROPPING THEIR SHIELDS AGAIN, MISTER SPOCK!

PERHAPS THEY'RE ENDEAVORING TO SURRENDER. ANY COMMUNICATIONS YET, LIEUTENANT?

STILL NO RESPONSE, MISTER--

LOOK!

19

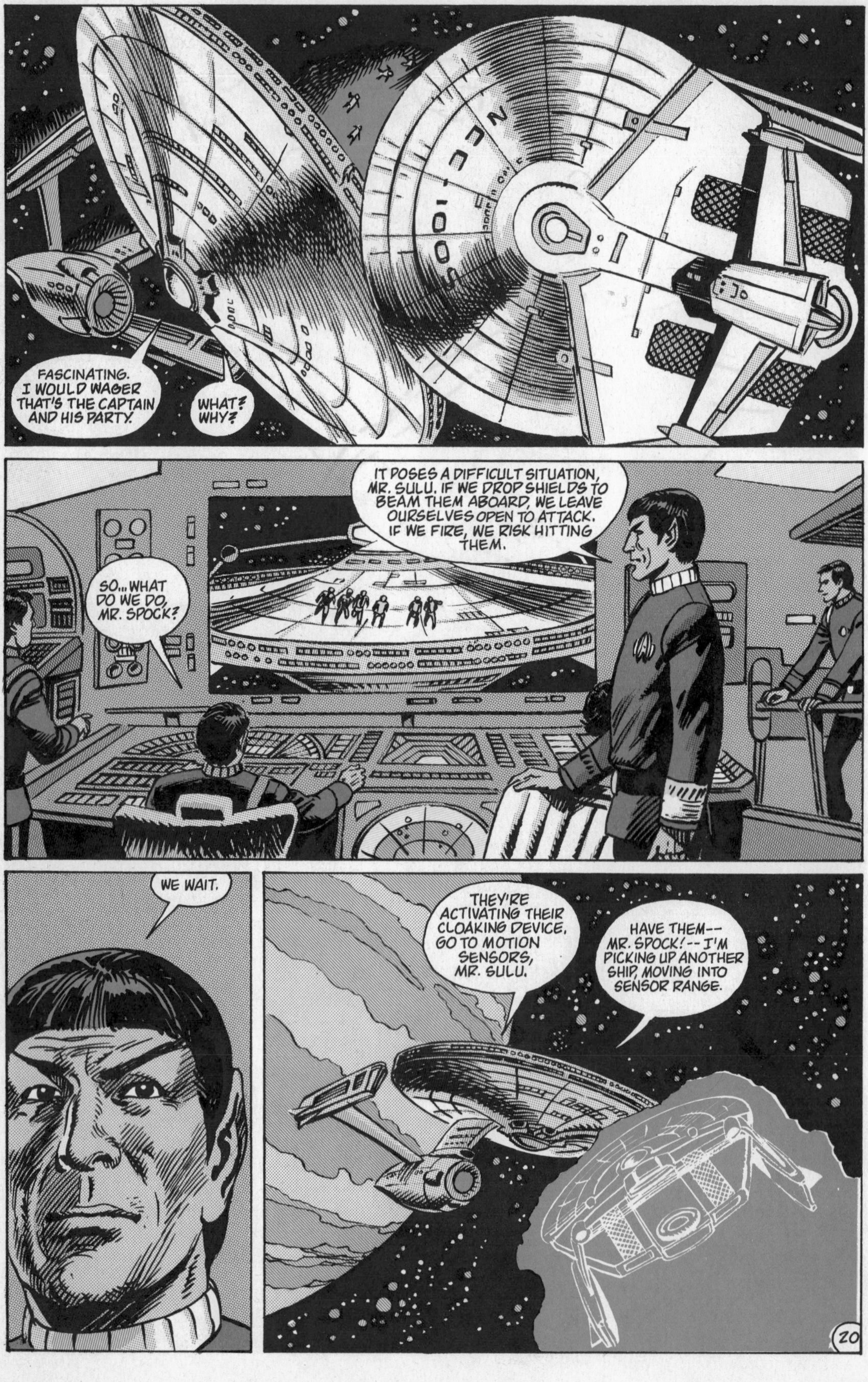
FASCINATING. I WOULD WAGER THAT'S THE CAPTAIN AND HIS PARTY.
WHAT? WHY?
IT POSES A DIFFICULT SITUATION, MR. SULU. IF WE DROP SHIELDS TO BEAM THEM ABOARD, WE LEAVE OURSELVES OPEN TO ATTACK. IF WE FIRE, WE RISK HITTING THEM.
SO... WHAT DO WE DO, MR. SPOCK?
WE WAIT.
THEY'RE ACTIVATING THEIR CLOAKING DEVICE. GO TO MOTION SENSORS, MR. SULU.
HAVE THEM-- MR. SPOCK! -- I'M PICKING UP ANOTHER SHIP, MOVING INTO SENSOR RANGE.
20

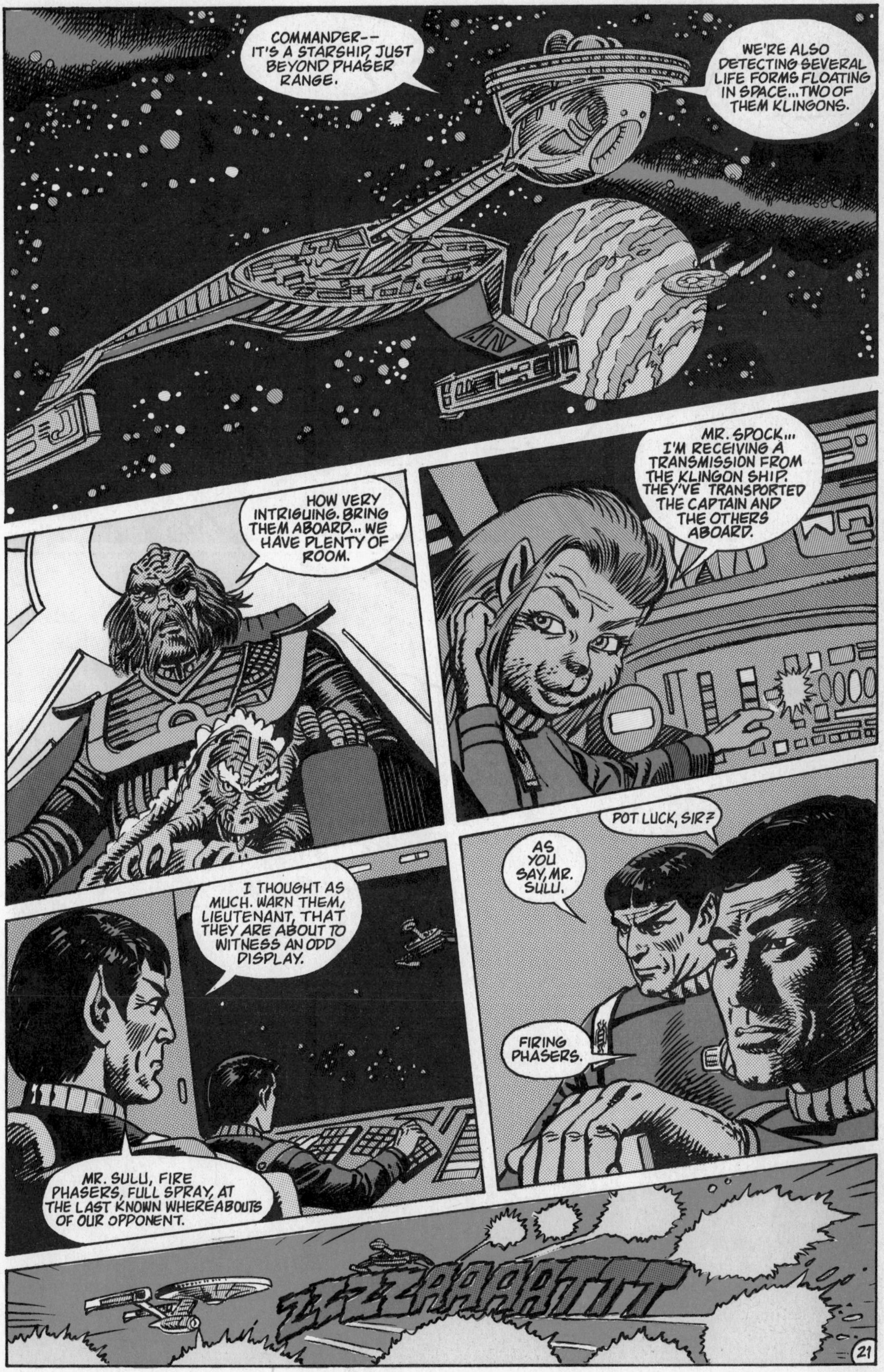
COMMANDER-- IT'S A STARSHIP, JUST BEYOND PHASER RANGE.
WE'RE ALSO DETECTING SEVERAL LIFE FORMS FLOATING IN SPACE...TWO OF THEM KLINGONS.
HOW VERY INTRIGUING. BRING THEM ABOARD... WE HAVE PLENTY OF ROOM.
MR. SPOCK... I'M RECEIVING A TRANSMISSION FROM THE KLINGON SHIP. THEY'VE TRANSPORTED THE CAPTAIN AND THE OTHERS ABOARD.
I THOUGHT AS MUCH. WARN THEM, LIEUTENANT, THAT THEY ARE ABOUT TO WITNESS AN ODD DISPLAY.
MR. SULU, FIRE PHASERS, FULL SPRAY, AT THE LAST KNOWN WHEREABOUTS OF OUR OPPONENT.
POT LUCK, SIR?
AS YOU SAY, MR. SULU.
FIRING PHASERS.
ZZZZAAAARRTTTTT
21

CAPTAIN'S LOG, STARDATE 8988.9. WE HAVE BEEN BEAMED ABOARD A KLINGON BATTLE CRUISER WHERE THE COMMANDER KRON, IS ALLOWING ME TO COMMUNICATE WITH MY SHIP.

"...PHASER BARRAGE PROVED INEFFECTIVE, SIR. IT IS MY BELIEF THAT THEY HAVE LEFT THE AREA.

NO DOUBT WHEN THEY SAW MY SHIP THEY FLED IN TERROR. YOU ARE WELCOME TO RETURN TO YOUR SHIP AT YOUR LEISURE, CAPTAIN.

YOU ARE... REMARKABLY HOSPITABLE, COMMANDER KRON.

MAKE NO MISTAKE. HAD I KNOWN ONE OF THE KLINGONS I DETECTED WAS THE LEGENDARY TRAITOR, KONOM, I WOULD HAVE SHOT YOU MYSELF. BUT, WHAT'S DONE IS DONE.

FIFTEEN MINUTES, CAPTAIN. THAT IS HOW LONG YOU HAVE TO GIVE ME, AND THROUGH ME THE EMPEROR, A FULL REPORT.

GIVE YOUR COORDINATES TO YOUR SHIP AND TAKE THIS... THING... WITH YOU.

BUT... HE'S ONE OF YOUR PEOPLE. HOW CAN YOU--

MY PEOPLE? MY DEAR EARTHER, THIS HALF-BREED, MUTATED FREAK IS HARDLY ONE OF MINE.

BUT THEN, WHAT ELSE WOULD YOU EXPECT WHEN A HUMAN AND A KLINGON MATE...EXCEPT A FREAK?

22

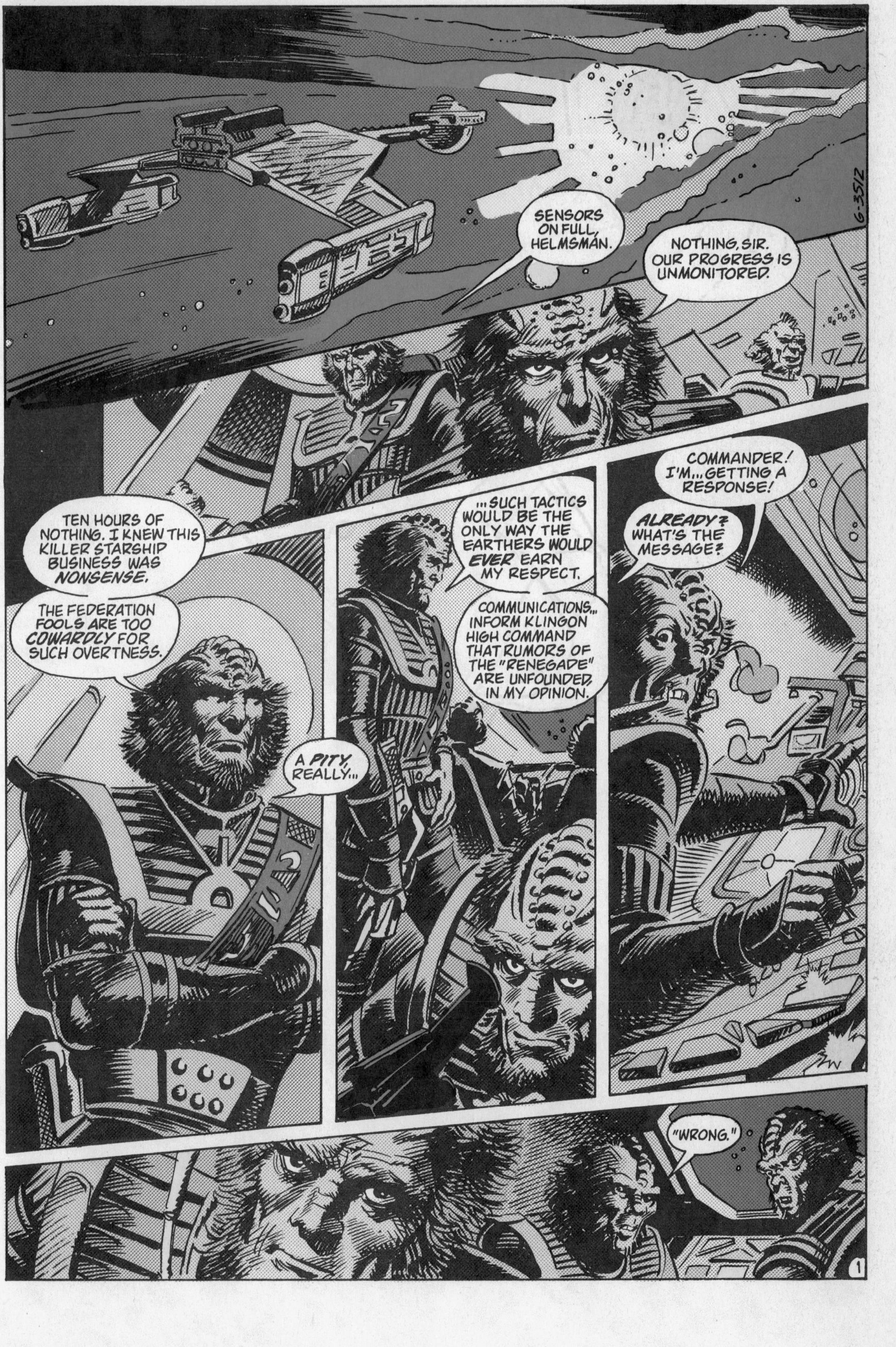

SENSORS ON FULL, HELMSMAN.
NOTHING, SIR. OUR PROGRESS IS UNMONITORED.
TEN HOURS OF NOTHING. I KNEW THIS KILLER STARSHIP BUSINESS WAS NONSENSE.
THE FEDERATION FOOLS ARE TOO COWARDLY FOR SUCH OVERTNESS.
A PITY, REALLY...
...SUCH TACTICS WOULD BE THE ONLY WAY THE EARTHERS WOULD EVER EARN MY RESPECT.
COMMUNICATIONS... INFORM KLINGON HIGH COMMAND THAT RUMORS OF THE "RENEGADE" ARE UNFOUNDED, IN MY OPINION.
COMMANDER! I'M... GETTING A RESPONSE!
ALREADY? WHAT'S THE MESSAGE?
"WRONG."

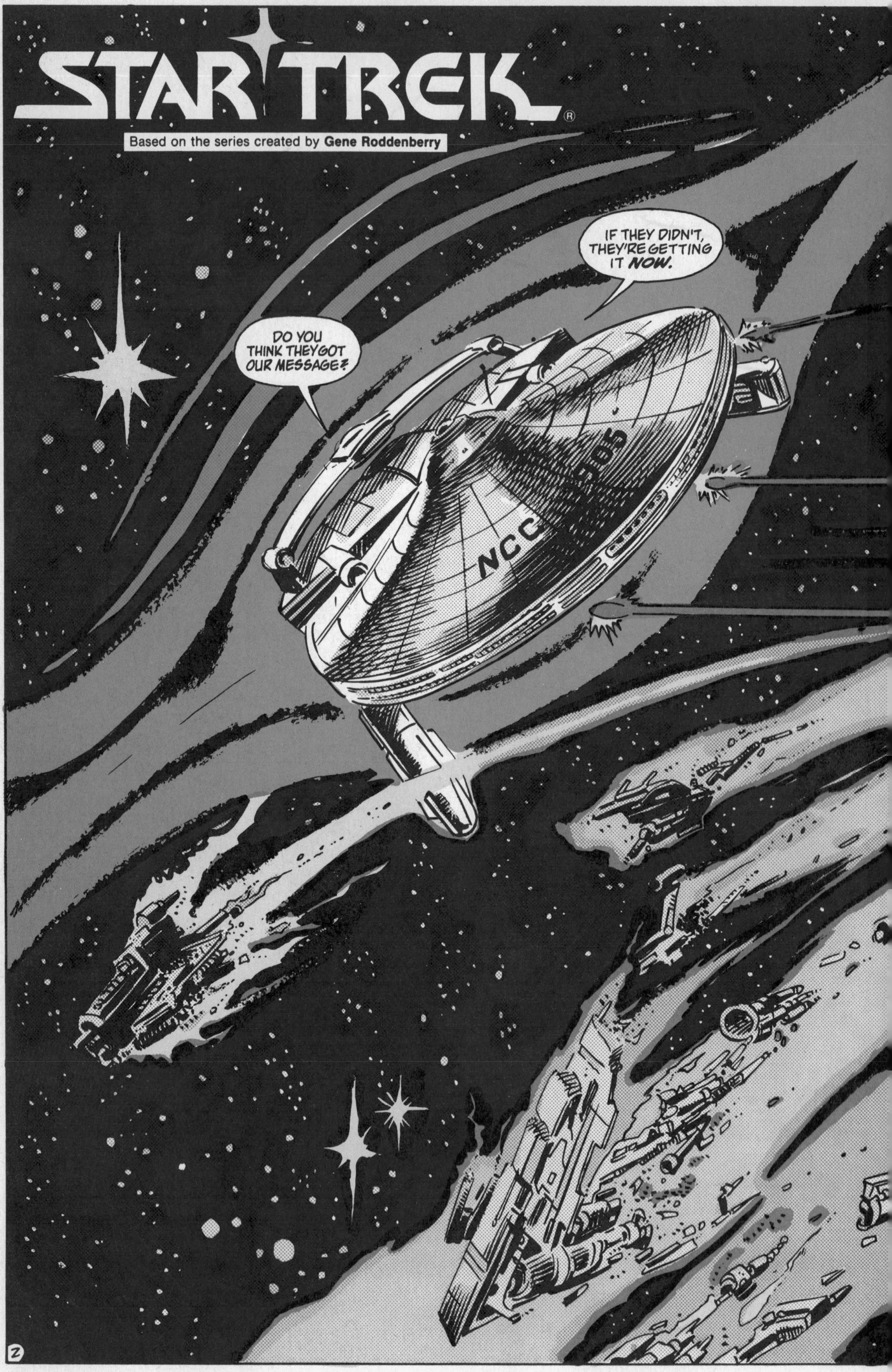
STAR TREK
Based on the series created by Gene Roddenberry
DO YOU THINK THEY GOT OUR MESSAGE?
IF THEY DIDN'T, THEY'RE GETTING IT NOW.
NCC
2

MARRIAGE OF INCONVENIENCE

PETER DAVID *	TOM SUTTON *	RICARDO VILLAGRÁN
WRITER	PENCILLER	INKER
HELEN VESIK *	MICHELE WOLFMAN *	ROBERT GREENBERGER
LETTERER	COLORIST	KLINGON EMPEROR

A FEW MORE SHOTS OUGHT TO FINISH THEM.

CAPTAIN ZAIR, SIR, I'M GETTING *ANOTHER* OUTGOING TRANSMISSION.

TELLING OF THEIR *DESTRUCTION* AT *OUR* HANDS?

YES SIR. I CAN *JAM* IT IF YOU WISH.

NOW WHY IN THE *WORLD* SHOULD WE WANT TO DO *THAT*?

THEY'RE *RETURNING* FIRE, CAPTAIN.

STILL SOME FIGHT LEFT, EH?

FIRE BOUNCING OFF OUR *SHIELDS*, SIR. NO DAMAGE. THEY STILL HAVEN'T MANAGED TO PULL SHIELDS TOGETHER.

THEN LET'S *NOT* GIVE THEM THE *OPPORTUNITY*, MELCHIOR.

4

IT'S *DESTROYED*.

MY CAREER. MY *LIFE*. TOTALLY BLOWN TO BITS.

BUT IT'S *NOT* MY FAULT. WHY CAN'T KIRK *UNDERSTAND* THAT?

SURE I SAID THINGS, *DID* THINGS... BUT I WAS *DRUNK*. HE *KNOWS* THAT.

SOMEONE SPIKED THE *PUNCH*. *THAT'S* THE ONLY ANSWER. THAT'S WHY I ATTACKED KONOM AT THE PARTY.

I WAS *TRYING*, DAMMIT. TRYING TO FORGET HE'S A STINKING KLINGON. BUT I GET *THIS* ROTTEN BREAK.

AND THE NEXT THING I KNOW KIRK'S ALL *OVER* ME. HOW CAN I *TELL* ANYONE? HOW--

BEARCLAW? YOU *OKAY*?

I'M FINE. WHAT DO *YOU* CARE?

WHAT? BILL, WHAT'S *HAPPENED*? *SOMETHING* MUST HAVE HAPPENED TO MAKE YOU LIKE THIS.

5

NOTHING HAPPENED. HAVEN'T YOU HEARD? I'M ALWAYS LIKE THIS.

NOW IF YOU'LL *EXCUSE* ME...

HEY! EXCUSE ME.

WHAT'S *YOUR* PROBLEM?

DON'T BE UPSET, MEESTER SULU...

HE'S ONLY BEING BEARCLAW.

SO WHAT EES GOING ON VIZ YOU AND *M'RESS*?

OOOOOH, DON'T *ASK*.

IT'S ALL THAT *KLINGON'S* FAULT. THAT ROTTEN KONOM.

I'D *LOVE* TO GET MY HANDS ON A FEW KLINGONS RIGHT NOW...

6

GET THE HELL OUT OF MY--

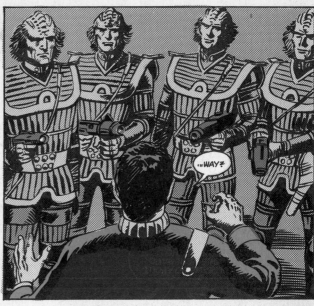

"...WAY?

NOW MEN... YOUR CAUTION IS *LAUDABLE* BUT *MISPLACED*.

I'M SURE ADMIRAL KIRK WOULD HARDLY ALLOW GUESTS TO BE ATOMIZED BY ONE OF HIS CREW. *WOULD* YOU, ADMIRAL?

7

IT'S RATHER UNLIKELY, COMMANDER KRON...

AS UNLIKELY AS MY PERMITTING *ANYONE* TO THREATEN ONE OF MY CREWMEMBERS.

I'VE ALLOWED YOU TO BRING WEAPONS ABOARD MY SHIP... BUT KEEP THEM HOLSTERED OR I'LL HAVE TWO SECURITY GUARDS ASSIGNED TO EVERY ONE OF YOURS.

AND IT'S "CAPTAIN" KIRK.

REDUCTION IN RANK?

IN THE KLINGON EMPIRE, THAT'S TANTAMOUNT TO DEMANDING *SUICIDE* FOR THE SHAMED OFFICER.

IN *MY* INSTANCE IT WAS A COMMENDATION FOR A JOB WELL DONE.

THIS WAY, PLEASE.

THANK YOU FOR STANDING UP FOR ME, SIR. DOES THIS MEAN YOU'VE... *RECONSIDERED* ABOUT TRANSFERRING ME OFF THE ENTERPRISE?

IT DOES *NOT*.

8

WELL, WHATEVER THIS LITTLE FELLOW *IS*, HE'S GOT NORMAL KLINGON VITAL SIGNS... WHATEVER *THOSE* ARE.

NO OFFENSE, KONOM.

NONE *TAKEN*, DOCTOR. IS HE... A CHILD?

AS NEAR AS I CAN TELL, HE'S *FULL GROWN*. AT LEAST AS FULL GROWN AS HE'LL *GET*.

NO *HURT*?

NO. *NO ONE'S* GOING TO HURT YOU. WHAT'S YOUR *NAME*?

MORON.

NO, THAT'S NOT A NAME.

WHAT IS NAME?

A NAME IS SOMETHING LIKE "NANCY" OR "KONOM". SOMETHING YOUR FRIENDS CALL YOU.

WHAT IS "FRIEND"?

IS IT *TRUE*, DOCTOR? THAT HE'S... SOME SORT OF HALF-BREED, BETWEEN *HUMAN* AND *KLINGON*?

PROBABLY. LOVE BETWEEN A HUMAN AND A KLINGON IS EXTREMELY RARE. MY GUESS IS THAT A KLINGON FORCED HIMSELF ON A HUMAN FEMALE *HE*... WAS THE RESULT.

THEN AGAIN, I UNDERSTAND KLINGONS *DON'T* NORMALLY TAKE PRISONERS.

TRUE, BUT WE SOMETIMES... ADOPT *PETS*.

NANCY...I THINK WE HAVE TO--

NANCY?

"WHERE DID SHE GO?"

SICK BAY

OH, *NANCY!* I'M *GLAD* YOU'RE HERE. I WAS LOOKING OVER THE DRESS I'M SUPPOSED TO WEAR AS MAID OF HONOR.

I KNOW WE'D CONSIDERED FUSCIA, AND THEN CHANGED TO AQUAMARINE. BUT NOW I'M THINKING OF GOING...

...BACK TO THE FUSCIA. NANCY, WHAT'S *WRONG?*

NOTHING.

THIS IS *RIDICULOUS.* I'M SPENDING THE DAY ASKING PEOPLE WHAT'S WRONG, AND HAVING THEM LIE TO ME.

I *THOUGHT* YOU CAME IN HERE TO TALK ABOUT THE WEDDING...

THERE ISN'T GOING TO BE A WEDDING!!

LIFE WAS EASIER WHEN PEOPLE *LIED* TO ME.

10

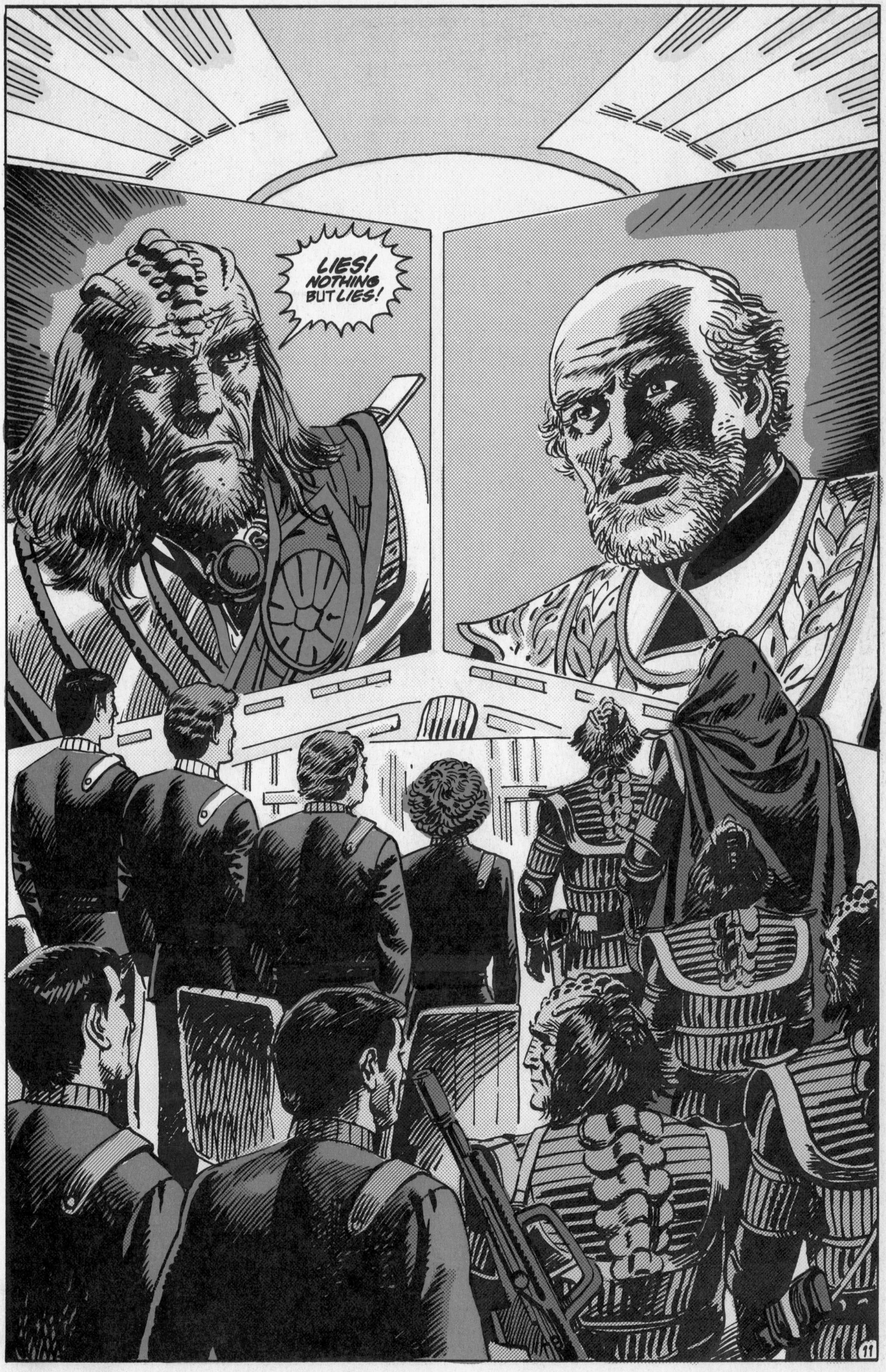
LIES! NOTHING BUT LIES!
11

EMPEROR KAHLESS, HYSTERICAL ACCUSATIONS ARE *NOT* THE ANSWER TO OUR DIFFICULTIES.

NOR ARE THE PATHETIC EXCUSES *YOU'VE* OFFERED TO BE CONSIDERED ANSWERS. DO YOU *SERIOUSLY* EXPECT ME TO BELIEVE THAT YOU HAVE NOT AUTHORIZED THIS SUPPOSED "RENEGADE'S" "ACTIVITIES"?

EMPEROR, I AM FRANKLY HURT TO HAVE OUR WORD SO *CAVALIERLY* IGNORED.

YOUR WORD! THE WORD OF A FEDERATION WHO HAS ADMITTEDLY ENGAGED IN ESPIONAGE... INCLUDING AT LEAST *ONE* KNOWN MISSION PERFORMED BY "CAPTAIN" KIRK.

SINS OF THE PAST RETURN TO *HAUNT* US.

IT WOULD SEEM THEY NEVER *LEFT.*

LET'S NOT *KID* EACH OTHER, EMPEROR. NEITHER OF US IS VIRGINAL WHEN IT COMES TO UNKIND DEEDS. NOW WE CAN EITHER CITE CHAPTER AND VERSE OF RESPECTIVE INFRACTIONS...

OR WE CAN WORK TOGETHER TO FORESTALL *FURTHER* MISUNDER-STANDINGS.

MISUNDERSTANDINGS?! OVER A HUNDRED KLINGONS ON MIRAUD ARE *DEAD,* AND THE DEATH WEAPON WAS A FEDERATION SHIP! YOU CALL *THAT* A MIS-UNDERSTANDING?

YOUR WORSHIP...

WHAT. *WHAT DID YOU SAY?*

UH OH. I DON'T LIKE THE LOOKS OF THIS.

12

IT SEEMS WE HAVE *ANOTHER...* "MISUNDERSTANDING".

THE KLINGON BATTLE CRUISER *FURY* HAS BEEN LOST WITH ALL HANDS.

THE FINAL MESSAGE STATED THAT A FEDERATION STARSHIP APPEARED FROM NOWHERE AND DESTROYED THEM.

KIRK.... MY *BROTHER* WAS SECOND IN COMMAND ON THE *FURY.*

WOULD YOU CARE TO CLARIFY THIS "MISUNDERSTANDING"?

EMPEROR KAHLESS.... COMMANDER KRON... I UNDERSTAND YOUR ANGER, BUT I'VE ALREADY TOLD YOU ALL I *KNOW.*

THE RELIANT-CLASS STARSHIP CALLED "RENEGADE" KILLED THE INHABITANTS OF THE KLINGON SCIENCE OUTPOST ON MIRAUD. WE INTERCEPTED A DISTRESS CALL FROM MIRAUD AND, UPON ARRIVAL...

..."DISCOVERED A SINGLE SURVIVOR, WHO IS NOW IN OUR SICKBAY... AND THREE MEMBERS OF THE *CREW* OF THE RENEGADE.

WE WERE TRANSPORTED UP TO THE RENEGADE SHIP AND I FOUND IT WAS BEING COMMANDED BY CAPTAIN *PHIL BURROUGHS*, NOW BEING CALLED *CAPTAIN ZAIR* BY HIS CREW.

UPON UNSUCCESSFULLY ENGAGING THE ENTERPRISE, THE RENEGADE PUT US IN ENVIRONMENT SUITS AND BEAMED US INTO SPACE AS A DELAYING TACTIC.

WE WERE *SAVED* BY COMMANDER KRON, AND THEN AGREED TO HAVE THIS BRIEFING WITH ALL CONCERNED PARTIES.

BUT TOSSING *INSULTS* AROUND WON'T MAKE THINGS ANY BETTER.

13

YOU'VE PASSED OVER SOME *DETAILS*, CAPTAIN. SUCH AS THAT THIS RENEGADE WAS EQUIPPED WITH A CLOAKING DEVICE THAT SUPPOSEDLY YOUR TECHNOLOGY *COULDN'T* PENETRATE.

HOW *CONVENIENT*. DO YOU ACTUALLY EXPECT US TO *BELIEVE* THAT?

BUT *OF COURSE*. OBVIOUSLY TECHNOLOGY THAT IS *BEYOND* OUR CURRENT PARAMETERS IS INVOLVED.

OTHERWISE HOW WOULD ONE EXPLAIN THE DEMISE OF THE FURY? CERTAINLY NO SHIP OF *RESPECTABLE* KLINGONS COULD FALL PREY SO EASILY TO A SINGLE STARSHIP.

SO EITHER THE FURY WAS MANNED BY *INCOMPETENTS*, OR THE CAPTAIN'S CLAIMS HAVE MERIT. THOSE ARE THE *LOGICAL* ALTERNATIVES.

SO HOW DO WE GO ABOUT FINDING THIS RENEGADE STARSHIP WITH THE IMPENETRABLE CLOAKING DEVICE?

14

ELIZABETH? HAVE YOU SEEN NANCY ANY--

NC-19118

--WHERE.

NANCY.

KONOM.

WELL? ARE YOU TWO GOING TO JUST STAND THERE SHOWING YOUR MASTERY OF EACH OTHER'S NAMES?

NANCY... I HOPE THAT I DIDN'T OFFEND YOU SOME--

NO. NO, KONOM, IT'S NOT THAT. YOU KNOW WHAT IT IS.

YOU SAW HIM. YOU KNOW I'M WORRIED ABOUT... "MORON". THAT HE'S THE PRODUCT OF A KLINGON AND HUMAN MATING.

CHILDREN, KONOM. WE HADN'T DISCUSSED IT, EVEN CONSIDERED IT. FRANKLY, I WASN'T SURE IT WAS POSSIBLE.

AND YOUR CAREER? AREN'T PREGNANT WOMEN ROTATED OUT OF STARFLEET?

NOT ALWAYS, AND THAT'S NOT THE POINT KONOM. I'M YOUNG. I'M NOT READY TO DECIDE ABSOLUTELY IF I WILL OR WON'T HAVE CHILDREN.

BUT IF YOU MARRY ME, YOU'LL ALREADY BE MAKING THAT CHOICE? IS THAT IT?

NANCY, WE DON'T KNOW THAT FOR CERTAIN.

EXACTLY!

15

HOW CAN WE GET MARRIED IF THERE'S *ANYTHING* THAT'S SO *UNCERTAIN*?

I THOUGHT THAT MANY THINGS WERE *POSSIBLE* WHERE *LOVE* WAS CONCERNED.

IT SEEMS I WAS *MISTAKEN.* THAT'S UNDER-STANDABLE, I SUPPOSE.

WE KLINGONS AREN'T KNOWN FOR OUR *EXPERTISE* IN LOVE.

HEY! WERE YOU JUST COMING FROM *ELIZABETH'S* QUARTERS?

THAT'S RIGHT.

WHAT WERE YOU DOING IN THERE?

TALKING ABOUT *MATING.*

WHAT?!

YOU HEARD ME.

ELIZABETH!

...AND SO, *EXTRAPOLATING* FROM THE COORDINATES OF THE *FURY'S* DESTRUCTION AND THE INITIAL SAVAGING OF *MIRAUD*...

...THERE WOULD APPEAR TO BE TWO LOGICAL TARGETS... AND ONE SOMEWHAT *ILLOGICAL* ONE... FOR THE RENEGADE'S *NEXT* ASSAULT.

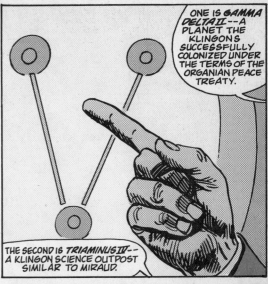

ONE IS *GAMMA DELTA II*--A PLANET THE KLINGONS SUCCESSFULLY COLONIZED UNDER THE TERMS OF THE ORGANIAN PEACE TREATY.

THE SECOND IS *TRIAMINUS IV*-- A KLINGON SCIENCE OUTPOST SIMILAR TO MIRAUD.

THE ONLY OTHER KLINGON-INFLUENCED PLANET IN THE QUADRANT IS *ENDICOR*--A PARTIALLY DEVELOPED PLANET WHICH BOTH THE FEDERATION AND EMPIRE ARE STILL *COMPETING* FOR.

IT IS SOMEWHAT "OUT OF THE WAY" FOR THE RENEGADE, AND ALSO CONTRARY TO THE APPARENT PURE ANTI-KLINGON BIAS THE RENEGADE DISPLAYS.

UNLIKELY OR *NO*, I WANT *FULL* PROTECTION FROM THE FEDERATION ON *ALL* POSSIBLE TARGETS, UNTIL SUCH TIME THAT WE CAN GET MORE OF OUR *OWN* BATTLE CRUISERS INTO THE TARGETED AREA.

IF YOUR CLAIMS OF INNOCENCE ARE *TRUE*, YOU'LL DO *WHATEVER* IS NECESSARY TO ACT IN OUR INTEREST.

WE WILL DO WHATEVER IS *POSSIBLE*, EMPEROR...

...BUT THE ENTERPRISE IS THE ONLY SHIP IN THE QUADRANT. UNTIL WE CAN GET MORE OF THE FLEET *OUT* THERE KIRK AND KRON WILL HAVE TO WORK *TOGETHER* TO KEEP THIS SITUATION UNDER *CONTROL*.

17

CAPTAIN, COUNT YOUR FINGERS.

I ALREADY HAVE.

CAPTAIN'S LOG,
STAR DATE 8994.6
HAVING REACHED AN
UNEASY ALLIANCE WITH
COMMANDER KRON, THE
ENTERPRISE IS ENROUTE
TO TRIAMINUS IV, WHILE
COMMANDER KRON'S
SHIP IS GOING TO
GAMMA DELTA II.

THE UNLIKELY TARGET OF ENDICOR WILL BE PUT UNDER GUARD AS SOON AS A SHIP IS AVAILABLE.

HOWEVER, EVEN AS WE PREPARE OURSELVES FOR THE UNUSUAL TASK OF AIDING THE KLINGONS, WE ARE CONTINUING TO PURSUE THE RENEGADE QUESTION FROM OTHER DIRECTIONS.

ACCORDING TO CAPTAIN BURROUGHS' LAST COMMUNICATION WITH STARFLEET, HE WAS ON A ROUTINE MISSION TO THE PLANET OMICRON CETI IV--THE FARMING COMMUNITY. NEITHER CAPTAIN BURROUGHS NOR THE SHIP, THE ZEPHYR, HAS BEEN HEARD FROM IN APPROXIMATELY TWO WEEKS.

SO IT'S YOUR GUESS THAT THE ZEPHYR IS NOW THE RENEGADE.

"GUESS" CAPTAIN?

FORGIVE HIM, SPOCK. HE MISSPOKE-- THE STRAIN OF COMMAND AND ALL THAT

I HAD PRESUMED AS MUCH.

18

SO IT WOULD BE INTERESTING TO GO TO OMICRON CETI IV TO SEE IF WE CAN DISCOVER WHAT HAPPENED THERE THAT CHANGED PHIL BURROUGHS.

IT WOULD BE THE LOGICAL APPROACH. IT IS BETTER TO ACT THAN TO REACT.

BUT IF WE DO THAT, IF WE GO AGAINST WHAT WE AGREED TO, THE KLINGONS WILL ASSUME THAT WE'RE CROSSING THEM UP SOMEHOW.

AND IF THAT HAPPENS, ALL HELL COULD BREAK LOOSE.

ALL HELL HAS BROKEN LOOSE *BEFORE*, BONES, AND WE'VE ALWAYS MANAGED TO *STITCH* IT BACK *TOGETHER*.

YES, BUT HOW LONG BEFORE WE RUN OUT OF *THREAD?*

KIRK TO BRIDGE.

BRIDGE. *SULU* HERE.

MR. SULU, HAVE A SHUTTLE CRAFT WITH *WARP SLED* READIED. I WANT A TEAM ASSEMBLED TO MAKE A VISIT TO OMICRON CETI IV WHILE *WE* PROCEED TO TRIAMINUS.

KIRK OUT.

JIM...YOU REALIZE YOU HAVE NO IDEA WHAT KIND OF *DANGER* YOU MAY BE SENDING THAT TEAM INTO.

IF THERE'S A *GOOD* KIND OF DANGER, DOCTOR I'VE YET TO *ENCOUNTER* IT.

19

47

BRIDGE TO CAPTAIN.

KIRK HERE.

A CLARIFICATION, SIR. THE SHUTTLE-CRAFT TEAM--WILL YOU BE MAKING THE ASSIGNMENTS OR ARE WE LOOKING FOR VOLUNTEERS?

SIR, I SAID...

VOLUNTEERS AT FIRST, MR. SULU. PREFERABLY THOSE WITHOUT MATES OR CHILDREN.

KONOM? LOOK, I STILL WANT TO BE FRIENDS. CAN'T WE BE FRIENDS?

KONOM? DON'T JUST LET ME STAND OUT HERE.

KONOM?

KONOM, WHERE ARE--

GONE ON SUICIDE MISSION. BE BACK LATER...

THIS LIFE OR NEXT.

20

CAPTAIN! CAN I SPEAK TO YOU FOR A MOMENT?

OF COURSE, MISTER BEARCLAW.

I'D LIKE TO VOLUNTEER FOR THE MISSION.

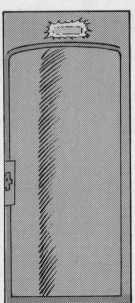

AND THAT'S MY FINAL WORD ON IT. UNDERSTOOD?

UNDERSTOOD...

...SIR.

STATUS OF THE SHUTTLE LAUNCH, MISTER SULU?

THE COPERNICUS IS BEING PREPPED AND WILL BE READY TO LAUNCH IN FIVE MINUTES, SIR.

FINE. LET'S SEE THE DUTY ROSTER.

FERGUSON, O'NEILL, CASTILLE--GOOD, HAVING A MENTITE ABOARD WILL BE HANDY...

WILKINS, BLOEMKER, KONOM... KONOM?

HE WAS VERY INSISTENT, SIR.

ALL RIGHT. HAVE THEM ASSEMBLE IN THE HANGER BAY IN THREE MINUTES.

21

SO THAT WILL BE YOUR ASSIGNMENT. I HAVE NO IDEA WHAT TO TELL YOU TO EXPECT.

ALL WE KNOW IS THAT *OMICRON CETI IV* WAS THE *LAST* KNOWN LOCATION OF THE *ZEPHYR* BEFORE SHE WENT ROGUE. YOUR SHUTTLECRAFT WILL BE EQUIPPED WITH A SIGNAL BEACON, SET ON AUTOMATIC, SO WE CAN *FIND* YOU.

OR SO, BY ITS CESSATION, YOU CAN TELL WE'VE BEEN *DESTROYED*.

OPTIMISTIC AS *ALWAYS*, CASTILLE.

WE WILL BE BACK IN TOUCH WITH YOU AS SOON AS POSSIBLE. GOOD LUCK.

KONOM, A *MOMENT* PLEASE

KONOM, ARE YOU *CERTAIN* YOU WANT TO TAKE ON SUCH A TRICKY ASSIGNMENT, SO SHORTLY BEFORE YOUR MARRIAGE? WHAT IF...?

AT THIS POINT, CAPTAIN, NANCY HAS MADE IT CLEAR THAT A WEDDING IS *NOT* A CONSIDERATION.

I AM....SADDENED. BUT *NOT* SURPRISED. NANCY'S LOVE FOR ME ALWAYS SEEMED TOO *GOOD* TO BE *TRUE*.

22

KONOM, I *DON'T* WANT A DEPRESSED CREWMAN ON THIS MISSION.

OUT OF THE *QUESTION,* CAPTAIN. AS I *ALWAYS* HAVE--EVEN WHEN I WAS PART OF THE KLINGON EMPIRE, THAT FIRST TIME WE MET--I WILL CONTINUE TO ACT IN THE BEST INTERESTS OF THE ENTERPRISE.

MAY I *GO* NOW, SIR?

ON YOUR WAY. AND KONOM...I'LL TALK TO NANCY, IF YOU WISH.

NO. THANK. YOU.

HANGAR BAY

HEY *FERGUSON.* I'M TAKING YOUR PLACE.

WHAT? WHY?

YOUR MOTHER'S DEAD. JUST CAME OVER *SUBSPACE.*

OH MY GOD.

SHUTTLECRAFT *COPERNICUS,* PREPARE FOR LAUNCH.

23

SHUTTLECRAFT AWAY.

A *SHAME* ABOUT FERGIE'S MOTHER, BEARCLAW.

WHAT ABOUT FER--? OH, YEAH.

LOG OF THE RENEGADE, NEW STAR DATE 8901.8. FIRST MATE MELCHIOR MAKING THE ENTRY.

WE ARE EN ROUTE TO OUR NEXT TARGET WHILE, AT THIS MOMENT, CAPTAIN ZAIR IS ONCE AGAIN IN A LOCKED ROOM SESSION WITH OUR MYSTERIOUS BACKERS.

WE PRAY, AS ALWAYS, THAT HE EMERGES IN A GOOD MOOD.

CAPTAIN

PSSSHT

ZZZT

HE'S IN A GOOD MOOD.

HUZZAH!

HOORAY!

HURRAY FOR CAPTAIN ZAIR!

24

COMMUNICATIONS WITH THE *COGNOSCENTI* WENT WELL?

AS *WELL AS* COULD BE *EXPECTED.*

YOU SEEM IMPATIENT, CAPTAIN.

PATIENCE IS FOR ACCOUNTANTS AND LIBRARIANS, MELCHIOR.

THE COGNOSCENTI TELL ME THEY'RE *PLEASED* AT THE WAY I'M STIRRING UP HOSTILITIES BETWEEN THE FEDERATION AND THE KLINGONS.

BUT THEY CONTINUE TO GIVE ME THEIR TECHNOLOGY IN DRIPS AND DRABS. LIKE THIS ADVANCED CLOAKING DEVICE, AND THE MODIFICATIONS MADE TO OUR ESCAPE POD.

WHY DO THEY ONLY OFFER *TANTALIZING GLIMPSES* OF WHAT THEY CAN GIVE ME?

PERHAPS THEY'RE CONCERNED YOU'D USE THE POWER TO *TURN* ON THEM.

GOOD POINT.

AND NOT AN *UNFOUNDED* CONCERN. HOW LONG UNTIL WE REACH OUR NEXT TARGET?

FIFTY-ONE MINUTES.

GOOD. MY TRIGGER FINGER IS GETTING ITCHY.

25

OMICRON CETI IV AHEAD, MR. KONOM.

"MR.," KONOM? HOW *CIVILIZED* OF YOU, BEARCLAW. BRING US INTO ORBIT. BLOEMKER, ANY LIFE FORM READINGS?

NOT AT ALL.

THAT'S NOT EXACTLY *PROMISING.* CASTILLE, I'D LIKE YOU TO--

I KNOW, I KNOW. I'M MENTALLY *BROADCASTING* NOW.

ANY SENTIENT MIND, NO MATTER HOW UNTRAINED, WILL PICK-UP MY BROADCAST ON A SUBLIMINAL LEVEL AND *RESPOND.*

GOING LOWER MIGHT *FACILITATE* THINGS.

ALL RIGHT. IF NOTHING ELSE, WE MAY PICK UP SOMETHING VISUALLY.

CAPTAIN'S LOG, STARDATE 8996.7. WE ARE PRESENTLY IN ORBIT AROUND *TRIAMINUS IV.* MOTION SENSORS ON *MAXIMUM,* ALTHOUGH WE ARE CURRENTLY NOT ON RED ALERT.

RELATIONS REMAIN...*CORDIAL...* BETWEEN OURSELVES AND THE PLANETARY RESIDENTS.

AND WE EXPECT YOU NOT TO *BUDGE* FROM ORBIT UNTIL THIS SITUATION IS STRAIGHTENED OUT.

GOVERNOR KORT, YOU *KNOW* THAT WE WILL ACT IN YOUR BEST INTEREST.

WE KNOW NO SUCH *THING.*

26

I can ASSURE you that the ENTERPRISE will be doing its duty in our commitment to this planet. KIRK OUT.

You know, BONES, I keep thinking about how. The ORGANIANS once said that KLINGONS and EARTHMEN would someday be allies.

NOT in THIS generation, JIM.

WELL... maybe in the NEXT one.

STARS! PRETTY!

YES, that's RIGHT. They're PRETTY.

KONOM OUT THERE?

YES. Somewhere out in the STARS.

You know... you seem so SMALL. And then I look out at the stars, where there's one tiny SPECK that's KONOM... and I realize how SMALL we ALL are in space.

GOD, I MISS him.

FORGIVE my INTRUSION, ENSIGN...

OH! MISTER SPOCK, I--

AND similarly, please PARDON my NEXT question.

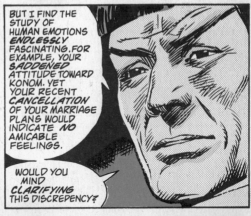

BUT I find the study of human emotions ENDLESSLY FASCINATING. For example, your SADDENED attitude toward KONOM. YET your recent CANCELLATION of your marriage plans would indicate NO AMICABLE feelings.

WOULD you MIND CLARIFYING this DISCREPENCY?

You KNOW about our BREAKING UP?

As you SAY, ENSIGN... EVERYTHING is small in space. Even the COMMUNITY of a STARSHIP.

27

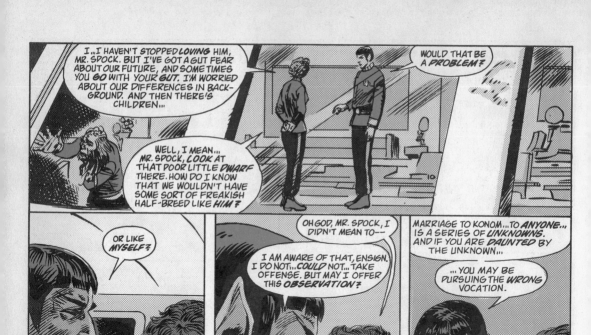

I...I HAVEN'T STOPPED *LOVING* HIM, MR. SPOCK. BUT I'VE GOT A GUT FEAR ABOUT OUR FUTURE, AND SOMETIMES YOU *GO* WITH YOUR *GUT.* I'M WORRIED ABOUT OUR DIFFERENCES IN BACK-GROUND. AND THEN THERE'S CHILDREN...

WOULD THAT BE A *PROBLEM?*

WELL, I MEAN... MR. SPOCK, *LOOK* AT THAT POOR LITTLE *DWARF* THERE. HOW DO I KNOW THAT WE WOULDN'T HAVE SOME SORT OF FREAKISH HALF-BREED LIKE *HIM?*

OR LIKE *MYSELF?*

I AM AWARE OF THAT, ENSIGN. I DO NOT...*COULD* NOT... TAKE OFFENSE. BUT MAY I OFFER THIS *OBSERVATION?*

OH GOD, MR. SPOCK, I DIDN'T MEAN TO--

MARRIAGE TO KONOM...TO *ANYONE*... IS A SERIES OF *UNKNOWNS.* AND IF YOU ARE *DAUNTED* BY THE UNKNOWN...

...YOU MAY BE PURSUING THE *WRONG* VOCATION.

IF YOU'LL *EXCUSE* ME, I'M NEEDED ON THE BRIDGE. THE INHABITANTS OF TRIAMINUS ARE STILL CONCERNED THAT THEY WILL BE ATTACKED SHORTLY, AND THE *CAPTAIN* IS--

ENDICOR. ENDICOR NEXT.

MORON HEARD *BAD* ONES SAY, AFTER THEY MAKE HEAVE-HO WITH OTHER KLINGON. *ENDICOR* NEXT TARGET.

28

THIS IS *MADNESS!* YOU'RE LEAVING YOUR POST AT THIS PLANET TO PURSUE INFORMATION GIVEN YOU BY THIS GENETIC *THROWBACK?*

YOU'LL *HANG* FOR THIS, KIRK!

SIR, I HAVE BEEN HANGED SO OFTEN I HAVE PERMANENT *ROPE* BURNS ON MY NECK.

BUT I'M *STILL HERE*, BECAUSE I'VE LEARNED IN CASES LIKE THIS--

--THAT SOMETIMES YOU HAVE TO GO WITH YOUR *GUT.*

UH... *EXACTLY.*

"MR. SULU, WARP FACTOR EIGHT."

VISUAL SIGHTING, MR. KONOM. AND IT DOESN'T LOOK *GOOD.*

HOW ABOUT THAT? WE AGREE *AGAIN*, BEARCLAW. TAKE US *DOWN*, MISTER O'NEILL.

SHUTTLE LOG, STARDATE 8996.9. KONOM, SHUTTLE COMMANDER REPORTING. WE HAVE MADE PLANETFALL ON OMICRON CETI IV. BUT FROM THE LACK OF LIFE READINGS...

I'D HAVE TO SAY THAT THIS PLACE APPEARS *DEAD.*

29

KONOM, HERE'S SOME MORE BODIES...AND *THIS* ONE IS WEARIN' A FLEET UNIFORM.

MY GUESS IS THAT THAT'S ONE OF THE *ZEPHYR'S ORIGINAL* CREW.

YOU KNOW WHAT IT MIGHT BE. BURROUGHS HAD HIS ENTIRE CREW BEAM DOWN, AND THEN WITH SHIP'S WEAPONS, LAID WASTE TO *EVERYONE!*

BUT THAT'S *INSANE.* WHY WOULD--

PHASER FIRE! *RUN!*

ZZZZAAATT!

YAAARRGH!

YOU... *SAVED ME?* WHY?

BECAUSE *YOU* GOT US INTO THIS, AND I'LL BE DAMNED IF YOU'RE GOING TO *DIE* AND LEAVE *US* BEHIND.

BUT THERE WERE NO LIFE READINGS! *HOW--*

THAT'S HOW.

ANDROIDS.

30

ENDICOR DEAD AHEAD, SIR.

DEAD IS RIGHT.

LOCK PHASERS ON THE MAIN KLINGON OUTPOSTS. BE SURE NOT TO COME *ANYWHERE* NEAR FEDERATION TARGETS.

THE *SELECTIVE* DESTRUCTION WILL *CONFIRM* FOR THE KLINGONS THAT THE FEDERATION IS INDEED SUPPORTING OUR EFFORTS.

AND AS THE FEDERATION AND EMPIRE *DESTROY* EACH OTHER, MY REVENGE WILL --

OH NO!

SIR! WE'VE COME OUT OF WARP SPACE ON A *COLLISION COURSE* WITH RENEGADE!

EVASIVE MANEUVERS! ALL HANDS, *BRACE* FOR *IMPACT*!

31

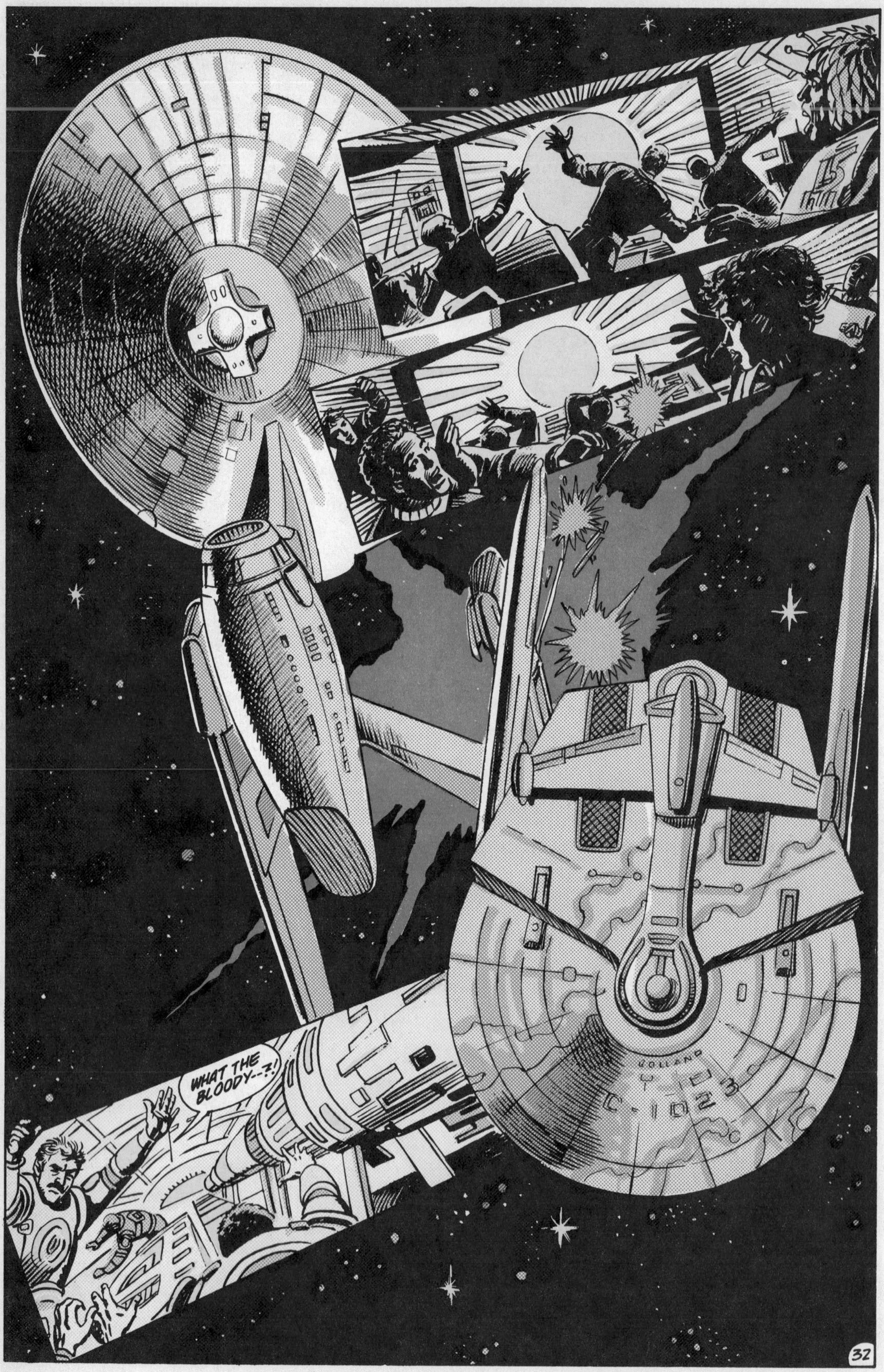
WHAT THE BLOODY--?!
C-1023
32

SECURITY SQUADS A, B AND C, TO MAIN TRANSPORTER ROOM! TRANSPORTER ROOM, LOCK ON RENEGADE'S ENGINEERING SECTION!

DEFLECTORS *UP!* WE *CAN'T!* WE'RE TANGLED WITH THE ENTERPRISE! SHE'S INSIDE OUR FIELD AREA!

I'LL *FIRE* ON HER!

NO! YOU COULD BLOW *HER* UP AND TAKE US *WITH* HER!

MELCHIOR! SEND A TEAM TO THE TRANSPORTER ROOM AND--

CAPTAIN TOR! THEY'VE *TRANSPORTED* INTO THE ENGINE ROOM! THEY'VE--

B AND C SQUADS! CONVERGE ON THE BRIDGE! ALPHA SQUAD, MOP UP *HERE!* AND SOMEBODY SHOOT *THAT* THING UP THERE, IT MUST BE THE CLOAKING DEVICE!

STERNO! I WANT YOU ON *POINT. MOVE!*

33

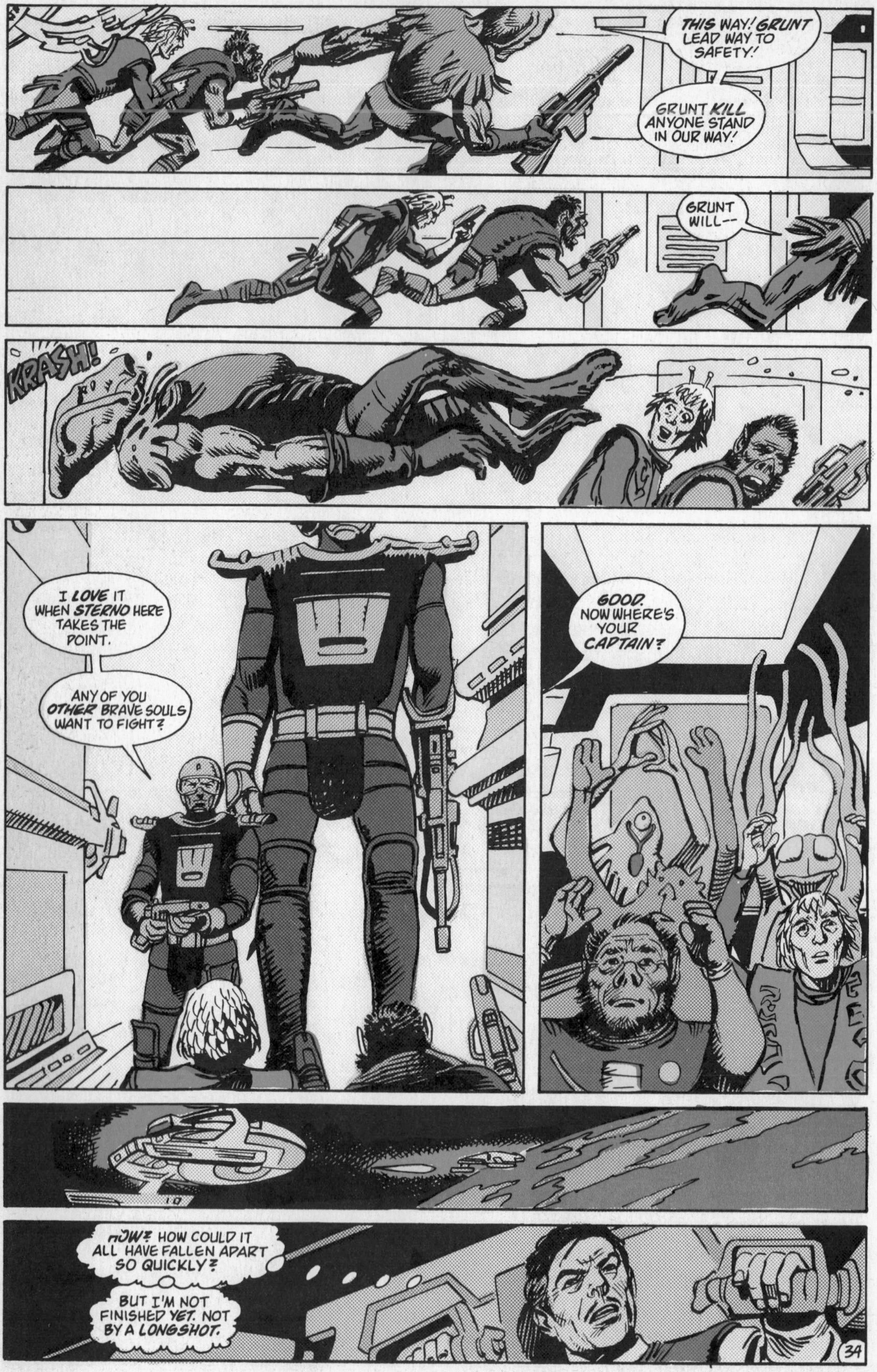
THIS WAY! GRUNT LEAD WAY TO SAFETY!
GRUNT KILL ANYONE STAND IN OUR WAY!
GRUNT WILL--
KRASH!
I LOVE IT WHEN STERNO HERE TAKES THE POINT.
ANY OF YOU OTHER BRAVE SOULS WANT TO FIGHT?
GOOD. NOW WHERE'S YOUR CAPTAIN?
HOW? HOW COULD IT ALL HAVE FALLEN APART SO QUICKLY?
BUT I'M NOT FINISHED YET. NOT BY A LONGSHOT.
34

SHUTTLECRAFT LAUNCHED FROM THE *RENEGADE*, SIR!

TRACTOR BEAMS, MR. SULU.

ALREADY *TRYING*, CAPTAIN! AND THE CRAFT IS -- SHAKING *LOOSE* OF THEM.

WHAT? BUT THAT'S *IMPOSSIBLE!* HOW--

SIR, MESSAGE FROM THE SECURITY CREW ON THE RENEGADE. THEY'VE ROUNDED UP EVERYONE-- EXCEPT THE *CAPTAIN.*

I CAN *GUESS* WHERE HE IS. MR. SULU, SLOW REVERSE THRUST. DISENGAGE US FROM RENEGADE AND *PURSUE* THAT SHUTTLECRAFT. I SUSPECT I KNOW WHERE IT'S GOING--OMICRON CETI III.

CRAZIEST THING, HITTING A SHIP AND SENDING A BOARDING PARTY. *NEXT* THING YOU KNOW WE'LL BE SWINGING ACROSS ON ROPES LIKE PIRATES.

WHERE'S YOUR SENSE OF *ADVENTURE,* DOCTOR?

DOWN THE DRAIN WITH THE ROMULAN ALE YOU CONFISCATED.

YAAA-HAH! THAT'S THE *LAST* OF THEM.

LOOK! A SHUTTLECRAFT COMING IN FOR A LANDING! AND IT'S SURE NOT ONE OF *OURS!*

IT CAME DOWN NEAR THOSE BUILDINGS ABOUT A HALF-MILE OFF! ALL OF YOU, *SPREAD OUT!* TRACK IT DOWN-- MAYBE IT'S A RENEGADER COME HOME TO *ROOST.*

35

THE ANDROIDS MUST HAVE BEEN HERE... TO *KILL* ANYONE WHO CAME DOWN AND SAW WHAT HAPPENED HERE.

NICE.

K'ONOM! YOU'RE ALL RIGHT!

THANKS TO *BEARCLAW* HERE.

I JUST WANTED TO PROVE... I *BELONG.*

WHERE *YOU* BELONG, BEARCLAW, IS THE *BRIG!*

BREEP!

HOLD ON A MOMENT.

KIRK HERE.

OH, *CAPTAIN. HI.* BLOEMKER HERE. I'M IN A BUILDING THEY USED FOR FREEZER STORAGE. I THINK I'VE *FOUND* PHIL BURROUGHS... JUDGING FROM THE *PICTURES* I'VE SEEN.

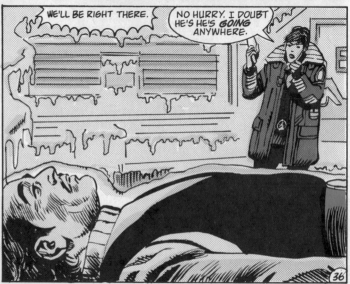

WE'LL BE RIGHT THERE.

NO HURRY. I DOUBT HE'S HE'S *GOING* ANYWHERE.

36

64

CAPTAIN'S LOG SUPPLEMENTAL. IT WOULD SEEM THE RENEGADE AFFAIR IS *OVER*—BUT TOO MANY QUESTIONS ARE STILL HANGING FOR ME TO FEEL *GOOD* ABOUT THIS. AND THE LAST BIT OF CONFUSION IS CONTRIBUTED BY *DOCTOR McCOY.*

HE'S *DEAD* ALL RIGHT, JIM. BUT MORE THAN *THAT...*

"CAPTAIN ZAIR" HERE HAS BEEN DEAD FOR *TWO WEEKS.*

THIS IS GOING TO LOOK *MARVELOUS* IN MY REPORT.

COME ON, JIM. WHERE'S YOUR SENSE OF *ADVENTURE?*

DRY UP, DOCTOR.

THAT SHOULD MAKE IT FEEL BETTER. KONOM...I *MISSED* YOU.

THAT'S GOOD TO HEAR.

I'VE BEEN DOING SOME *THINKING.*

SOME THINKING ABOUT WHAT IT WOULD BE LIKE *WITHOUT* YOU. AND MAYBE...WE *WOULD* BE TAKING LOTS OF CHANCES GETTING MARRIED. LOTS OF THINGS MIGHT *NOT* WORK OUT.

BUT I'VE REALIZED THAT THE ONE CHANCE THAT I *DON'T* WANT TO TAKE IS THE CHANCE OF LOSING YOU. AND...

NO, NANCY. I'VE BEEN THINKING, TOO. I THINK WE SHOULD *FORGET* THE IDEA OF MARRIAGE. THERE'S JUST TOO MUCH *AGAINST* US.

THAT'S WHAT *I* THINK.

YOU *DO?*

I *DO.*

HOW ABOUT *YOU?*

OH, I DO DEFINITELY...

I *DO.*

37

65

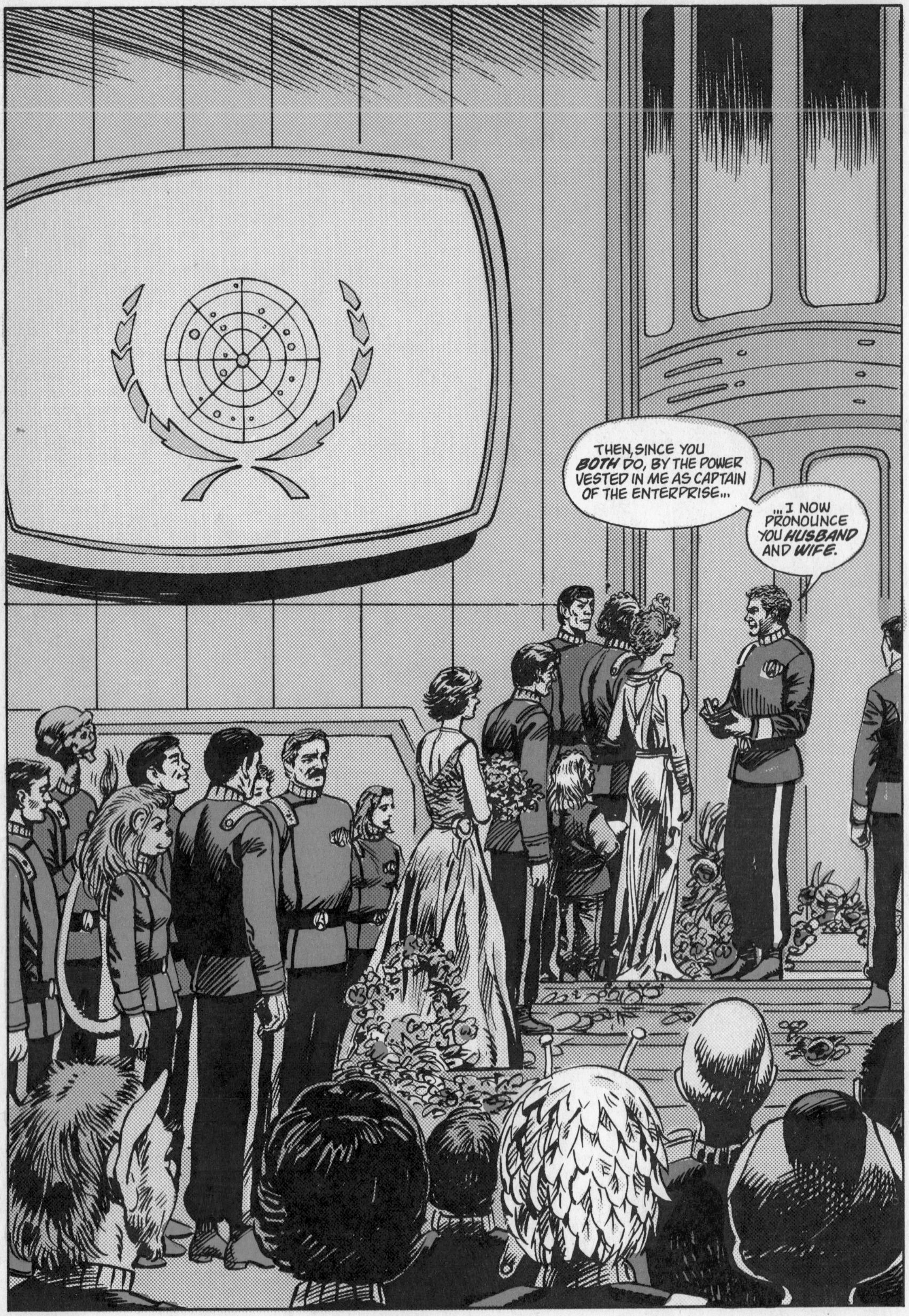
THEN, SINCE YOU BOTH DO, BY THE POWER VESTED IN ME AS CAPTAIN OF THE ENTERPRISE...
...I NOW PRONOUNCE YOU HUSBAND AND WIFE.

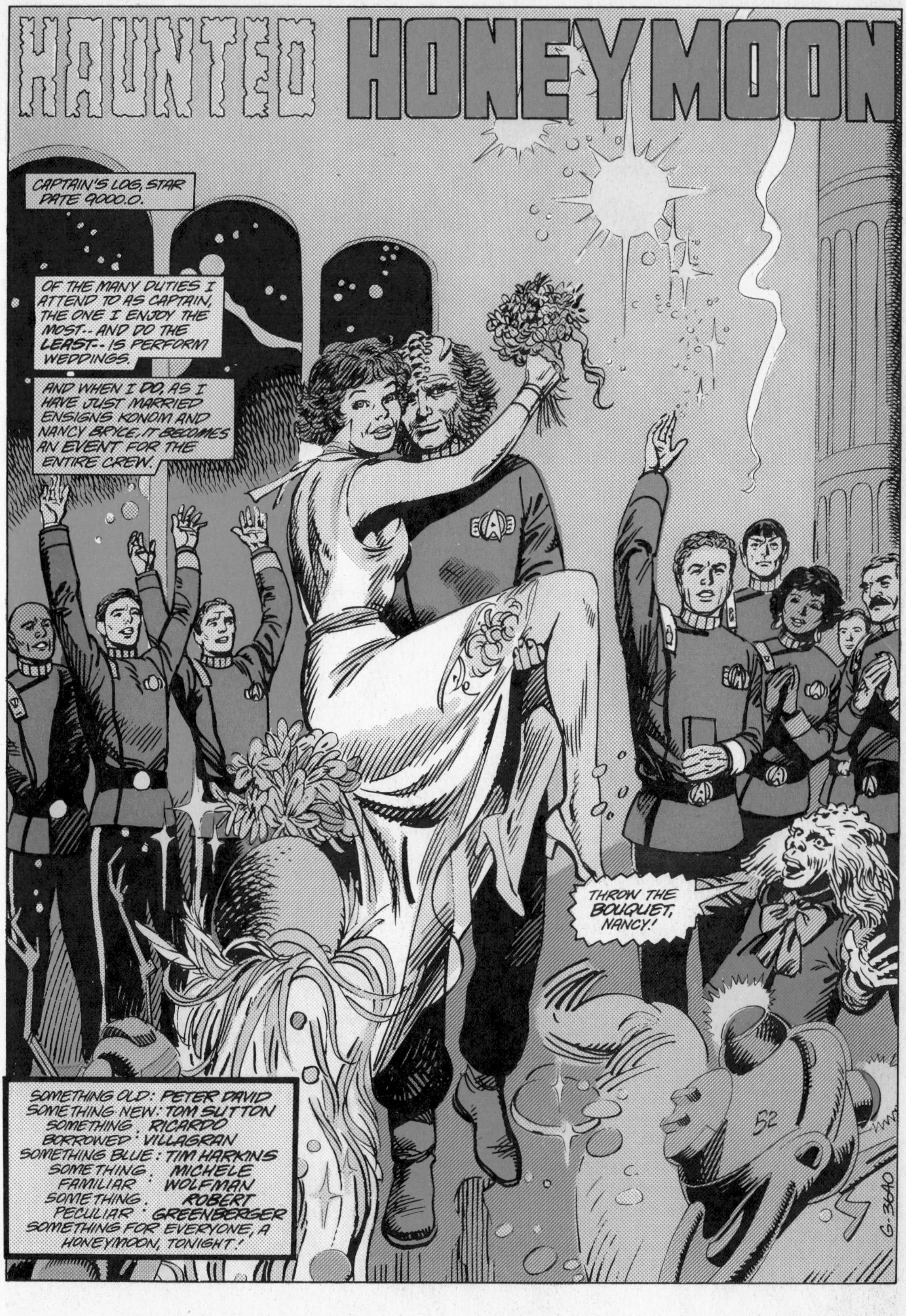
HAUNTED HONEYMOON
CAPTAIN'S LOG, STAR DATE 9000.0.
OF THE MANY DUTIES I ATTEND TO AS CAPTAIN, THE ONE I ENJOY THE MOST-- AND DO THE LEAST-- IS PERFORM WEDDINGS.
AND WHEN I DO, AS I HAVE JUST MARRIED ENSIGNS KONOM AND NANCY BRYCE, IT BECOMES AN EVENT FOR THE ENTIRE CREW.
THROW THE BOUQUET, NANCY!
SOMETHING OLD: PETER DAVID
SOMETHING NEW: TOM SUTTON
SOMETHING BORROWED: RICARDO VILLAGRAN
SOMETHING BLUE: TIM HARKINS
SOMETHING FAMILIAR: MICHELE WOLFMAN
SOMETHING PECULIAR: ROBERT GREENBERGER
SOMETHING FOR EVERYONE, A HONEYMOON, TONIGHT!

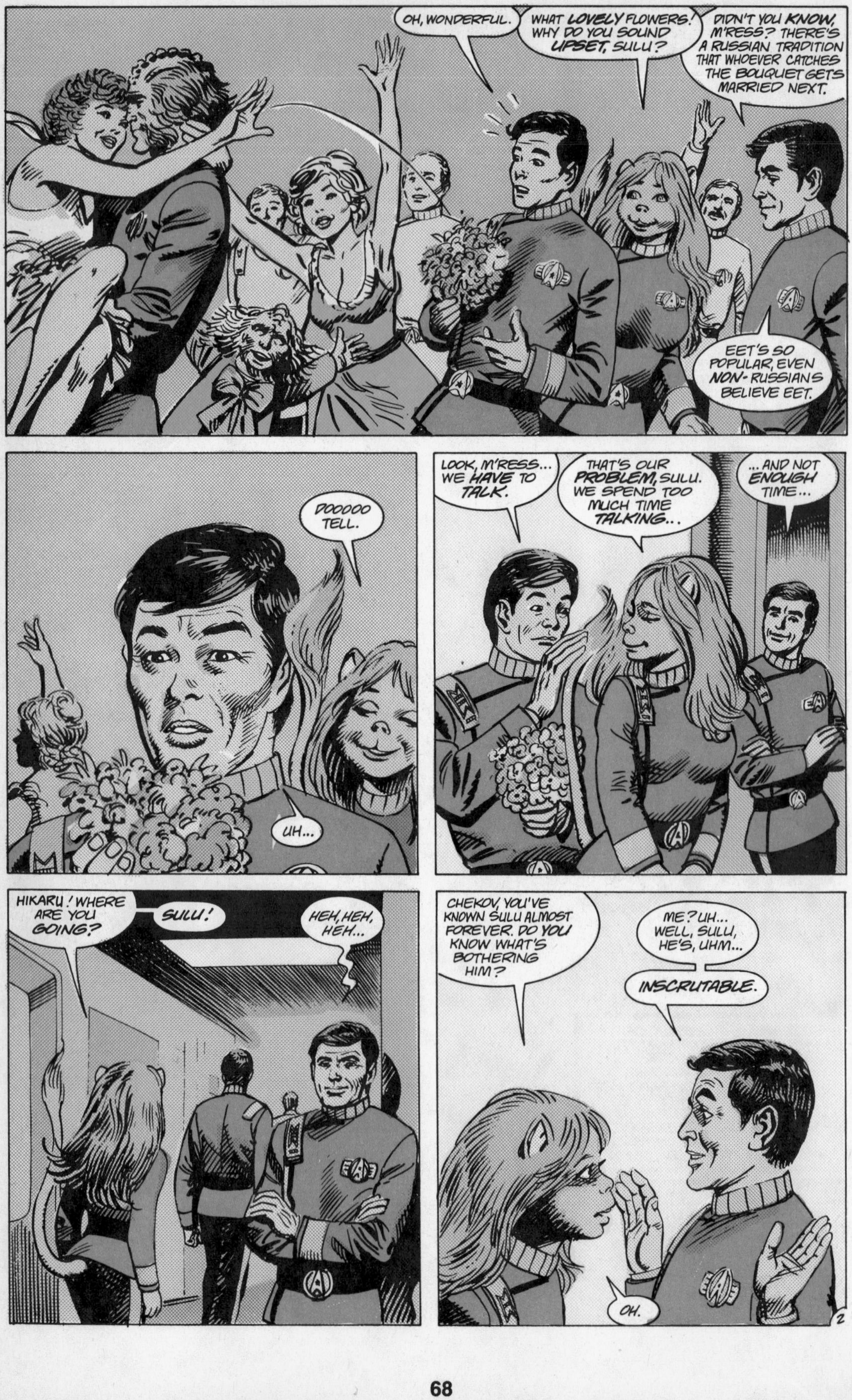
OH, WONDERFUL.
WHAT LOVELY FLOWERS! WHY DO YOU SOUND UPSET, SULU?
DIDN'T YOU KNOW, M'RESS? THERE'S A RUSSIAN TRADITION THAT WHOEVER CATCHES THE BOUQUET GETS MARRIED NEXT.
EET'S SO POPULAR, EVEN NON-RUSSIANS BELIEVE EET.
DOOOOO TELL.
UH...
LOOK, M'RESS... WE HAVE TO TALK.
THAT'S OUR PROBLEM, SULU. WE SPEND TOO MUCH TIME TALKING...
...AND NOT ENOUGH TIME...
HIKARU! WHERE ARE YOU GOING?
SULU!
HEH, HEH, HEH...
CHEKOV, YOU'VE KNOWN SULU ALMOST FOREVER. DO YOU KNOW WHAT'S BOTHERING HIM?
ME? UH... WELL, SULU, HE'S, UHM...
INSCRUTABLE.
OH.
2

WILLIAM BEARCLAW! YOU'RE THE ONLY PERSON WITHIN TEN METERS WHO ISN'T GRINNING. YOU'VE GOT TO TELL ME WHAT'S BOTHERING YOU!

LOOK, ELIZABETH, I --

I BELIEVE I CAN ANSWER YOUR QUESTION, ENSIGN SHERWOOD.

MR. BEARCLAW HERE IS PROBABLY CONCERNED HE'LL BE COURT-MARTIALED.

OH, DISOBEYING A DIRECT ORDER, INSUBORDINATION, STOWING AWAY ON A SHUTTLECRAFT--

COURT-MARTIALED! FOR WHAT?!

SIR.

LOOK, CAPTAIN, EVERYTHING I DID, I DID BECAUSE I WANTED TO IMPRESS YOU, SIR.

THAT'S ALL. I WANTED TO SHOW YOU I COULD MAKE A VALUABLE CONTRIBUTION.

AND I DID. I SAVED THE LIFE OF THE KLINGON WHO JUST GOT MARRIED. DOESN'T THAT COUNT FOR SOMETHING?

IT SHOULDN'T. THEN AGAIN, I'VE ALWAYS HAD A SOFT SPOT FOR BRAVERY MOTIVATED BY DETERMINED STUPIDITY. OR VICE VERSA.

FOR THAT REASON, I WILL NOT INITIATE COURT-MARTIAL PROCEEDINGS.

BUT IF YOU THINK YOUR BONEHEAD MANEUVER WAS YOUR TICKET BACK INTO MY GOOD GRACES, YOU'RE SADLY MISTAKEN.

STARFLEET HAS APPROVED MY TRANSFER REQUEST FOR YOU. AT FIRST OPPORTUNITY, YOU'RE GONE, MISTER.

BILL...

BILL...LET ME TALK TO HIM. MAYBE...

NO.

NO. SOMETIMES, YOU REACH A POINT WHERE WORDS JUST DON'T CUT IT ANYMORE.

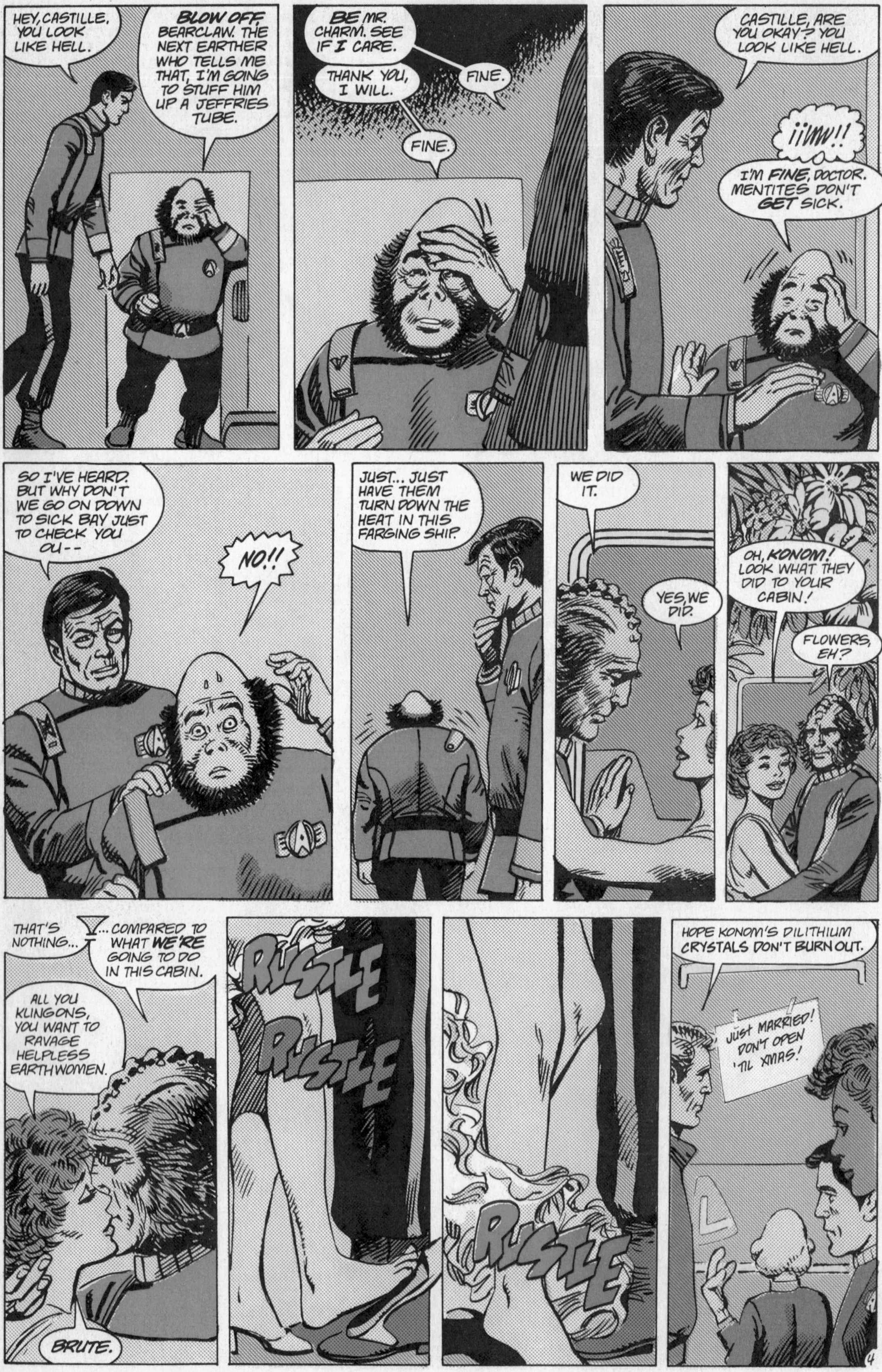
HEY, CASTILLE. YOU LOOK LIKE HELL.
BLOW OFF, BEARCLAW. THE NEXT EARTHER WHO TELLS ME THAT, I'M GOING TO STUFF HIM UP A JEFFRIES TUBE.
BE MR. CHARM. SEE IF I CARE.
FINE.
THANK YOU, I WILL.
FINE.
CASTILLE, ARE YOU OKAY? YOU LOOK LIKE HELL.
¡¡UUW!!
I'M FINE, DOCTOR. MENTITES DON'T GET SICK.
SO I'VE HEARD. BUT WHY DON'T WE GO ON DOWN TO SICK BAY JUST TO CHECK YOU OU--
NO!!
JUST... JUST HAVE THEM TURN DOWN THE HEAT IN THIS FARGING SHIP.
WE DID IT.
YES, WE DID.
OH, KONOM! LOOK WHAT THEY DID TO YOUR CABIN!
FLOWERS, EH?
THAT'S NOTHING...
...COMPARED TO WHAT WE'RE GOING TO DO IN THIS CABIN.
ALL YOU KLINGONS, YOU WANT TO RAVAGE HELPLESS EARTHWOMEN.
BRUTE.
RUSTLE
RUSTLE
RUSTLE
HOPE KONOM'S DILITHIUM CRYSTALS DON'T BURN OUT.
JUST MARRIED! DON'T OPEN 'TIL XMAS!
4

ENTERPRISE MEDICAL LOG; STAR DATE 9000.1. WE HAVE RENDEZVOUSED AS SCHEDULED WITH THE MEDICAL TRANSPORT SHIP WEINSTEIN...

THE WEINSTEIN HAS TRANSPORTED OVER A SHIPMENT OF SERUM THAT IS DESPERATELY NEEDED FOR A PLAGUE RAVAGING THE PLANET CHAPIN ONE. IT SHOULD BE A RELATIVELY ROUTINE MISSION...

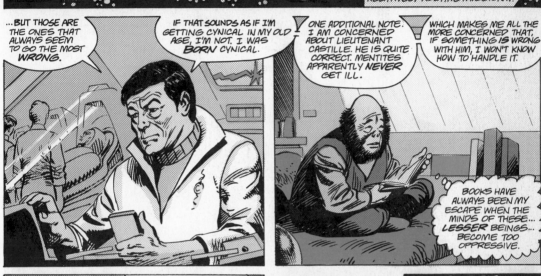

...BUT THOSE ARE THE ONES THAT ALWAYS SEEM TO GO THE MOST **WRONG.**

IF THAT SOUNDS AS IF I'M GETTING CYNICAL IN MY OLD AGE, I'M NOT. I WAS **BORN** CYNICAL.

ONE ADDITIONAL NOTE. I AM CONCERNED ABOUT LIEUTENANT CASTILLE. HE IS QUITE CORRECT. MENTITES APPARENTLY **NEVER** GET ILL.

WHICH MAKES ME ALL THE MORE CONCERNED THAT, IF SOMETHING IS WRONG WITH HIM, I WON'T KNOW HOW TO HANDLE IT.

BOOKS HAVE ALWAYS BEEN MY ESCAPE WHEN THE MINDS OF THESE... **LESSER** BEINGS... BECOME TOO OPPRESSIVE.

BUT NOW I CAN'T EVEN CONCENTRATE ON **THAT.** WHAT'S HAPPENING?

DANTE
INFERNO

DECLINE AND FALL OF THE ROMAN EMPIRE

I'M THE STRONGEST TELEPATH ON THIS SHIP AND IT'S LIKE MY **OWN** MIND IS CLOSED TO ME.

HAVE TO REST. JUST... JUST **REST.**

I DO NOT HAVE TO TELL YOU THAT **TIME** IS OF THE ESSENCE ON THIS MISSION.

MAY I POINT OUT, CAPTAIN, THAT YOU JUST DID.

THERE WILLNA BE A PROBLEM, SIR. MUH **ENGINES** WILL--

EMPHASIS, MR. SPOCK. **EMPHASIS.**

5

?

CAPTAIN?

CAPTAIN, ARE YOU QUITE ALL RIGHT?

MUH...

MUH... MISTER SPOCK... ARE YOU A PENGUIN?

NOT THAT I AM AWARE OF, SIR.

PENGUIN?

EXCUSE ME. I'M, UH...

I'M GOING TO... EXCUSE ME.

THERE'S AN OLD GAG THAT GOES "ARE YOU A TURTLE?" IS THAT WHAT THE CAPTAIN WAS DOING?

I DINNA THINK HE WAS JOKING, MR. SULU. HE LOOKED AS IF HE'D SEEN A... A...

A PENGUIN.

6

72

BRIDGE.

HOLD THE *LIFT!*

SULU! NOW ISN'T *THIS* A BIT OF LUCK?

M'RESS, I'M IN KIND OF A *HURRY...*

SLOW DOWN, YOU'LL LIVE LONGER.

CLICK

ALSO I'M HOLDING US BETWEEN FLOORS SO WE CAN CHAT.

NOW *OUT* WITH IT, SULU. WHY ARE YOU AVOIDING ME?

AND NO MORE PUSSY-FOOTING AROUND.

LISTEN, M'RESS... THAT TIME AT THE BACHELOR PARTY SHOULD *NEVER* HAVE HAPPENED. I WAS DRUNK, WASN'T *THINKING* STRAIGHT.

WHO *CARES* WHY IT HAPPENED? IT DID.

I'M HUMAN, YOU'RE CAITIAN. IT MAKES ME *UNCOMFORTABLE.* I MEAN, WHEN DID YOU LAST SEE A *SUCCESSFUL* INTERSPECIES RELATIONSHIP?

ENSIGN KONOM

JUST MARRIED! DON'T OPEN 'TIL XMAS!

ALL RIGHT, *BESIDES* THEM.

BUT SULU, WHO SAID *ANYTHING* ABOUT A RELATIONSHIP? CAN'T WE JUST *FOOL AROUND?*

RELAX! THIS ISN'T THE 20th CENTURY, YOU KNOW.

BREEP BREEP

7

STATUS REPORT, MR. AREX. WHY ARE WE ON RED ALERT?

BECAUSE OF *THAT*, MR. SULU!

HOLY...

IT MUST BE *MILES* LONG! WHERE DID IT *COME* FROM?

IT WAS... IT WAS JUST *THERE!*

M'RESS, SENSOR READINGS.

NOTHING.

NOTHING? PERMIT *ME*, LIEUTENANT.

APPARENTLY IT JUST MATERIALIZED FROM *NOWHERE*, CAPTAIN.

A CLOAKING DEVICE? BUT THE POWER NEEDED TO CLOAK IT WOULD BE... BE...

A *LOT*.

THANK YOU, ENSIGN.

UHURA...

ALREADY *TRYING*, SIR. NO ANSWER ON ANY HAILING FREQUENCY.

CAPTAIN, I'VE *COMPLETED* MY SENSOR SWEEP.

GOOD, SPOCK. NO *OFFENSE*, M'RESS, BUT *SPOCK* HAS THE *EXPERIENCE*. READINGS, SPOCK?

NOTHING, SIR.

8

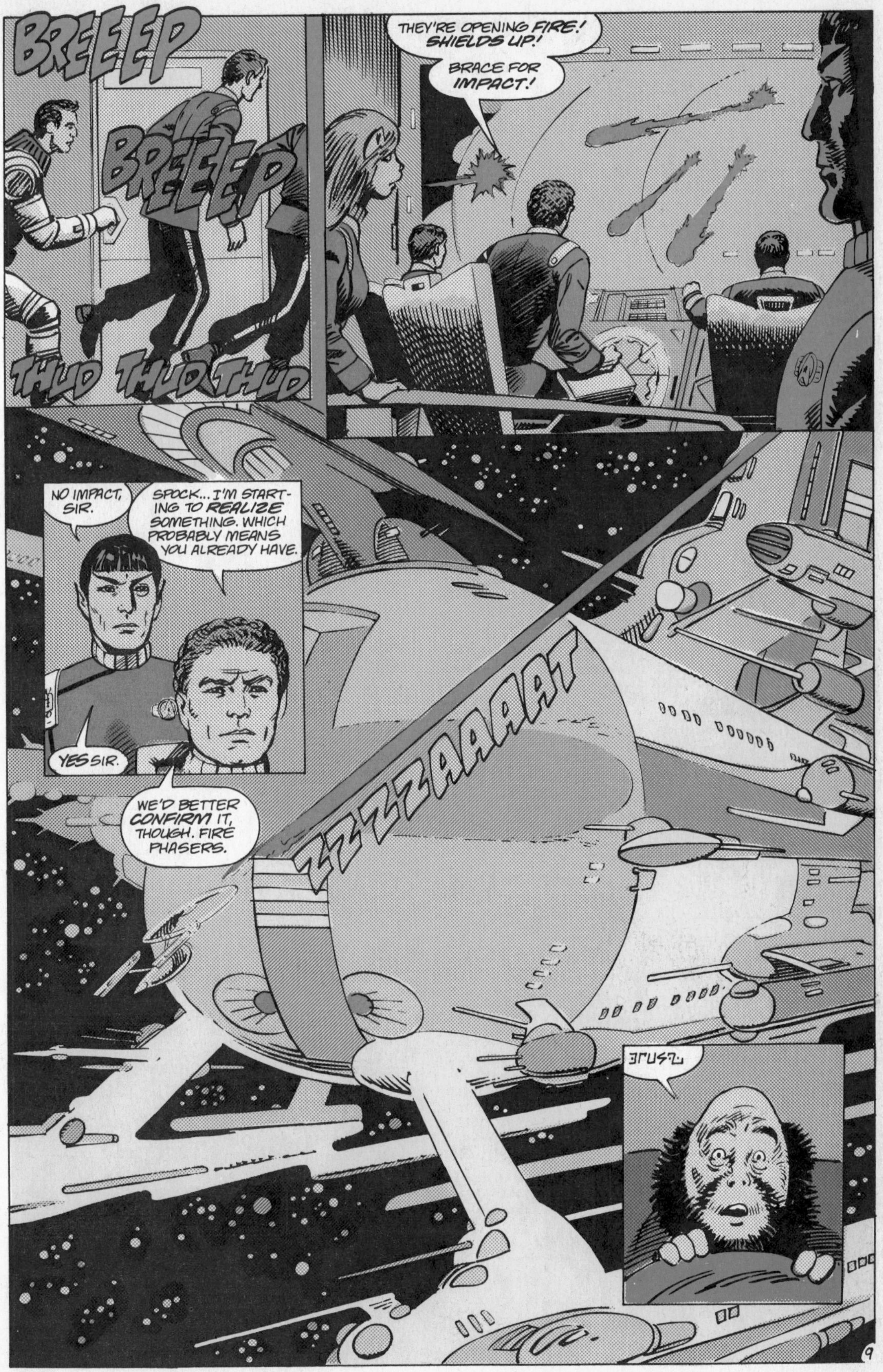
BREEEP
BREEEP
THUD THUD THUD
THEY'RE OPENING FIRE! SHIELDS UP!
BRACE FOR IMPACT!
NO IMPACT, SIR.
SPOCK... I'M STARTING TO REALIZE SOMETHING. WHICH PROBABLY MEANS YOU ALREADY HAVE.
YES SIR.
WE'D BETTER CONFIRM IT, THOUGH. FIRE PHASERS.
ZZZZAAAAAT

SECURE FROM GENERAL QUARTERS. CANCEL RED ALERT.

OPINIONS, MR. SPOCK?

IT'S... GONE.

IN THE EARTH VERNACULAR, SIR, I BELIEVE WE'VE BEEN "HAD!"

BRE-EEP BREE*

JUST MARRIED! DON'T OPEN 'TIL XMAS!

JUST MARRIED! DON'T OPEN 'TIL XMAS!

KONOM...did you HEAR something?

Like what?

Nothing. FORGET IT.

MARRIED! DON'T OPEN XMAS!

ENSIGN KONOM

HEY, *CASTILLE*, REMATCH TONIGHT IN THE BOWLING ALLEY?

CASTILLE?

WONDER WHAT'S WITH *HIM?*

FIFTEEN MINUTES AND I'M OFF SHIFT.

NO ONE WILL CARE IF I JUST CRUISE THESE LAST--

WHAT IN--?!

CASTILLE! HELP!!

HELP!

Mmmfbhh--

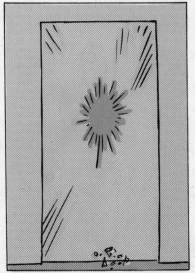

BURP!

77

BLOCK YOUR EARS

HEY! HOLD THE TURBOLIFT!

GRRRARRR

HE SAID THERE WAS A *WHAT* IN THE TURBOLIFT?

A THREE-HEADED DOG, KEPTIN. AND REPORTS ARE COMING FROM ALL OVER THE *SHIP*.

EVERYTHING FROM MONSTERS TO ANIMATED FURNITURE.

FULL SECURITY *ALERT*, MR. CHEKOV. PHASERS SET ON STUN.

SOMEONE OR *SOMETHING* IS ON THIS SHIP CAUSING THESE ILLUSIONS, AND I WANT THE SOURCE FOUND.

STAY *TIGHT*, PEOPLE. STERNO, I WANT *YOU* UP FRONT.

12

YOUR SQUAD *FIND* ANYTHING, APPEL?

NOTHING, HAZZARD. OF COURSE, IT WOULD HELP IF WE KNEW WHAT WE WERE *LOOKING* FOR.

JIM... HAVE THEM ROUND UP *CASTILLE.*

HE'S A PROJECTING TELEPATH. HE *COULD* BE BEHIND THIS, IF ANYONE IS.

BUT, WHY, BONES?

I DON'T KNOW.

ENGINEERING

CHIEF ENGINEER

CAPTAIN. THIS IS SCOTT IN ENGINEERING.

YES, MR. SCOTT?

THERE'S SECURITY MEN ALL *OVER* THE PLACE, CAPTAIN. AH WOULD DEARLY LOVE TO KNOW WHAT'S *HAPPENING.*

IF YE'LL BE NEEDING MUH ENGINES FOR EMERGENCY *MANEUVERS,* AH COULD USE A--

13

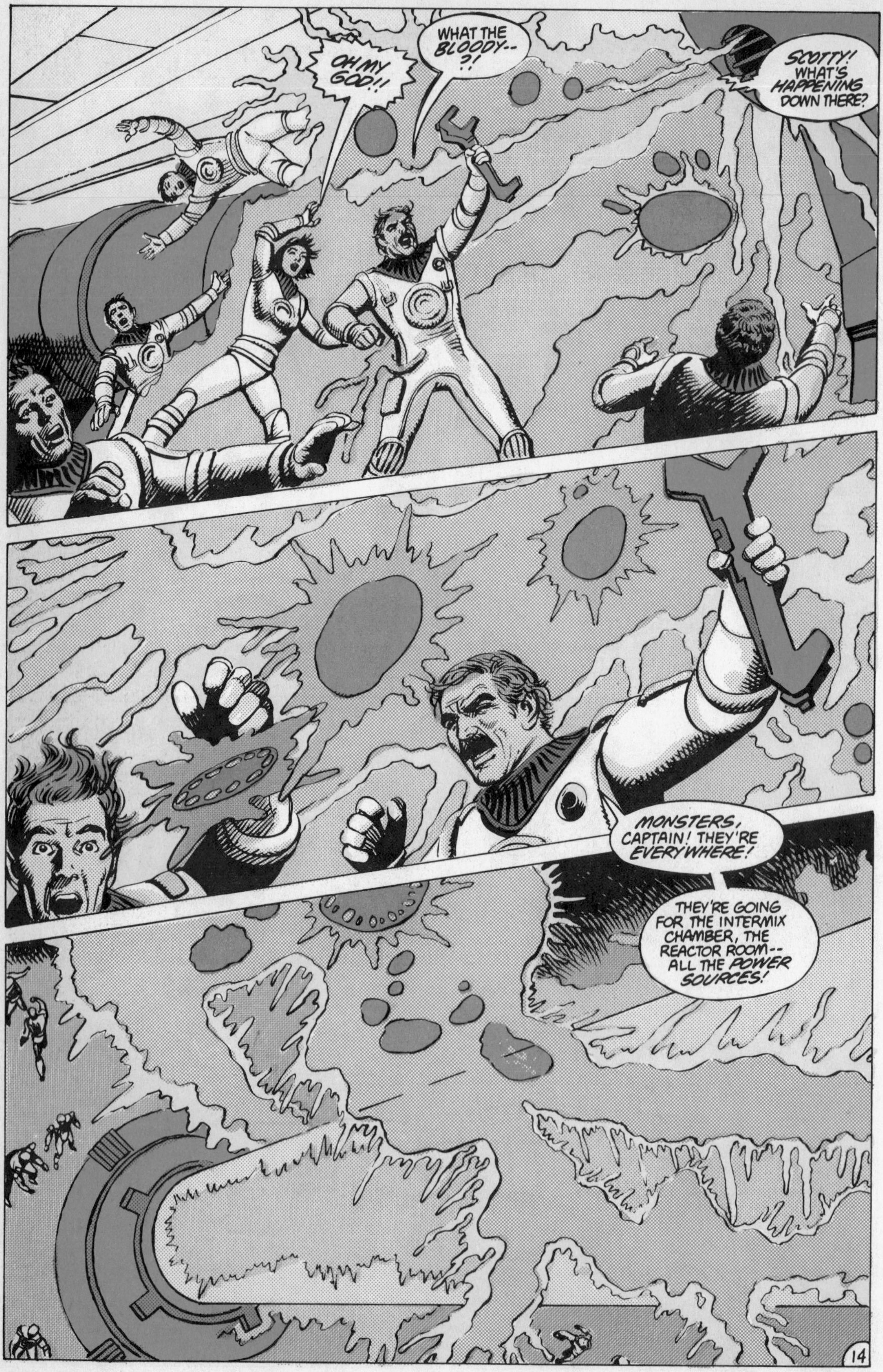
OH MY GOD!!
WHAT THE BLOODY-- ?!
SCOTTY! WHAT'S HAPPENING DOWN THERE?
MONSTERS, CAPTAIN! THEY'RE EVERYWHERE!
THEY'RE GOING FOR THE INTERMIX CHAMBER, THE REACTOR ROOM-- ALL THE POWER SOURCES!
14

THEY'RE LEECHING OFF THE POWER-- GETTING *BIGGER!*

AH GOTTA SHUT DOWN THE SYSTEMS BEFORE IT'S *TOO LATE!*

SCOTTY! *WAIT!!*

KEPTIN! POWER LEVELS DROPPING ALL OVER THE--

--SHIP.

ENGINEERING

PHASER RIFLES, ON STUN OR WE'LL KILL OUR OWN PEOPLE

BLOEMKER, STERNO-- FIRE INTO THE *CREATURE!*

15

WAIT! NOT HIM! DON'T--

IT HAS MR. SCOTT!

Unnnhh!

CAPTAIN'S LOG, STAR DATE 9000.2. PANDEMONIUM HAS GRIPPED THE SHIP. BIZARRE ILLUSIONS HAVE SPRUNG TO LIFE. SECURITY FORCES HAVE CONVERGED ON ENGINEERING TO FIGHT MONSTERS THAT MR. SCOTT CLAIMED WERE ATTACKING.

16

IT IS MY *BELIEF* THAT WHATEVER THEY'RE ENCOUNTERING *ISN'T REALLY THERE.*

BUT THESE *ILLUSIONS* ARE SO *OVERPOWERING* THAT THEY COMPLETELY *CONVINCE* THE VICTIM OF THEIR *REALITY.* THEY IMAGINE THEMSELVES TO BE *ATTACKED.* THEY "SEE" *EACH OTHER* IN THE CREATURE'S CLUTCHES--AND ACT *ACCORDINGLY.*

AND IF THERE'S AS MUCH *FIRE-POWER* FLYING AROUND DOWN THERE AS I *BELIEVE* THERE TO BE--

17

--THEN ULTIMATELY IT WON'T MAKE ANY DIFFERENCE *WHAT* THEY BELIEVE. THE PHASER BLASTS WILL BE QUITE *REAL,* AND WITH WILD SHOTS THEY COULD DECOMMISSION EACH OTHER.

POWER IS DOWN ALL OVER THE *SHIP.* TURBOLIFTS ARE FROZEN. WE'RE STRUGGLING TO BRING AUXILIARY POWER ON LINE, BUT PHASER BLASTS IN ENGINEERING MAY HAVE HIT SYSTEMS CONTROLS AND MONITERING SECTIONS. WE'RE RIDING A *BLIND HORSE.*

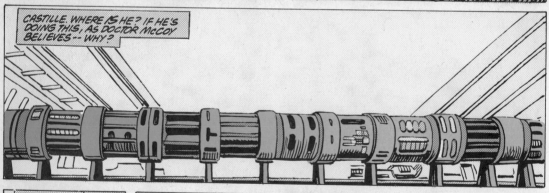

CASTILLE. WHERE IS HE? IF HE'S DOING THIS, AS DOCTOR McCOY BELIEVES -- *WHY?*

HAS HE LOST HIS *MIND?*

T DECK

UKꟼNOϴႶ

BOTANICA GARDEN

ᘓUᙅᘓᗋꝀ VOV

18

SECURITY TO *BRIDGE.* I'VE SPOTTED LIEUTENANT CASTILLE. HE'S HEADING INTO THE BOTANICAL GARDENS.

LIEUTENANT! I HAVE ORDERS TO ARREST YOU AND BRING YOU TO THE *BRIDGE.*

NOW, LIEUTENANT. DON'T FORCE ME TO--

LIEUTENANT!

DAEV

NYAAH.

AAAH

AAAARR

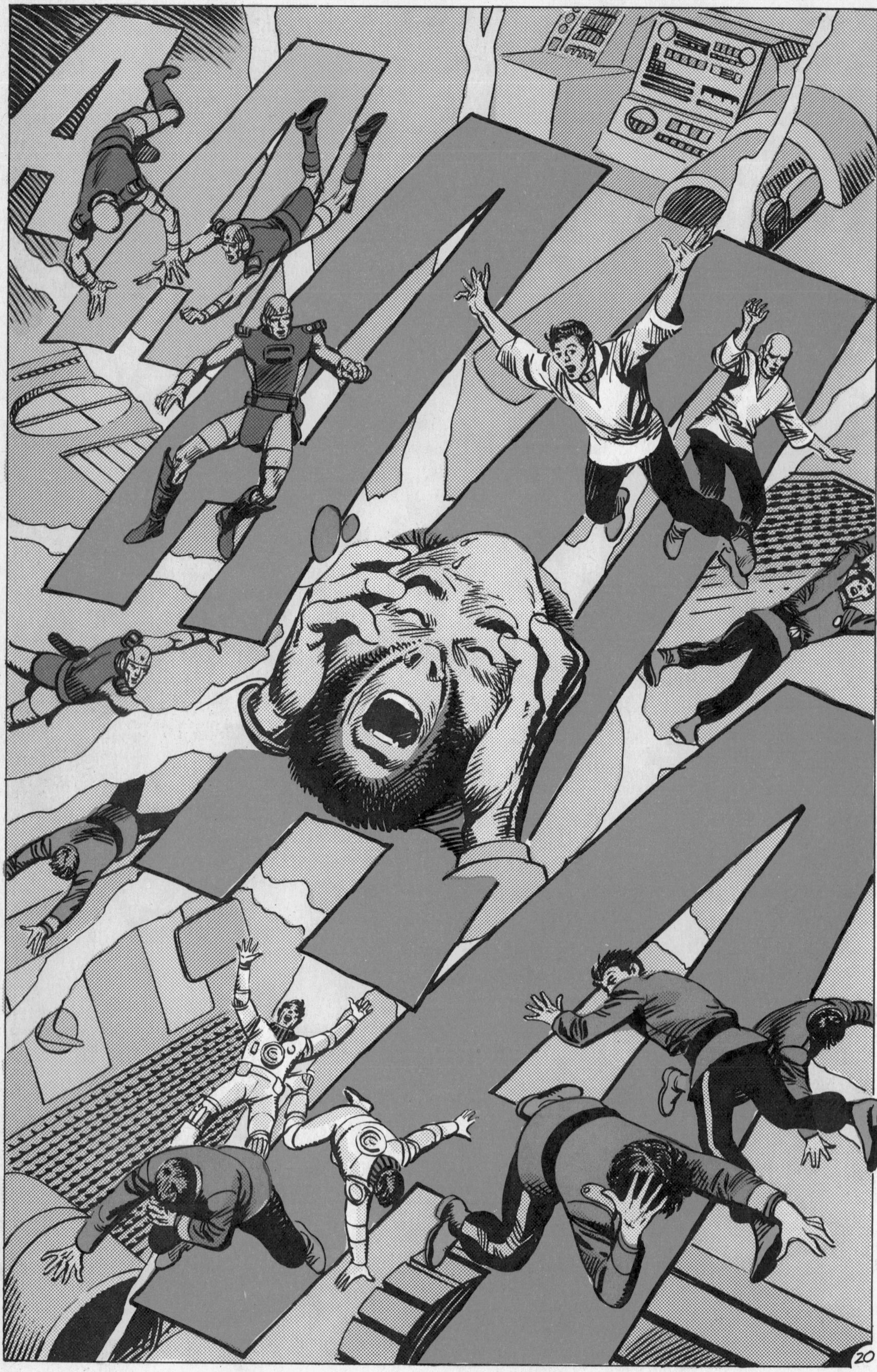

Unnnhh...

SPOCK! WHAT'S--

A A A A A A A A A A A A A A A

WHAT... WHAT... THE HELL WAS THAT?

CAPTAIN... NO RESPONSE FROM ANY OF THE LOWER DECKS.

ALL HANDS, REPORT. SPOCK, ARE YOU--

I AM... SOMEWHAT RECOVERED, CAPTAIN.

ANY THEORIES?

ALWAYS, CAPTAIN.

I BELIEVE THAT LIEUTENANT CASTILLE UNLEASHED SOME MANNER OF PSYCHIC BLAST, INCAPACITATING MOST OF THE CREW.

SINCE HE WAS REPORTED IN BOTANICAL, WE WERE THE LEAST AFFECTED, BEING FARTHEST AWAY. THE REST OF THE CREW WAS DOUBTLESS LESS FORTUNATE.

WE HAVE TO GET DOWN THERE, BRING HIM OUT OF IT.

IT WILL NOT BE EASY, SIR HE IS STILL PROJECTING ILLUSIONS--

COME ON, SPOCK, HOW DIFFICULT CAN IT-- HEY!

THERE! LIGHTS ON, KEP--

I'LL BE DAMNED.

21

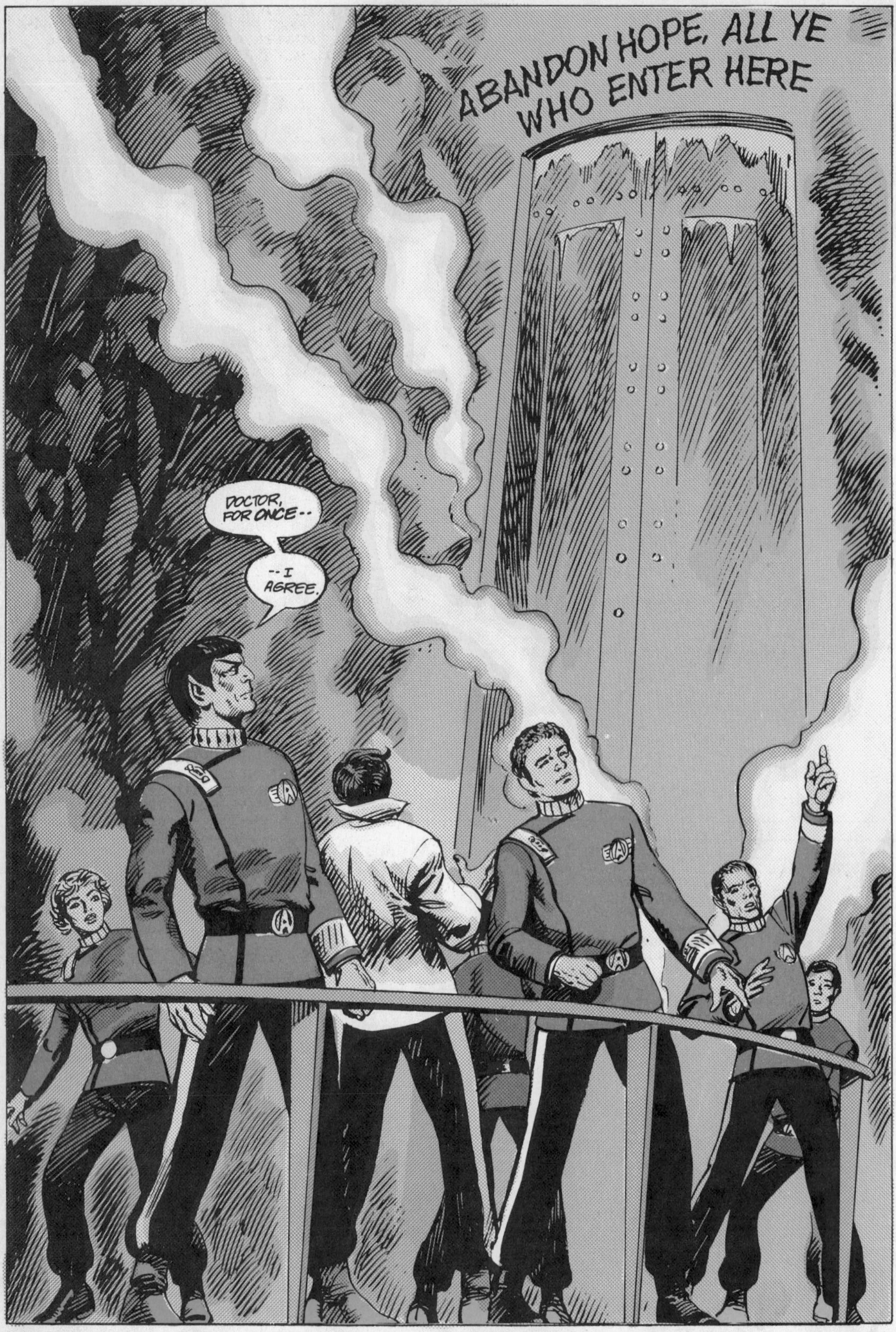

ABANDON HOPE, ALL YE WHO ENTER HERE
DOCTOR, FOR ONCE--
--I AGREE.

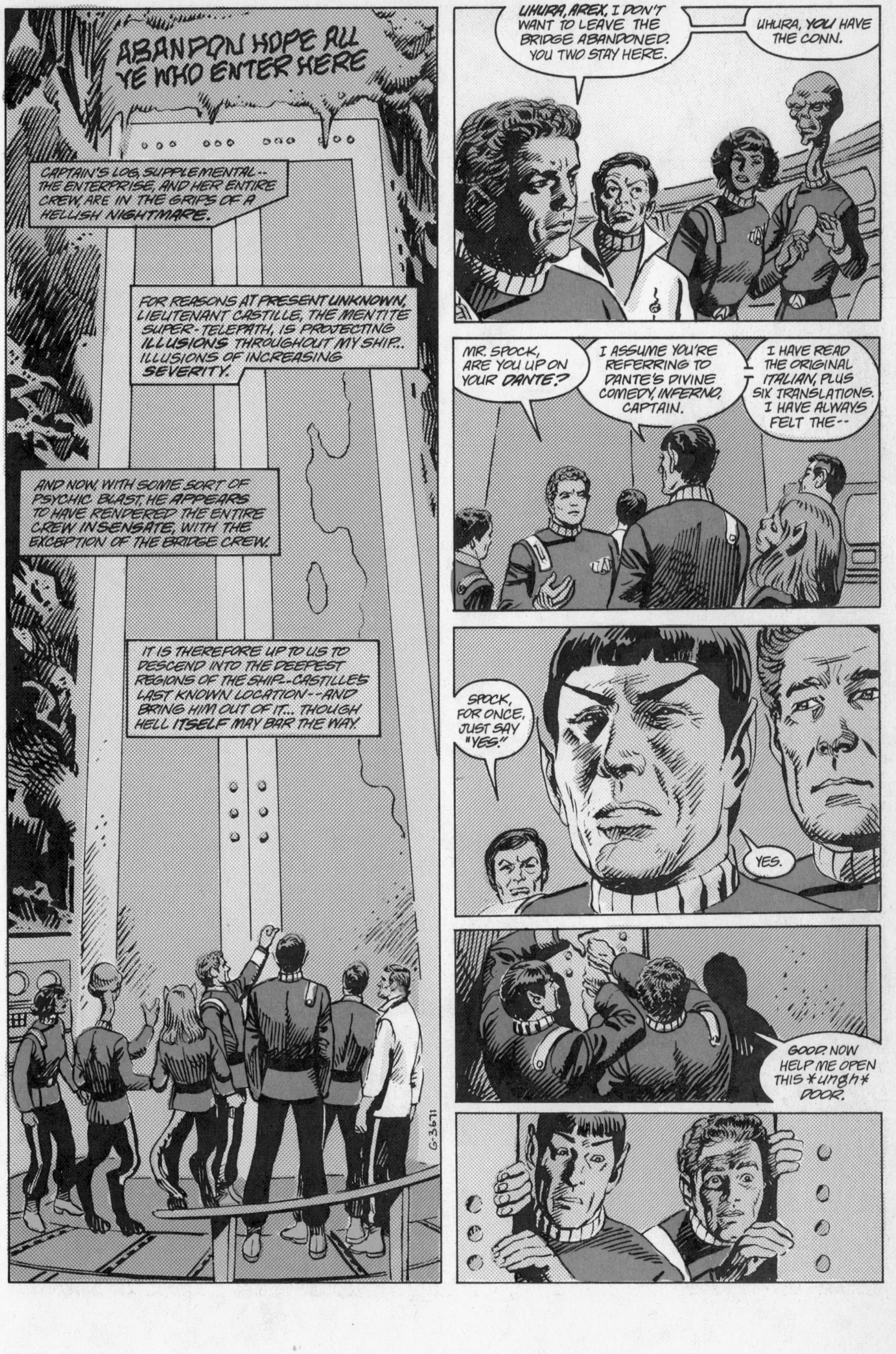
ABANDON HOPE ALL YE WHO ENTER HERE
CAPTAIN'S LOG, SUPPLEMENTAL-- THE ENTERPRISE, AND HER ENTIRE CREW, ARE IN THE GRIPS OF A HELLISH NIGHTMARE.
FOR REASONS AT PRESENT UNKNOWN, LIEUTENANT CASTILLE, THE MENTITE SUPER-TELEPATH, IS PROJECTING ILLUSIONS THROUGHOUT MY SHIP.. ILLUSIONS OF INCREASING SEVERITY.
AND NOW, WITH SOME SORT OF PSYCHIC BLAST, HE APPEARS TO HAVE RENDERED THE ENTIRE CREW INSENSATE, WITH THE EXCEPTION OF THE BRIDGE CREW.
IT IS THEREFORE UP TO US TO DESCEND INTO THE DEEPEST REGIONS OF THE SHIP--CASTILLE'S LAST KNOWN LOCATION--AND BRING HIM OUT OF IT... THOUGH HELL ITSELF MAY BAR THE WAY.
UHURA, AREX, I DON'T WANT TO LEAVE THE BRIDGE ABANDONED. YOU TWO STAY HERE.
UHURA, YOU HAVE THE CONN.
MR. SPOCK, ARE YOU UP ON YOUR DANTE?
I ASSUME YOU'RE REFERRING TO DANTE'S DIVINE COMEDY, INFERNO, CAPTAIN.
I HAVE READ THE ORIGINAL ITALIAN, PLUS SIX TRANSLATIONS. I HAVE ALWAYS FELT THE--
SPOCK, FOR ONCE, JUST SAY "YES."
YES.
GOOD. NOW HELP ME OPEN THIS *ungh* DOOR.

STAR TREK

HELL IN A HANDBASKET

YOUR GUIDES FOR TODAY:
PETER DAVID WRITER
TOM SUTTON AND
RICARDO VILLAGRAN ARTISTS
TIM HARKINS LETTERER
MICHELE WOLFMAN COLORIST
ROBERT GREENBERGER EDITOR

QUOTES FROM: THE DIVINE COMEDY OF DANTE ALIGHIERI: INFERNO, TRANSLATED BY ALLEN MANDELBAUM, © 1980 ALLEN MANDELBAUM. BY PERMISSION OF BANTAM BOOKS.

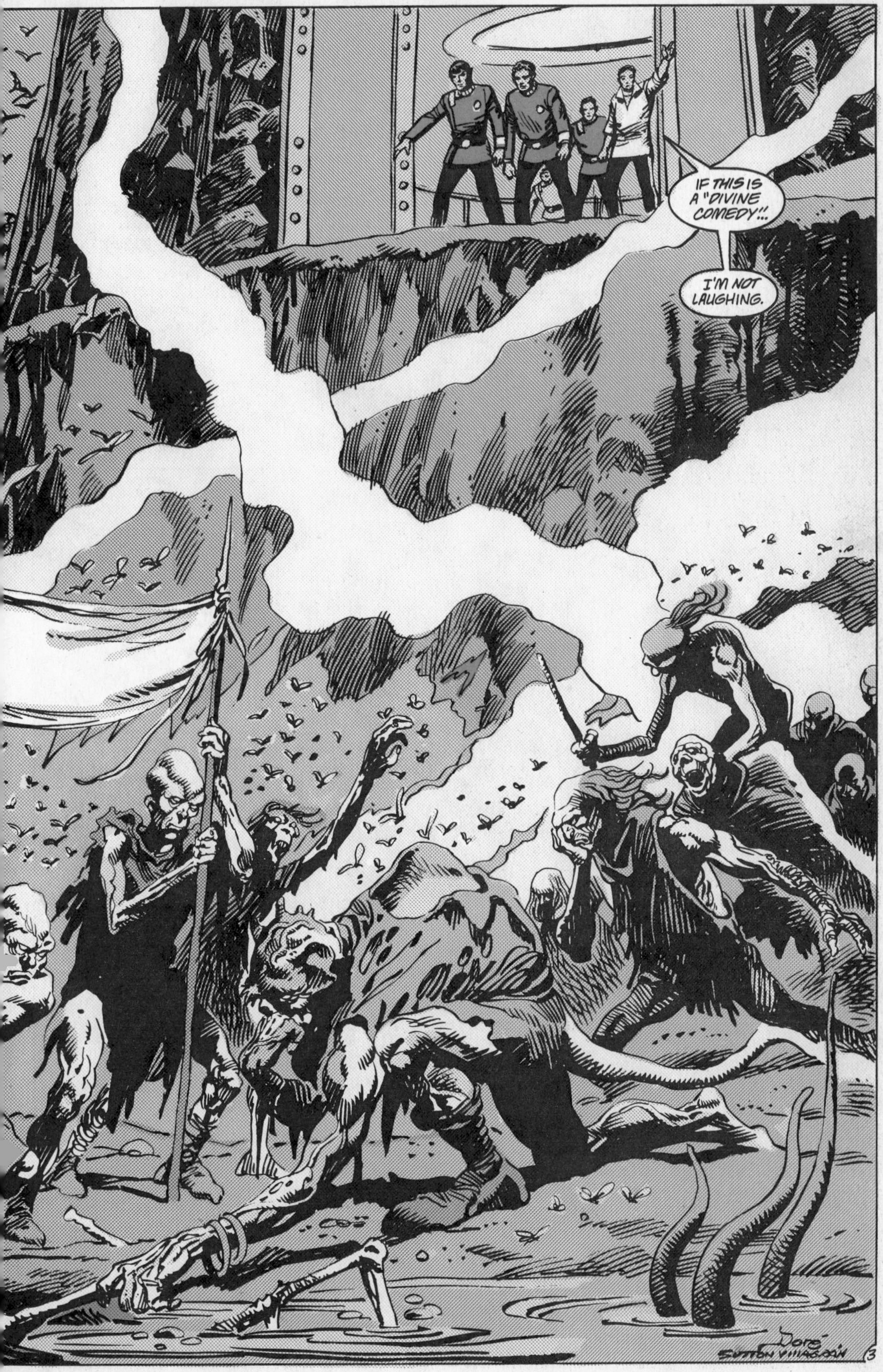
IF THIS IS A "DIVINE COMEDY"!!
I'M NOT LAUGHING.

THIS IS... THIS IS INSANE.

THERE'S NO... THERE'S NO POINT OF REFERENCE. I KNOW, INTELLECTUALLY, THAT I SHOULD BE LOOKING AT THE LOWER DECKS. BUT I CAN'T CONVINCE MY MIND OF THAT.

SPOCK... WHAT ARE YOU SEEING? CAN YOU CUT THROUGH IT, THE WAY YOU DID WITH THE MELKOTIANS?

NEGATIVE, SIR. WHATEVER CASTILLE IS DOING, IT'S FAR MORE INTENSE THAN THE MELKOTIAN ILLUSION-CASTING. I CANNOT PENETRATE IT.

PERHAPS CASTILLE'S PERSONAL BELIEF IN THIS SCENARIO IS MAKING THE DIFFERENCE.

OR MAYBE YOU'RE STILL NOT FIRING ON ALL THRUSTERS YET.

GENTLEMEN, WE HAVE NO CHOICE. WITH THE TURBOLIFTS OUT OF COMMISSION... WE WALK. AND TAKE WHAT COMES.

INCREDIBLE. I KNOW THAT WE'RE ACTUALLY CLIMBING DOWN LADDERS OR SLIDING THROUGH JEFFERIES TUBES-- BUT I CAN'T CONVINCE THE REST OF ME THAT THAT'S WHAT IS HAPPENING.

SPOCK... ANY IDEA WHAT DECK WE'RE ON?

DECK, SIR? NO. WE ARE, HOWEVER, ENTERING THE "NEUTRAL ZONE," SO TO SPEAK.

THAT PLACE WHERE SOULS WHO LIVED WITHOUT PRAISE OR BLAME-- THE NEUTRALS-- RESIDE.

WHAT IN THE... TANNER! MARTELL! SPOCK. THOSE ARE CREWMEN!

FASCINATING. CREWMEMBERS LOWER DOWN THAN THE BRIDGE, CLOSER TO THE BLAST'S SOURCE, MAY ACTUALLY BE A PART OF WHAT WE'RE WITNESSING.

THEY HAVE "JUDGED THEMSELVES," SO TO SPEAK, AND ASSIGNED THEM-SELVES A PLACE IN ONE OF THE NINE CIRCLES OF HELL.

4

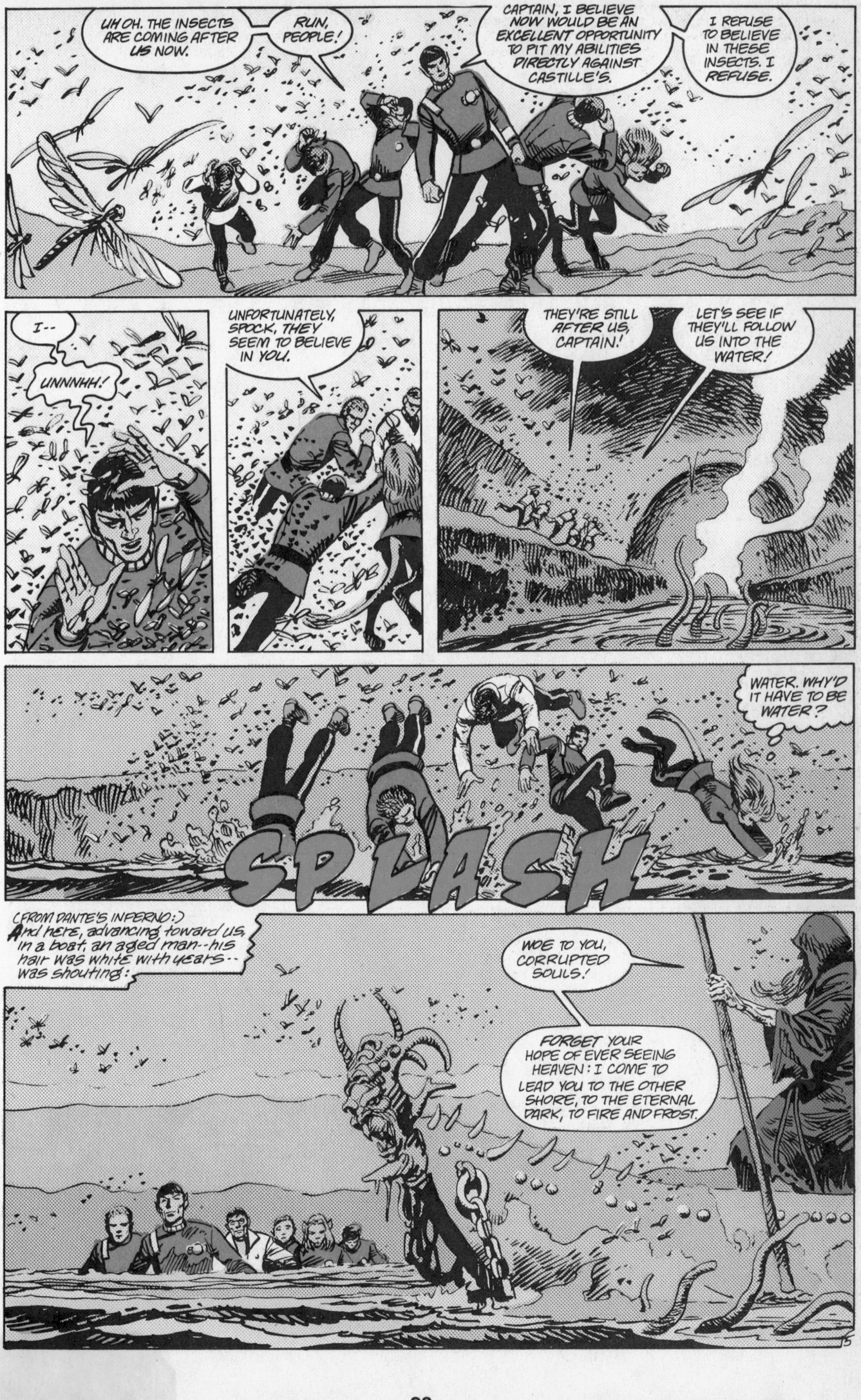
UH OH. THE INSECTS ARE COMING AFTER US NOW.
RUN, PEOPLE!
CAPTAIN, I BELIEVE NOW WOULD BE AN EXCELLENT OPPORTUNITY TO PIT MY ABILITIES DIRECTLY AGAINST CASTILLE'S.
I REFUSE TO BELIEVE IN THESE INSECTS. I REFUSE.
I--
UNNNHH!
UNFORTUNATELY, SPOCK, THEY SEEM TO BELIEVE IN YOU.
THEY'RE STILL AFTER US, CAPTAIN!
LET'S SEE IF THEY'LL FOLLOW US INTO THE WATER!
WATER. WHY'D IT HAVE TO BE WATER?
SPLASH
(FROM DANTE'S INFERNO:)
And here, advancing toward us, in a boat, an aged man--his hair was white with years--was shouting:
WOE TO YOU, CORRUPTED SOULS!
FORGET YOUR HOPE OF EVER SEEING HEAVEN: I COME TO LEAD YOU TO THE OTHER SHORE, TO THE ETERNAL DARK, TO FIRE AND FROST.
15

THIS, CAPTAIN, WOULD BE THE FERRYMAN ACROSS THE RIVER OF ACHERON...

"THE DEMON CHARON, WITH EYES LIKE EMBERS," TO QUOTE DANTE.

ANY PORT IN A STORM, MR. SPOCK.

I found myself upon the brink of an abyss, the melancholy valley containing thundering unending wailings.

JIM! OVER HERE!

STAY TIGHT, BONES! IF WE GET SEPARATED, WE COULD WANDER HERE IN LIMBO FOR AGES.

CHEKOV! SULU! SPOCK! M'RESS! FRONT AND CENTER!

SPOCK! REPORT!

THERE, SIR! I THINK.

That valley, dark and deep and filled with mist, is such that, though I gazed into its pit, I was unable to discern a thing.

SPOCK! I DON'T THINK HE HEARS US.

WITH THOSE EARS? I DON'T BELIEVE IT.

TRULY, PLATO, A GREAT TRAGEDY.

OH YES. JUST BECAUSE EUCLID, SOCRATES AND I WERE BORN BEFORE THE BIRTH OF CHRIST, WE'RE TRAPPED HERE IN LIMBO. TRULY UNJUST.

THEN AGAIN, SPOCK, YOU COULD JOIN US. BECOME OUR TRUE, JUST FRIEND.

IGNORE PLATO, MR. SPOCK. HE ALWAYS WANTS TO BE JUST FRIENDS.

6

94

SPOCK, GET OVER HERE NOW! THAT'S AN ORDER!

NOW HERE'S MY QUESTION...

NOT ANOTHER QUESTION, SOCRATES. WE'RE TIRED OF YOUR QUESTIONS, AREN'T WE, EUCLID?

YOU SHOULD TALK. ALWAYS BABBLING ABOUT "IDEALS." NEVER TRYING TO SEE THINGS FROM MY ANGLE.

STOP! NO IRRATIONAL BEINGS MAY APPROACH THE PHILOSOPHERS.

IN TRUTH, GENTLEMEN, I FIND ALL YOUR PRINCIPLES FASCINATING.

CLANG

I HAVE ENDEAVORED, PLATO, TO ACTUALLY STRIVE FOR THAT IDEALIZED STATE YOU SPEAK OF--THROUGH LOGIC. BUT IT SEEMS IMPOSSIBLE...

...IN LIFE. IS IT POSSIBLE IN AFTER-LIFE?

SECURITY CHIEF!

RIGHT HERE, KEPTIN. GOT A LEETLE LOST.

KRUNCH

BAM

SO NOTED. WHERE'S SULU?

RIGHT HERE, SIR! GRABBING A SWORD SOMEONE DROPPED.

CLANG

SULU! BEHIND YOU!

MMRRRAWRR

HOLY...

7

M'RESS, THAT'S ENOUGH!

M'RESS?

COME ON, SPOCK, YOU'VE GOT TO BE KIDDING.

YOU ACTUALLY THINK YOU'RE ON ANY KIND OF INTELLECTUAL PAR WITH *THESE GUYS*? THAT YOU CAN HOLD YOUR OWN FOR EVEN *A MINUTE*? WHO IN HELL DO YOU THINK YOU ARE?

DON'T LISTEN TO HIM, SPOCK!

WHO

DOCTOR McCOY, CONSIDERING YOUR INTELLECTUAL LEVELS ARE SCARCELY ABOVE PLANKTON, I WOULD HARDLY...

I WOULD... I...

DOCTOR... McCOY.

YOUR PARDON, DOCTOR. I... FORGOT MYSELF. A RATHER INSIDIOUS ILLUSION.

SPOCK! COME BACK!

I BELIEVE THE CAPTAIN WOULD SAY-- "I OWE YOU, BONES."

I'LL PUT IT ON THE TAB.

So I descended from the first enclosure down to the second circle, that which girdles less space but brief more great, that goads to weeping.

The hellish hurricane, which never rests, drives on the spirits with its violence, wheeling and pounding, it harasses them.

I learned that those who undergo this torment are damned because they sinned within the flesh, subjecting reason to the rule of lust.

8

There dreadful Minos stands, gnashing his teeth: examining the sins of those who enter. He judges and assigns as his tail twines.

LOOK OUT!!

SPOCK, WHERE ARE WE?!

YOUR PAST IS CATCHING UP WITH YOU, JIM.

WHERE THE LUSTFUL GO, SIR!

SULU!!

AND TO WHAT LEVEL SHALL MINOS CONSIGN YOU, LOST ONE?

OR SHALL YOU STAY HERE WITH THE LUSTFUL?

RRRR

SHOK

RRROOORRR

FOR A SECOND I THOUGHT YOU'D LET IT DRAG ME OFF.

WHEN HELL FREEZES OVER.

THIS WAY! THERE'S A GAP TOO NARROW FOR IT TO FOLLOW.

I HOPE.

I am in the third circle, filled with cold, unending, heavy and accursed rain; its measure and its kind are never changed.

Gross hailstones, water gray with filth, and snow come streaking down across the shadowed air; the earth, as it receives that shower, stinks.

WHAT DID THESE POOR DEVILS DO?

THEY'RE THE GLUTTONOUS.

YOU CAN'T BE SERIOUS.

LORD, I'LL NEVER STUFF MYSELF AT THANKSGIVING AGAIN.

THERE'S SOMETHING MOVING UP AHEAD!

GRRAWLL

WHAT'S THAT ?!

CERBERUS, DOCTOR. THE THREE-HEADED DOG.

THAT'S A DOG ?! WHAT ARE WE SUPPOSED TO DO, THROW HIM A BISCUIT ?

NOT A BISCUIT, DOCTOR.

DIRT.

DIRT ? HE EATS DIRT ?

I THOUGHT ONLY RABID DOGS EAT DIRT.

IF HE BITES YOU, DOCTOR, RABIES WILL BE THE LEAST OF YOUR CONCERNS.

Thus we made our way down to the fourth ditch, to take in more of that despondent shore where all the universe's ill is stored.

Justice of God! Who has amassed as many strange tortures and travails as I have seen? Why do we let our guilt consume us so?

BON APPETIT.

Here, more than elsewhere, I saw multitudes to every side of me; their howls were loud while, wheeling weights, they used their chests to push.

COME ON, PEOPLE. LET'S MOVE IT BEFORE THAT CREATURE WITH THE WHIP SEES US.

JIM, WE CAN'T JUST... JUST *LEAVE* THEM.

IT'S NOT REALLY *HAPPENING*, BONES.

I DON'T KNOW *WHAT'S REAL OR FANTASY* ANYMORE, JIM! BUT THESE ARE PEOPLE SUFFERING. YOU HEARD SPOCK! MAYBE EVEN *REAL CREWMEN* WHO, DEEP DOWN, THINK THEY DESERVE THIS.

I CAN'T JUST IGNORE SUFFERING PEOPLE!

BONES, I *UNDERSTAND.* BUT THE ONLY WAY WE CAN HELP THESE PEOPLE IS TO GET DOWN TO CASTILLE AND STOP HIM FROM CONJURING UP ANY *MORE* OF THIS.

NOW ARE YOU COMING OR NOT?

COMING.

We crossed the circle to the other shore; we reached a foaming watercourse that spills into a trench formed by its overflow... forming a swamp that bears the name of Styx.

And I, who was intent on watching it, could make out muddied people in that slime, all naked and their faces furious.

The kindly master told me: "Son, now see the souls of those whom anger has defeated... the wrathful and the sullen..."

CAPTAIN!

OH MY GOD. BEARCLAW.

CAPTAIN, I'M SORRY FOR EVERYTHING I DID. FORGIVE ME.

JIM, COME ON! IT MIGHT NOT EVEN BE HIM!

CAPTAIN, PLEASE!

I... I...

KEPTIN, COME ON!

NO!! HE'S MINE!

IF YOU CAN'T FORGIVE ME, THEN JOIN ME DOWN HERE!

GET HIM!

DRAG HIM DOWN!

CHEKOV! HOLD--

YOWTCH!

--ON!

13

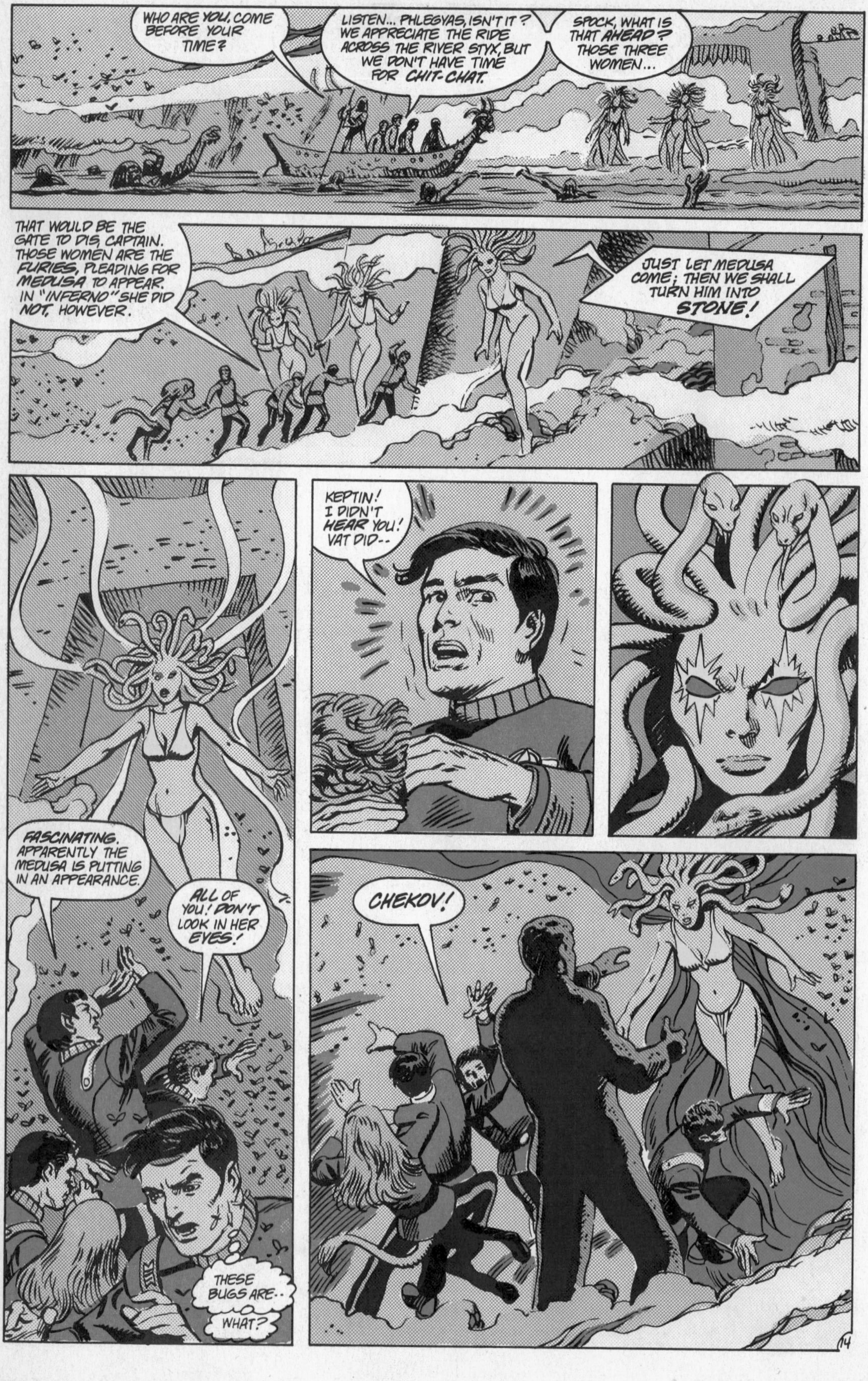
WHO ARE YOU, COME BEFORE YOUR TIME?
LISTEN... PHLEGYAS, ISN'T IT? WE APPRECIATE THE RIDE ACROSS THE RIVER STYX, BUT WE DON'T HAVE TIME FOR CHIT-CHAT.
SPOCK, WHAT IS THAT AHEAD? THOSE THREE WOMEN...
THAT WOULD BE THE GATE TO DIS, CAPTAIN. THOSE WOMEN ARE THE FURIES, PLEADING FOR MEDUSA TO APPEAR. IN "INFERNO" SHE DID NOT, HOWEVER.
JUST LET MEDUSA COME; THEN WE SHALL TURN HIM INTO STONE!
FASCINATING. APPARENTLY THE MEDUSA IS PUTTING IN AN APPEARANCE.
ALL OF YOU! DON'T LOOK IN HER EYES!
THESE BUGS ARE.. WHAT?
KEPTIN! I DIDN'T HEAR YOU! VAT DID--
CHEKOV!
14

LET ME GO, YOU WITCH! I'M WARNING YOU, I KNOW KARATE!...

SULU!

DON'T NEED MY EYES. I HEAR WHERE HIS SWORD FELL...

...AND MY SENSE OF SMELL WILL DO THE REST.

I'M COMING, SULU!

CH OP

EXCELLENT, M'RESS. YOU KNEW BEHEADING THE MEDUSA IS THE ONLY WAY TO DEFEAT HER.

UH... ACTUALLY I WAS... UH...

...AIMING FOR HER LEG.

M'RESS... ILLUSION OR NO, THE DANGER HERE LOOKS PRETTY REAL... AND I JUST WANTED TO SAY...

...THANKS.

AH. I BELIEVE MR. CHEKOV IS ABOUT TO REJOIN US.

KRAK

...YOU SAY?

15

As soon as I had entered, I looked about. I saw, on every side, a spreading plain of lamentation and atrocious pain.

SPOCK?

ARCH-HERETICS, SIR.

I'M SORRY I ASKED!

The place that we had reached for our descent along the bank was alpine; what reclined upon that bank would, too, repel all eyes.

OBVIOUSLY WE'VE ENTERED THE SEVENTH CIRCLE.

RRROOWRP

OBVIOUSLY. SPOCK, HOW DO YOU SUGGEST WE DEAL WITH THAT?

PERHAPS A NERVE PITCH WILL SUFFICE.

THEN AGAIN, PERHAPS NOT.

AND NOW CENTAURS ARE AIMING AT US.

GET READY TO BREAK RIGHT, KEEPING THE MINOTAUR BETWEEN US AND THEM. AND...

THWUK

THWUK THWUK

NOW!

MY GOD, SPOCK, IS THAT RIVER MADE OF... BLOOD?

YES, SIR. THAT'S THE PHLEGETHON.

FURTHER ALONG SHOULD BE A POINT THAT CAN ACTUALLY BE FORDED.

16

CAPTAIN'S LOG, STARDATE UNKNOWN. WE'VE LOST ALL TRACK OF TIME AS WE DESCEND FURTHER INTO THE INFERNO. BUT TIME IS SOMETHING WE DON'T HAVE...

A PLAGUE-RIDDEN PLANET URGENTLY NEEDS OUR HELP.. HELP WE CANNOT PROVIDE UNTIL WE HAVE RECLAIMED THE ENTERPRISE.

I AM HAUNTED BY DOUBTS. THESE ILLUSIONS ARE SO POWERFUL, THEY'VE INFILTRATED OUR VERY MINDS.

WHAT IF OUR DESCENT ITSELF IS ILLUSION? WHAT IF WE'RE NOWHERE NEAR THE LOWER SECTIONS OF THE SHIP?

BUT WE HAVE NO CHOICE. NONE.

AND MEANTIME, OUR EFFORTS ARE BEGINNING TO TAKE AN OVERWHELMING TOLL.

CAN'T... CAN'T DO IT ANYMORE.

TOO MUCH SUFFERING. TOO MUCH... EVERYTHING. CAN'T DO IT...

CAN'T...

URKH...

JIM! WHAT'RE WE MOVING SO SLOW FOR?

LET'S PICK UP THE PACE!

17

And after that I saw a thousand faces, made doglike by the cold; for which I shudder.. and always will--when I face frozen fords.

HOW ABOUT *THAT?* HELL REALLY *HAS* FROZEN OVER.

THIS IS THE NINTH RING, ISN'T IT? WHERE *LUCIFER* LIVES?

WHEN HE SEES *SPOCK,* HE'LL THINK IT'S A FAMILY REUNION.

YOUR HUMOR IS ILL-*TIMED,* DOCTOR.

YES, CAPTAIN, IT IS INDEED THE HOME OF LUCIFER... THE MAIN FORCE OF HELL. ALSO THE HOME OF *TRAITORS,* AS THESE FROZEN SOULS WILL *ATTEST.*

TRAITORS? SPOCK, THIS IS *MADNESS.*

LOOK THERE! THAT'S ENSIGN BLOEMKER, A SECURITY GUARD. WHO WAS *SHE* EVER A TRAITOR TO?

CAPTAIN, YOU SOUND *UPSET.*

UPSET? UPSET! OF COURSE I'M UPSET!

HOW MUCH MORE DO MY *SHIP, MY PEOPLE,* HAVE TO BE PUT THROUGH?

BLOEMKER! YOU'RE NO *TRAITOR!* WAKE UP!

THAT'S AN *ORDER!*

CAPTAIN, *PLEASE!*

IT'S.. YES. OKAY.

ARE YOU ALL *RIGHT,* SIR?

YES, MR. SPOCK. YOUR PARDON.

IT'S BEEN A HELL OF A DAY.

O reader, do not ask of me how I grew faint and frozen then-- I cannot write it.

18

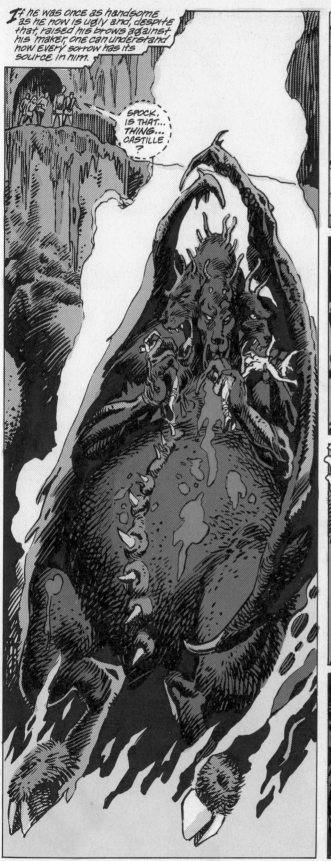

If he was once as handsome as he now is ugly and, despite that, raised his brows against his maker, one can understand how every sorrow has its source in him.

SPOCK, IS THAT... THING... CASTILLE?

IT IS QUITE POSSIBLE.

CASTILLE! LUCIFER! THIS IS --

RRRRUMBLE

MORE MEAT.

MORE SOULS.

19

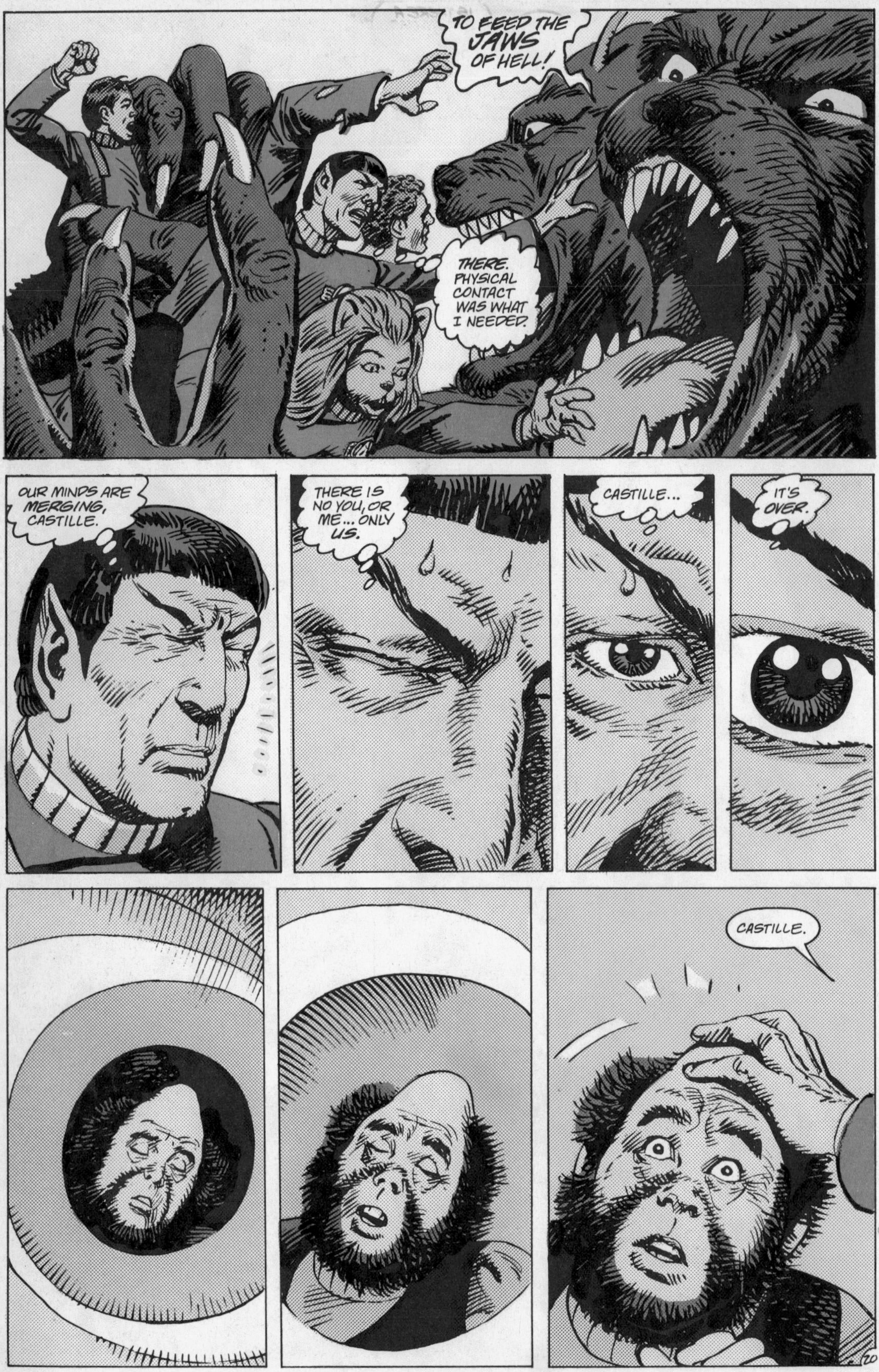
TO FEED THE JAWS OF HELL!
THERE. PHYSICAL CONTACT WAS WHAT I NEEDED.
OUR MINDS ARE MERGING, CASTILLE.
THERE IS NO YOU, OR ME... ONLY US.
CASTILLE...
IT'S OVER.
CASTILLE.
20

UH...

IS THERE A PROBLEM?

BOTANICAL GARDENS

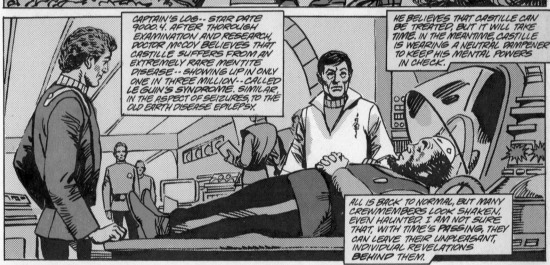

CAPTAIN'S LOG -- STAR DATE 9000.4. AFTER THOROUGH EXAMINATION AND RESEARCH, DOCTOR MCCOY BELIEVES THAT CASTILLE SUFFERS FROM AN EXTREMELY RARE MENTITE DISEASE -- SHOWING UP IN ONLY ONE IN THREE MILLION -- CALLED LE GUIN'S SYNDROME. SIMILAR, IN THE RESPECT OF SEIZURES, TO THE OLD EARTH DISEASE EPILEPSY.

HE BELIEVES THAT CASTILLE CAN BE TREATED, BUT IT WILL TAKE TIME. IN THE MEANTIME, CASTILLE IS WEARING A NEUTRAL DAMPENER TO KEEP HIS MENTAL POWERS IN CHECK.

ALL IS BACK TO NORMAL, BUT MANY CREWMEMBERS LOOK SHAKEN, EVEN HAUNTED. I AM NOT SURE THAT, WITH TIME'S PASSING, THEY CAN LEAVE THEIR UNPLEASANT, INDIVIDUAL REVELATIONS BEHIND THEM.

I HOPE I'M SURE.

NOK N'OK

OH... HI, CAPTAIN. SOMETHING WRONG?

NOT AT THE MOMENT, ENSIGN. IT'S JUST THAT THE CREW'S HAD A TRAUMATIC EXPERIENCE AND, UHM...

ARE YOU AND KONOM ALL RIGHT?

TRAUMATIC? UHH... WELL, I GUESS. I MEAN, WE'VE BEEN SLEEPING A WHILE, AND WHEN WE'RE NOT SLEEPING WE'VE BEEN--

RIGHT. CARRY ON.

IT IS COMFORTING TO KNOW, HOWEVER, THAT SOME THINGS REMAIN IMPERVIOUS TO MENTAL ASSAULT - INCLUDING THE SINGLE-MINDEDNESS OF HONEYMOONERS.

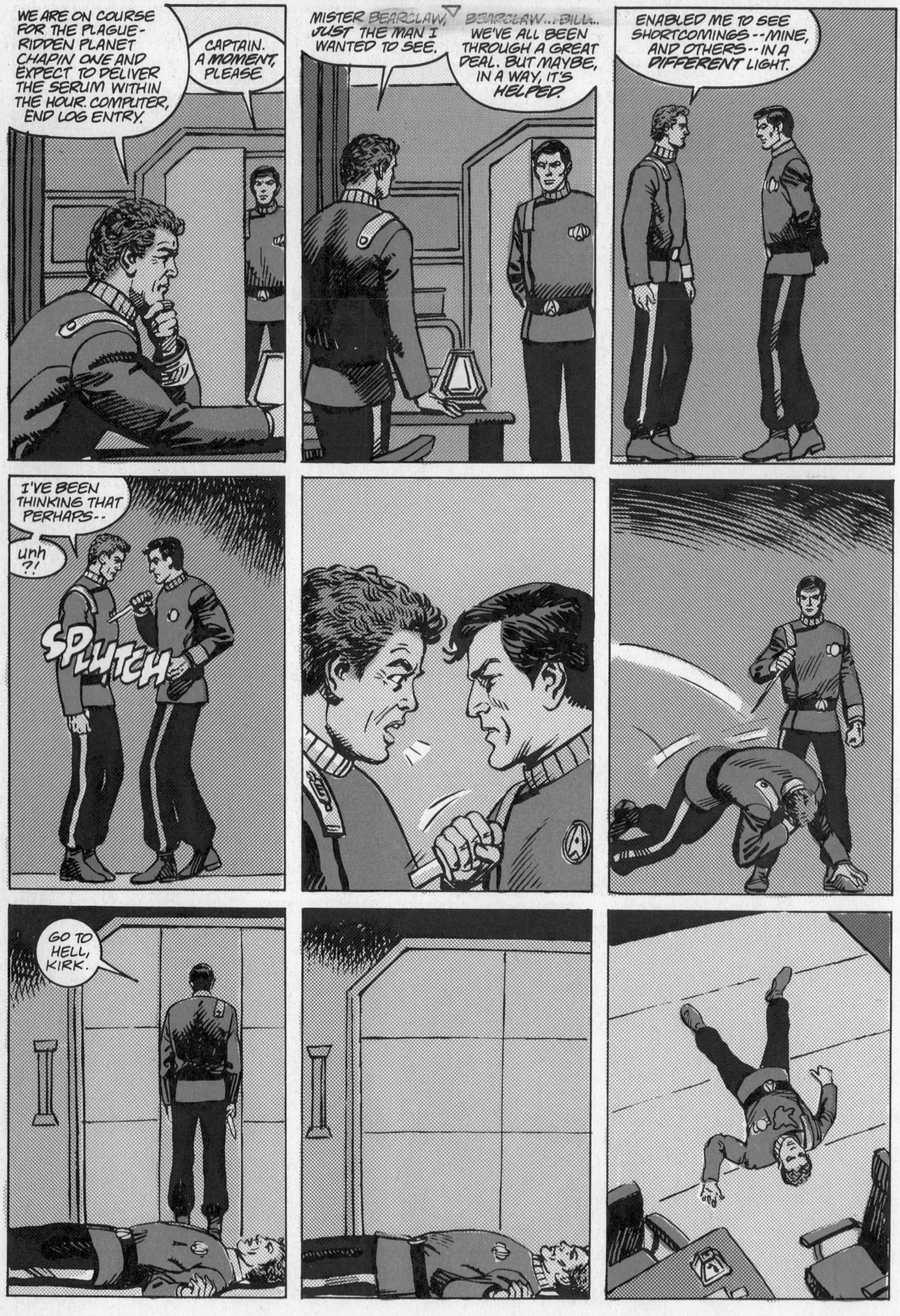
WE ARE ON COURSE FOR THE PLAGUE-RIDDEN PLANET CHAPIN ONE AND EXPECT TO DELIVER THE SERUM WITHIN THE HOUR. COMPUTER, END LOG ENTRY.
CAPTAIN. A MOMENT, PLEASE.
MISTER BEARCLAW, JUST THE MAN I WANTED TO SEE.
BEARCLAW... BILL... WE'VE ALL BEEN THROUGH A GREAT DEAL. BUT MAYBE, IN A WAY, IT'S HELPED.
ENABLED ME TO SEE SHORTCOMINGS--MINE, AND OTHERS--IN A DIFFERENT LIGHT.
I'VE BEEN THINKING THAT PERHAPS--
unh ?!
SPLUTCH
GO TO HELL, KIRK.

CAPTIAN'S LOG... ...FINAL ENTRY...

SO... SO MUCH BLOOD.

SO LITTLE TIME.

6-3756

~~EVERYDAY~~... WAS VERY THOROUGH. STABBED ME. SEALED THE DOOR.

THAT TOOK FORESIGHT. HALLMARK OF A GOOD OFFICER.

HE'S COME A LONG WAY I SHOULD BE PROUD.

AM I... DYING?

CAN'T BE. MY LIFE ISN'T FLASHING BEFORE MY EYES.

TERMINAL. GOT TO GET TO TERMINAL.

CALL FOR HELP ALMOST THERE. ALMOST TO... TERMINAL...

...TERMINAL. GOT TO ALMOST THERE.

I'M... I'M...

...TERMINAL.

KLUD!

CAN'T... LET IT END THIS WAY. I MUST...

... I MUST...

I MUST DOWN TO THE SEAS AGAIN, TO THE LONELY SEA AND THE SKY, AND ALL I ASK IS A TALL SHIP AND A STAR TO STEER HER BY, AND THE WHEEL'S KICK AND THE WIND'S SONG AND THE WHITE SAIL'S SHAKING, AND A GRAY MIST ON THE SEA'S FACE AND A GRAY DAWN BREAKING.

I MUST DOWN TO THE SEAS AGAIN, FOR THE CALL OF THE RUNNING TIDE IS A WILD CALL AND A CLEAR CALL THAT MAY NOT BE DENIED.

I MUST DOWN TO THE SEAS AGAIN, TO THE VAGRANT GYPSY LIFE,

TO THE GULL'S WAY AND THE WHALE'S WAY WHERE THE WIND'S LIKE A WHETTED KNIFE;

AND ALL I ASK IS A MERRY YARN...

... FROM A LAUGHING FELLOW ROVER,

AND A QUIET SLEEP AND A SWEET DREAM...

... WHEN THE LONG TREK'S OVER.

JIM.

CONTACT DR. McCOY IN SICKBAY. A MEDICAL TEAM TO THE CAPTAIN'S QUARTERS.

IMMEDIATELY!

YES SIR!

SPOCK, WHAT THE DEVIL'S GOING ON?!

UHURA GETS US UP HERE TO JIM'S QUARTERS, AND NOW WE CAN'T EVEN GET THE BLASTED DOOR OPEN!

E14

IT'S SEALED SOMEHOW! WE'VE CALLED SECURITY TO BLAST IT OPEN.

IS JIM IN THERE? IS HE IN DANGER?

5

SPOCK, I SAID IT'S SEALED! TELL ME WHAT'S HAPPENING!

NOT NOW, DOCTOR.

BLAST IT, SPOCK, I HAVE TO KNOW WHAT'S GOING ON!

DOCTOR McCOY...

SHUT UP.

DOCTOR...

...YOUR SERVICES ARE REQUIRED.

OH MY GOD.

6

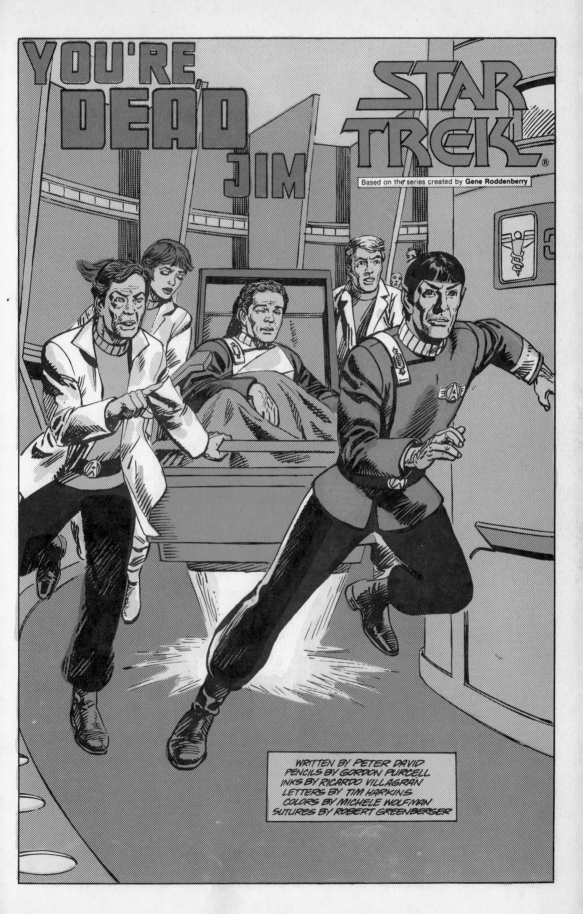

YOU'RE DEAD, JIM

STAR TREK

Based on the series created by **Gene Roddenberry**

WRITTEN BY PETER DAVID
PENCILS BY GORDON PURCELL
INKS BY RICARDO VILLAGRAN
LETTERS BY TIM HARKINS
COLORS BY MICHELE WOLFMAN
SUTURES BY ROBERT GREENBERGER

SOUNDS. RUNNING FEET. McCOY BARKING ORDERS.

WHAT'S HAPPEN--

...DAVID?

DAVID? IS IT-- YOU?

SURE IS, DAD. AND DON'T YOU WORRY.

WE'LL HAVE YOU FIXED UP AND PLAYING THE PIANO IN NO TIME.

HE'S CONSCIOUS! JIM, FOR CHRISSAKES, LIE DOWN!

BUT... I CAN'T PLAY THE PIANO...

IF YOU DON'T LIE DOWN, YOU WON'T LIVE TO LEARN!

IF YOU MEAN THE CAPTAIN BLEEDING TO DEATH, YEAH, I SAW IT...

...I'M JUST NOT SURE I BELIEVE IT.

HOLY KOLKER! BURNSIDE, YOU SEE THAT!?

8

I DON'T BELIEVE IT! HOW DID IT HAPPEN?

BEARCLAW! OPEN UP! ARE YOU IN THERE, BILL?

BEARCLAW

KNOK KICK

BILL, THANK HEAVENS! HAVE YOU HEARD?

I'VE BEEN SLEEPING.

WHAT'S UP?

THE CAPTAIN'S BEEN INJURED. THERE WAS SOME SORT OF ACCIDENT-- NOBODY KNOWS WHAT IT WAS!

THEY SAY HE MIGHT DIE!

GOOD RIDDANCE.

BILL.

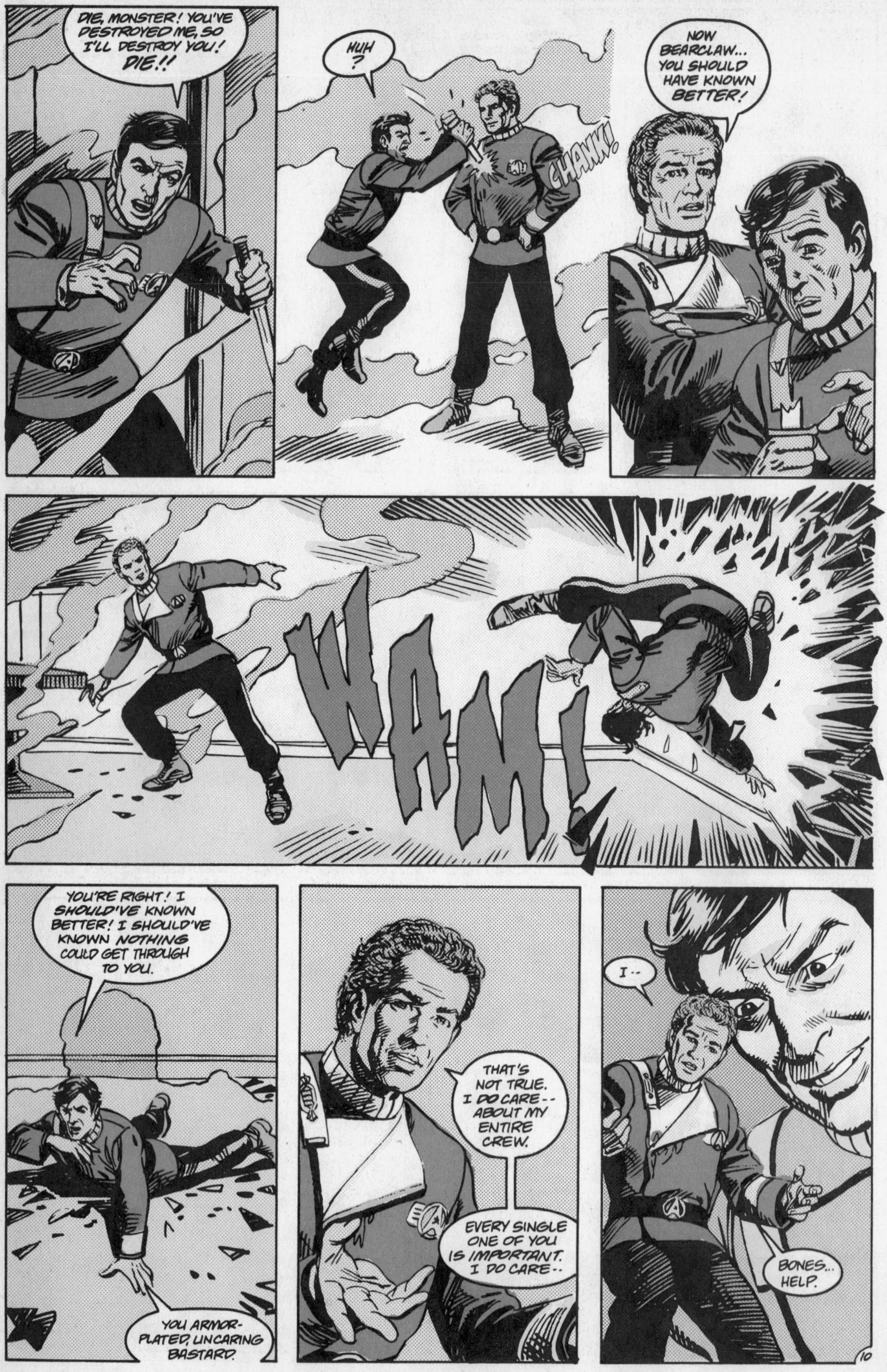

DIE, MONSTER! YOU'VE DESTROYED ME, SO I'LL DESTROY YOU! DIE!!
HUH ?
CHANK!
NOW BEARCLAW... YOU SHOULD HAVE KNOWN BETTER!
WAM!
YOU'RE RIGHT! I SHOULD'VE KNOWN BETTER! I SHOULD'VE KNOWN NOTHING COULD GET THROUGH TO YOU.
YOU ARMOR-PLATED, UNCARING BASTARD.
THAT'S NOT TRUE. I DO CARE-- ABOUT MY ENTIRE CREW.
EVERY SINGLE ONE OF YOU IS IMPORTANT. I DO CARE--.
I--
BONES... HELP.
10

PULSE AND RESPIRATION DROPPING, DOCTOR.

IF IT DROPS ANYMORE, IT'LL DISAPPEAR.

WE'LL HAVE TO CLEAR THE FLUID FROM HIS LUNGS, AND PRAY WE CAN REPAIR THE INTERNAL DAMAGE.

SHOULDN'T YOU BE ON THE BRIDGE, MR. SPOCK? ISN'T THAT THE *LOSICAL* PLACE FOR YOU TO BE?

YES, DOCTOR. THAT *IS* THE *LOSICAL* PLACE.

BUT YOU'RE NOT GOING THERE?

NO, DOCTOR.

THERE MAY BE HOPE FOR HIM AFTER ALL, JIM.

HEART RATE, BURKE?

"CAPTAIN'S LOG, STAR DATE 9000.8, HIKARU SULU ACTING COMMANDER. STILL NO WORD ON CAPTAIN KIRK'S STATUS. THE CONCERN HANGS OVER THE CREW, AND WE'RE FINDING IT IMPOSSIBLE TO TALK ABOUT, OR CONCENTRATE ON, ANYTHING ELSE."

THINK HE'LL BE OKAY?

I CAN'T IMAGINE HIS *NOT* BEING OKAY. NO MATTER HOW DIFFICULT THINGS HAVE GOTTEN, HE'S ALWAYS BEEN THERE.

BZZZZT

ALWAYS.

ENTER.

UHURA? I NOTICED YOU WEREN'T DOWN AT THE NEW YEAR'S EVE PARTY. THOUGHT I'D *CHECK* ON YOU.

YOU NOTICED I WASN'T THERE, SIR? 429 PEOPLE THERE AND YOU NOTICED THE MISSING 430th?

WHEN IT'S *YOU*, LIEUTENANT? YES.

12

UHURA... WOULD YOU LIKE TO TALK ABOUT IT?

I'M...

I'M THINKING OF LEAVING STARFLEET.

I SEE.

CAPTAIN, I WAS THE FIRST WOMAN IN MY FAMILY EVER TO TAKE INITIATIVE, TO TAKE CONTROL OF HER LIFE.

I TOOK MY NAME, UHURA-- "FREEDOM"-- SERIOUSLY. OVER MY FAMILY'S OBJECTIONS, I DECIDED TO MAKE A CAREER FOR MYSELF.

BUT I'VE BEEN DOUBTING MYSELF EVER SINCE.

I SECOND-GUESS MYSELF. I LOOK FOR ADVENTURE, BUT WHEN THERE'S TROUBLE I'M ALWAYS SO... SO FRIGHTENED.

IT'S AS IF MY WHOLE FAMILY IS STANDING THERE SAYING, "YOU WENT OFF AGAINST OUR WISHES, AND HERE'S YOUR REWARD.. YOU'LL GET TO DIE IN THE VACUUM OF SPACE, WITH NOTHING TO MARK YOUR PASSING OR TO SAY..."

"UHURA WAS HERE."

UHURA... WHAT DO YOU WANT FROM YOUR-SELF?

TO BE LIKE YOU, SIR. ALWAYS CONFIDENT, KNOW-ING YOU'VE MADE THE RIGHT DECISION. NEVER DOUBTING OR BEING AFRAID.

YOU KNOW THE FIRST THING THEY TEACH YOU IN CAPTAINS' SCHOOL, LIEUTENANT? THAT OFTEN THE DECISION YOU MAKE ISN'T HALF AS IMPORTANT AS THAT YOU MAKE ONE.

RIGHT OR WRONG, YOU STICK BY YOUR DECISION. IF YOU WAVER-- SHOW THE UNCERTAINTY THAT ALWAYS GNAWS AT YOU-- YOU ERODE YOUR CREW'S CONFIDENCE, AND YOUR OWN CONFIDENCE.

CAPTAIN, ARE YOU SAYING THAT-- DEEP INSIDE-- SOMETIMES YOU'RE AS FRIGHTENED AS I AM?

13

123

I'D NEVER SAY THAT.

HERE'S SOMETHING I HAVE ALWAYS VALUED: "WHEN YOU FOOL THE PEOPLE YOU FEAR, YOU'LL FOOL YOURSELF AS WELL".

DID YOU LEARN THAT FROM CAPTAINS' SCHOOL, TOO?

NO. RODGERS AND HAMMERSTEIN.

UHURA? YOU OKAY.

I'M FINE.

AND HE'LL BE FINE, TOO. I'M CERTAIN OF IT.

MEESTER SULU... A MOMENT OF YOUR TIME, PLEASE.

BONES! I FEEL GOOD AS NEW!

OBVIOUSLY MR. SCOTT ISN'T THE ONLY MIRACLE WORKER ON BOARD. GOOD JOB.

I'LL SEE YOU IN A BIT, BONES. SPOCK, COVER FOR ME ON THE BRIDGE.

...ERATIN ROOM

CHEER UP, M'RESS. I'M BACK NOW, SEE?

HMMM. SHE SEEMED PREOCCUPIED.

STABBED, MR. CHEKOV? ARE YOU SURE?

THAT EES WHAT MEESTER SPOCK SAID, BEFORE HE WENT INTO SICK BAY. I JUST TOLD MEESTER SULU. VE DON'T WANT TO PANIC THE CREW, SO VE VILL MAKE THE INITIAL INQUIRIES QUIETLY. I VANT YOU AN'D THE REST OF THE SECURITY TO VATCH FOR ANYTHING SUSPICIOUS.

LIKE DEAD BODIES, YOU MEAN?

MR. CHEKOV, YOU'VE KNOW THE CAPTAIN FOR LONGER THAN WE HAVE.

HONESTLY, WHAT DO YOU THINK HIS CHANCES OF PULLING THROUGH ARE?

FRANKLY, MEESTER KONOM, I'M NOT A GOOD ONE TO ASK. HE'S ALWAYS BEEN A LEETLE BEEGER THAN LIFE TO ME--

EVEN FROM THE WERY BEGINNING.

ENSIGN P.P. PAVEL CHEKOV REPORTING FOR DUTY, SIR.

WELCOME ABOARD

CHEKOV TAKE YOUR STATION

HE WAS LIKE A GIANT.

WELL, I REMEMBER THAT A SHEPHERD WITH A SLING KILLED A GIANT ONCE.

Y'KNOW, BLOEMKER, YOU'VE HAD A REAL ATTITUDE PROBLEM LATELY. KNOCK IT OFF. WE DON'T NEED DEFEATIST TALK. WE, AND THE CAPTAIN, NEED--

--A LONG VACATION. I'M FEELING SO TIRED. NEED TO TAKE IT EASY.

WANT TO GET AWAY FROM IT ALL, JIM?

WHAT IN THE--

16

SAM! MY GOD, IT'S BEEN AGES! COME IN HERE, YOU MUST BE FREEZING!

NAH. IT'S GREAT OUT HERE, LITTLE BROTHER.

COME OUT AND JOIN ME. JUST WATCH THE LIGHT AND COME TOWARD IT.

I--I CAN'T. I CAN'T GET OUT THERE.

OKAY, LITTLE BROTHER. NO HURRY. YOU'LL COME WHEN YOU'RE READY. I'VE GOT LOADS OF TIME.

"DOCTOR McCOY, TIME IS OF THE ESSENCE."

"WORK FASTER."

I KNOW THAT YOU THINK JUST BECAUSE YOU DIED ONCE THAT YOU'RE AN EXPERT, SPOCK, BUT YOU'RE WRONG.

BUT IF YOU THINK YOU CAN DO ANY DAMNED BETTER, THEN JUST JUMP IN ANYTIME.

DON'T WORRY, MR. SCOTT. HE'LL BE FINE. HE'S TOUGH. I'VE NEVER SEEN HIM WHERE HE'S NOT TOTALLY IN COMMAND.

IT SEEMS LIKE ONLY YESTERDAY THAT MR. SPOCK DIED IN THIS VERY CHAMBER-- ONLY TO BE MIRACULOUSLY BROUGHT BACK.

IF THE CAPTAIN DIES, THERE'LL BE NO VULCAN MIRACLES FOR HIM.

WHAT'S THAT YOU SAY, LAD?

17

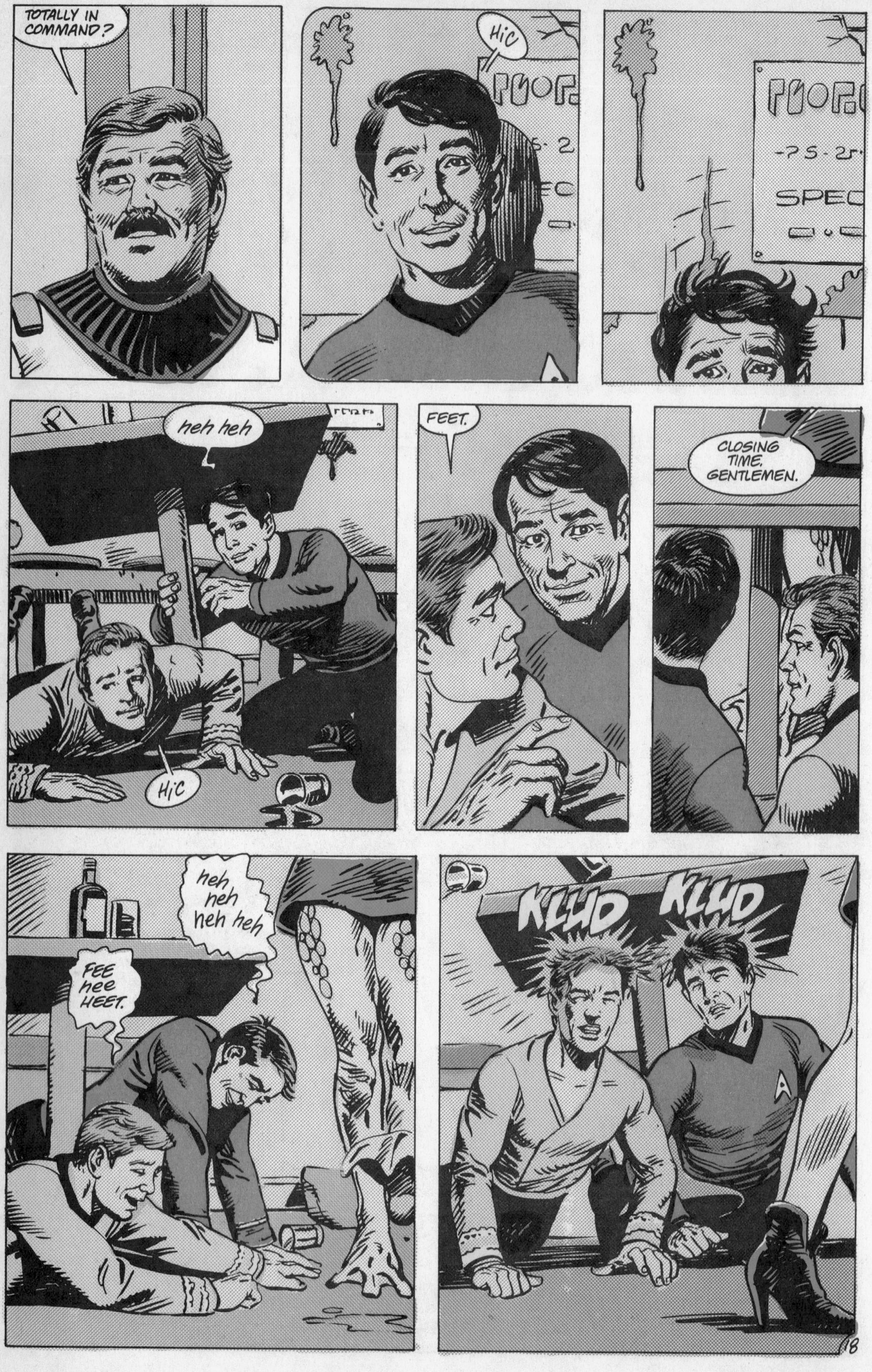
TOTALLY IN COMMAND?
HiC
heh heh
HiC
FEET.
CLOSING TIME, GENTLEMEN.
heh neh neh heh
FEE hee HEET.
KLUD KLUD

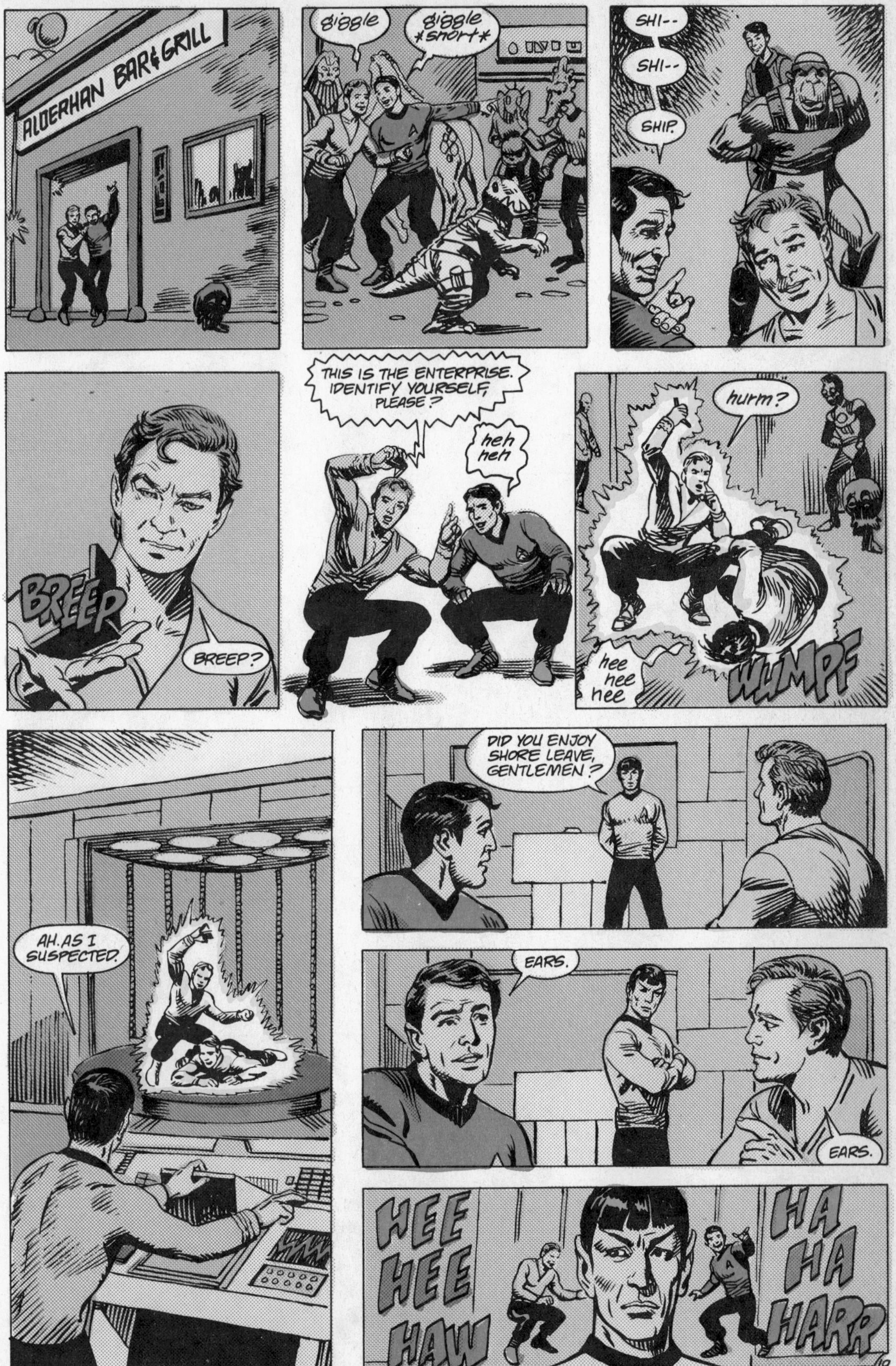
ALDERHAN BAR & GRILL
giggle
giggle *snort*
SHI--
SHI--
SHIP.
BREEP
BREEP?
THIS IS THE ENTERPRISE. IDENTIFY YOURSELF, PLEASE?
heh heh
hurm?
hee hee hee
WUMPF
AH. AS I SUSPECTED.
DID YOU ENJOY SHORE LEAVE, GENTLEMEN?
EARS.
EARS.
HEE HEE HAW
HA HA HARR
19

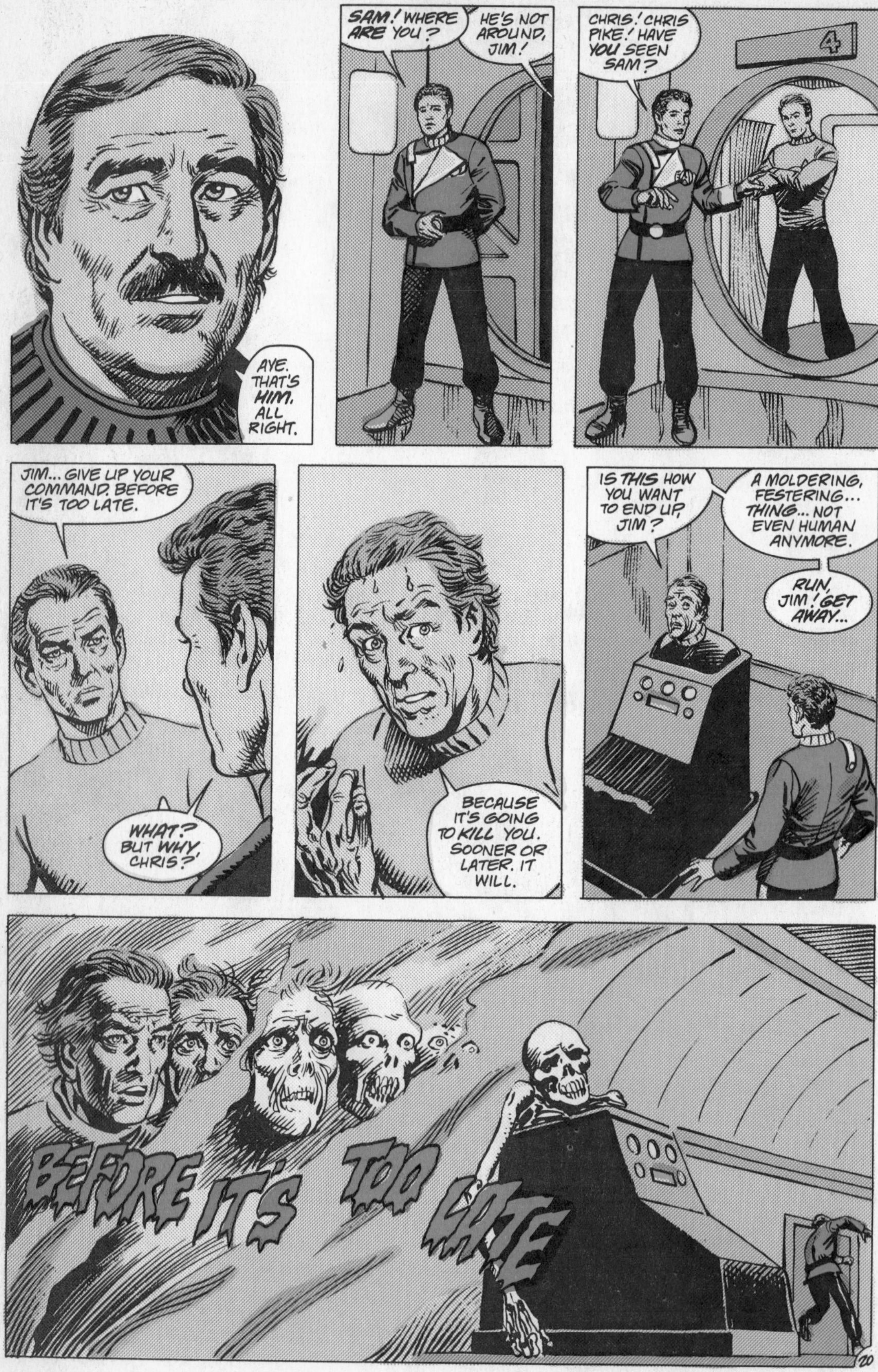
AYE. THAT'S HIM. ALL RIGHT.
SAM! WHERE ARE YOU?
HE'S NOT AROUND, JIM!
CHRIS! CHRIS PIKE! HAVE YOU SEEN SAM?
4
JIM... GIVE UP YOUR COMMAND. BEFORE IT'S TOO LATE.
WHAT? BUT WHY, CHRIS?
BECAUSE IT'S GOING TO KILL YOU. SOONER OR LATER. IT WILL.
IS THIS HOW YOU WANT TO END UP, JIM?
A MOLDERING, FESTERING... THING... NOT EVEN HUMAN ANYMORE.
RUN, JIM! GET AWAY...
BEFORE IT'S TOO LATE
20

BLAST IT, SPOCK, WHAT DO YOU WANT *NOW?*

MERELY TO TAKE YOU UP ON YOUR OFFER, DOCTOR.

WHAT OFFER? WAIT A MINUTE, SPOCK! WHAT'RE YOU --

SAM! SAM, WHERE *ARE* YOU?!

OUT HERE, JIM! THROUGH THE SHUTTLEBAY HANGER!

LOOK WHO I FOUND.. MY NEPHEW, DAVID! FINE SON YOU GOT HERE, JIM.

COME *JOIN* US, DAD. JUST FOLLOW THE LIGHT TO US.

DAVID... SAM... I THOUGHT I LOST YOU FOREVER.

YES. YES, SAVE ME A PLACE. I'M COMING.

CAPTAIN... JIM... IT'S TIME TO RETURN NOW.

BUT SPOCK... I'D JUST LIKE TO SPEND A LITTLE TIME WITH SAM AND DAVID. THERE'S NO *HARM* IN THAT.

TRUE, SIR. AND EVENTUALLY, YOU *WILL* BE ABLE TO SPEND AS MUCH TIME WITH THEM AS YOU WISH. BUT THERE ARE URGENT MATTERS THAT REQUIRE YOUR IMMEDIATE ATTENTION...

AND I WOULD BE REMISS IN MY DUTY IF I DID NOT REQUEST THAT YOU ATTEND TO THESE MATTERS.

AND *I* WOULD BE REMISS IF I DIDN'T ATTEND TO THEM.

COMING, MR. SPOCK.

DAVID, SAM... *ANOTHER* TIME, MAYBE?

SURE, JIM. ANOTHER TIME. WE'LL WAIT.

IT'S NOT LIKE WE HAVE MUCH ELSE TO DO.

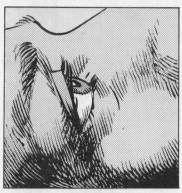

FINALLY. OPERATION'S OVER TWO HOURS AGO AND YOU FINALLY GET AROUND TO WAKING UP.

DON'T TRY TO TALK, JIM. IT WAS A NEAR THING. BUT WE SAVED YOU. ME AND MY VULCAN NURSE. NOW JUST REST AND--

PIKE.

PIKE, SIR? AS IN CAPTAIN PIKE?

NO, AS IN... I WANT BEARCLAW'S HEAD ON A PIKE.

132

OLD LOYALTIES

STAR TREK

WRITTEN BY :
    PETER DAVID
PENCILS BY :
    GORDON PURCELL
INKS BY :
    RICARDO VILLAGRÁN
LETTERS BY :
    TIM HARKINS
COLORS BY :
    MICHELE WOLFMAN
HEADACHES BY :
    ROBERT GREENBERGER

IMPRESSIVE, ISN'T IT, HEATHER ME LOVE? THE WAY WE DEVELOP *NEW* AND *IMPROVED* WAYS TO DESTROY EACH OTHER.

SAINTS, WHAT A *MASSACRE*.

I'VE SEEN WORSE.

AND DON'T CALL ME "ME LOVE." YOU KNOW I HATE THAT.

AS YOU WISH, ME LOVE.

I'D ALSO LIKE TO REMIND YOU THAT WE HAVE A **JOB** TO DO. A LITTLE **LESS** PHILOSOPHIZING AND A BIT **MORE** CONCENTRATION ON THAT JOB MIGHT BE IN ORDER.

WHERE?

IT TOOK THE FEDERATION YEARS TO ESTABLISH THIS COLONY, AND SOME LUNATIC IN A STARSHIP DESTROYS IT IN **MINUTES**.

NOW IF YOU FEDERATION SECURITY LEGION TYPES CAN FIGURE OUT WHY THAT "RENEGADE" SHIP DECIDED TO LAY WASTE TO OMICRON CETI IV, THEN **GREAT**. OTHERWISE, STAY OUT OF MY WAY.

NICE GUY.

HAVING A **BAD** DAY.

SEAN.

COME SEE SOMETHING WEIRD.

LORD KNOWS THERE'S ENOUGH **BODIES** AROUND HERE, BUT...

WHY'S THIS ONE **NAKED**?

MAYBE SOMEONE WANTED HER CLOTHES.

WHERE? WHERE WHAT?

WHERE HAVE YOU SEEN WORSE?

NOWHERE, ALL RIGHT? SATISFIED?

MR. PAUL, HOW IS THE CLEAN-UP GOING?

HOW DO YOU THINK IT'S GOING, MISS VAN HORNE?

ME TOO. I'M GOING TO EXPLORE A BIT.

FINE. I'LL BE CHECKING OUT THE FREEZER WHERE THEY FOUND THE LATE PHIL BURROUGHS.

A PUZZLE TO THE END, EH, PHIL? REPORTS SAID WHEN YOU WERE FOUND, YOU'D SHUFFLED OFF THIS MORTAL COIL TWO WEEKS PREVIOUS...

TWO WEEKS DURING WHICH YOU WERE WANDERING THE GALAXY IN A STOLEN STARSHIP.

I TRULY HATE A MYSTERY.

OH, YOU'RE A RIOT, SEAN.

COMMANDER! I'M ENSIGN KITTY FROM THE U.S.S. ENTERPRISE. STARFLEET INSTRUCTED US TO COME GET YOU.

IN THE MIDDLE OF THIS?

YES, SIR. THERE'S BEEN AN ATTEMPTED HOMICIDE ON BOARD THE ENTERPRISE AGAINST THE CAPTAIN.

FEDERATION POLICY IS THAT THE SECURITY LEGION IS TO INVESTIGATE SUCH INCIDENTS. YOU AND YOUR COMPANION WERE THE CLOSEST LEGIONNAIRES.

GOES AGAINST THE GRAIN TO START ONE JOB BEFORE FINISHING ANOTHER.

OUR ORDERS WERE SPECIFIC, SIR.

ALL RIGHT, MR. KITTY.

WE'LL HAVE TO BE SOLVING THE MYSTERY OF OMICRON CETI IV ANOTHER DAY.

LOOSEN UP, BEARCLAW. YOU'RE TOO STIFF.

YOU FALL, YOU COULD BREAK SOMETHING.

THE ONLY THING I'M GOING TO BREAK, HAZZARD, IS THE RECORD FOR KNOCKING YOU ON YOUR BUTT.

YOU PICKED A POOR TIME TO SCHEDULE A TRAINING SESSION FOR SECURITY PERSONNEL, BECAUSE I'M IN A REALLY BAD MOOD.

I'LL CONSIDER MYSELF WARNED.

HEEEYYY!!!

CHOK!

HOLY KOLKER. HE WASN'T KIDDING.

TO ME THIS IS PRACTICE, BUT TO HIM--

"HE'S GOT A LOT OF HOSTILITY HE'S WORKING OUT!"

THUNK!

THAT'S ENOUGH, BEARCLAW.

TAKE A MINUTE OR SO TO PULL YOURSELF TOGETHER.

5

NO! COME ON, DEFEND YOURSELF. I CAN *TAKE* IT.

DAMN YOU, I CAN *TAKE* IT! I CAN--

I SAID...

THAT'S ENOUGH.

SOMEONE TOSS ME A TOWEL FOR BEARCLAW'S NOSEBLEED?

THANKS, STERNO. NOW HOW ABOUT SOMEONE OF MORE *NORMAL* HEIGHT?

MEESTER BEARCLAW, EET EES MY DUTY TO PLACE YOU UNDER ARREST.

OH, HAR-DE-HAR.

ON WHAT CHARGE? LETTING MYSELF GET SUCKER-PUNCHED?

NO.

FOR THE ATTEMPTED MURDER OF KEPTAIN KIRK.

6

YOU CAN'T BE SERIOUS.

SURE, KIRK ISN'T MY FAVORITE PERSON--

THAT'S KEPTAIN KIRK TO YOU.

-- BUT THAT DOESN'T MEAN I'D TRY AND KILL THE "KEPTAIN"! WHO'S THE STINKING LIAR THAT ACCUSED ME?

THE KEPTAIN HIMSELF.

TAKE HIM, MEN.

NO! THIS IS CRAZY!

I'VE GOT TO FIND KIRK! CONVINCE HIM THAT--

BEARCLAW A WOULD-BE MURDERER. IMAGINE THAT.

BILL! GOOD LORD, WHAT HAPPENED?

HE'S UNCONSCIOUS! DID THIS HAPPEN IN *TRAINING* OR SOMETHING? GET HIM TO SICK BAY!

THE ONLY PLACE HE'S GOING IS THE *BRIG.*

THE *BRIG?* WHY?!

THAT'S WHERE YOU *USUALLY* PUT SOMEONE WHO TRIES TO *KILL* THE COMMANDING OFFICER AND RESISTS ARREST, TO *BOOT.*

THAT'S *ABSURD.* THERE MUST BE A *MISTAKE.*

CAPTAIN *HIMSELF* FINGERED HIM.

NICE *BOYFRIEND* YOU GOT THERE, SHERWOOD.

CUT HIM *LOOSE,* LIZ. HE'LL ONLY HURT YOUR *CAREER,* AND NO ONE'S GOING TO STAND UP FOR HIM.

I LEAVE YOU ALONE FOR *TWO MINUTES* AND YOU'RE TRYING TO STAND UP?!

DAMN IT, JIM, IT'S BAD ENOUGH WHEN YOU PULLED THIS SORT OF THING AS A *YOUNG* MAN.

BUT NOW YOU'RE AN *OLD* MAN AND YOU'RE STILL DOING IT!

JUST TESTING MY *LIMITS,* BONES.

YOUR LIMIT'S *DEATH,* AND YOU'RE PUSHING THAT.

BESIDES, LOOK WHO'S CALLING WHOM "OLD MAN."

HAH! I'LL LIVE ANOTHER 87 YEARS BECAUSE I TAKE *CARE* OF MYSELF.

COME ON, JIM. LIE *DOWN,* WILL YOU?

WHO DO YOU THINK YOU'RE *IMPRESSING?*

CAPTAIN! I NEED TO TALK TO Y--

WOW! YOU'RE UP AND AROUND ALREADY? I'M IMPRESSED!

OH, GREAT. NOW THERE'LL BE NO LIVING WITH HIM.

SOUR GRAPES, DOCTOR.

WHAT CAN I DO FOR YOU, ENSIGN?

9

CAPTAIN, I'VE JUST HEARD ABOUT BEARCLAW. THERE'S GOT TO BE SOME MISTAKE.

NO MISTAKE, ENSIGN SHERWOOD. I SAW WHAT I SAW AND, IN RETROSPECT, WHAT ANNOYS ME IS IN MY YOUNGER DAYS, I'D'VE WIPED THE FLOOR WITH HIM.

THAT'S ALL.

THAT'S ALL? THE WHOLE FILE?

CAN'T BE. THERE MUST BE SOMETHING I'M MISSING.

I MEAN, KIRK'S A BLOODY GENIUS FOR COMMANDING CREW LOYALTY...

I DON'T KNOW. FROM ALL I'VE READ, KIRK'S A REAL MAVERICK.

BENDING RULES WHENEVER HE CAN. A CAPTAIN SETS AN EXAMPLE FOR HIS CREW.

IF HE POINTS THE WAY TO ANARCHY, HE'S ONLY GOT HIMSELF TO BLAME.

ANARCHY'S ONE THING, HEATHER, ME LOVE... MURDER ANOTHER.

AND I'LL BE GETTING TO THE BOTTOM OF THIS, OR MY NAME ISN'T--

MORON.

LET MORON HELP MOVE FRIEND NANCY'S CLOTHES.

NO, THAT'S OKAY, MOR--

OH, KONOM, WE CAN'T KEEP CALLING HIM "MORON." THAT'S NOT A NAME.

I SUPPOSE.

HOW ABOUT KORG?

WHAT MEANS KORG?

"FIERCE ONE." HMM... DOESN'T QUITE FIT, DOES IT? HOW ABOUT...

NO, KORT ISN'T QUITE RIGHT, EITHER. KODOL? KULOS? KELROK? KUR?

HOW ABOUT BERNIE?

BERNIE? WHAT KIND OF STUPID NAME IS THAT?

I'LL HAVE YOU KNOW BERNIE IS MY FATHER'S NAME. AND--

LIKE NAME. LIKE BERNIE. CALL ME BERNIE.

OH, MARVELOUS. BERNIE THE KLINGON.

NANCY! KONOM! THE CAPTAIN'S ALWAYS LIKED YOU! MAYBE YOU CAN CONVINCE HIM.

LIZ, SLOW DOWN! CONVINCE HIM OF WHAT?

THAT BEARCLAW COULDN'T *POSSIBLY* HAVE TRIED TO KILL HIM.

Uhhh, WELL...

ELIZABETH, IT'S NOT THAT WE'RE *UNSYMPATHETIC* TO YOUR PLIGHT, BUT...

WELL, I UNDERSTAND THE CAPTAIN IS QUITE POSITIVE, AND--

AND THAT'S GOOD ENOUGH FOR YOU, HUH?

MY FRIENDS! HAH!

LIZ, WAIT!

DAMN. SHE DIDN'T TAKE IT ALL THAT WELL.

LIZ IS JUST GOING TO HAVE TO REALIZE, SOONER OR LATER, THAT BEARCLAW'S NAME IS *MUD* ON THIS SHIP.

NOT AS GOOD A NAME AS *BERNIE*.

COME ON, BOYAJIAN, YOU'VE GOT TO LET ME SEE HIM.

FORGET IT, SHERWOOD. YOU'RE WASTING YOUR TIME ON HIM.

LIZ!

LI-- YAARRGH!

BILL, THE FORCE FIELD!

ZZNNZZTT

12

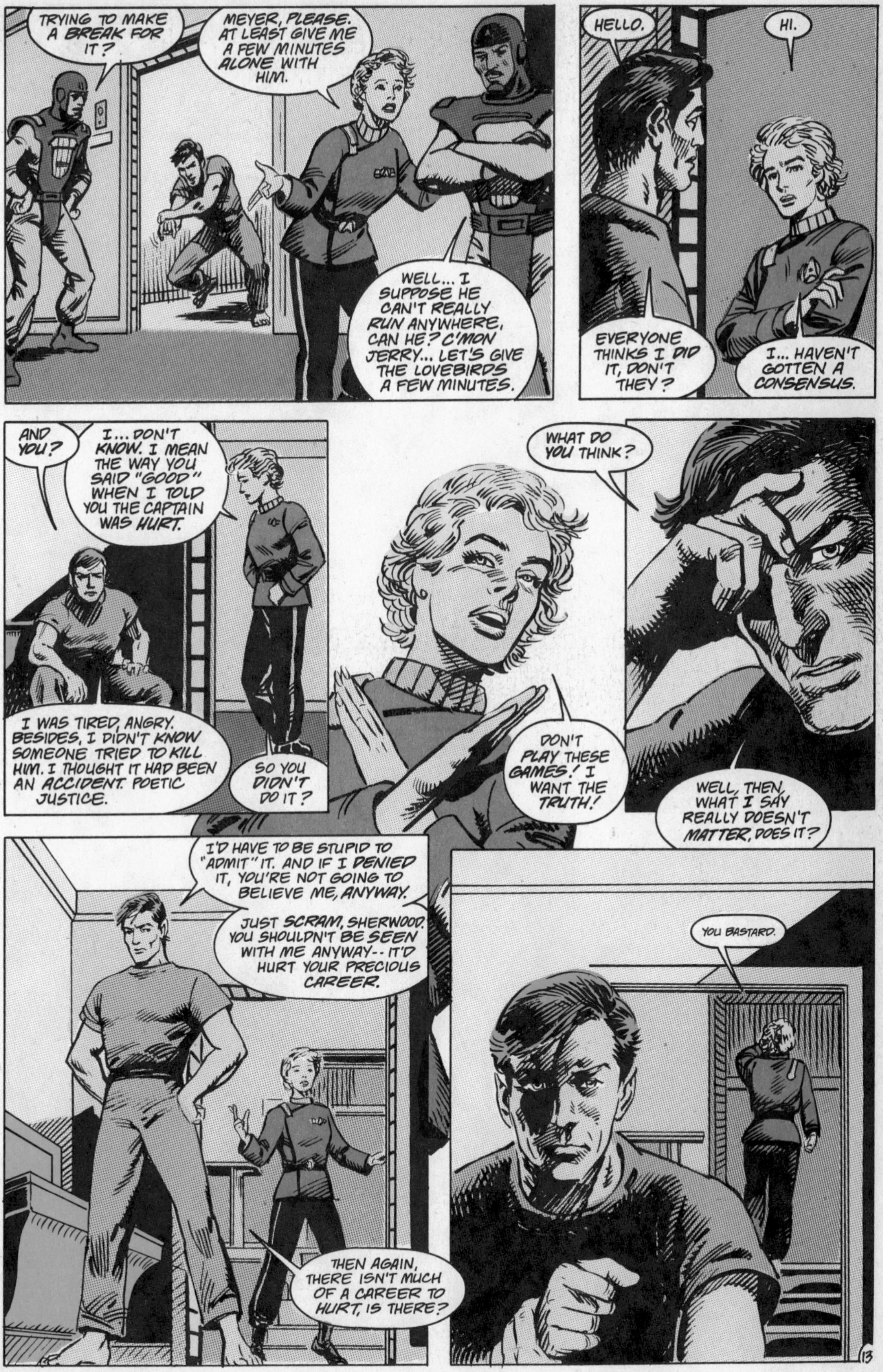
TRYING TO MAKE A BREAK FOR IT?
MEYER, PLEASE. AT LEAST GIVE ME A FEW MINUTES ALONE WITH HIM.
WELL... I SUPPOSE HE CAN'T REALLY RUN ANYWHERE, CAN HE? C'MON JERRY... LET'S GIVE THE LOVEBIRDS A FEW MINUTES.
HELLO.
HI.
EVERYONE THINKS I DID IT, DON'T THEY?
I... HAVEN'T GOTTEN A CONSENSUS.
AND YOU?
I... DON'T KNOW. I MEAN THE WAY YOU SAID "GOOD" WHEN I TOLD YOU THE CAPTAIN WAS HURT.
I WAS TIRED, ANGRY. BESIDES, I DIDN'T KNOW SOMEONE TRIED TO KILL HIM. I THOUGHT IT HAD BEEN AN ACCIDENT. POETIC JUSTICE.
SO YOU DIDN'T DO IT?
DON'T PLAY THESE GAMES! I WANT THE TRUTH!
WHAT DO YOU THINK?
WELL, THEN, WHAT I SAY REALLY DOESN'T MATTER, DOES IT?
I'D HAVE TO BE STUPID TO "ADMIT" IT. AND IF I DENIED IT, YOU'RE NOT GOING TO BELIEVE ME, ANYWAY.
JUST SCRAM, SHERWOOD. YOU SHOULDN'T BE SEEN WITH ME ANYWAY-- IT'D HURT YOUR PRECIOUS CAREER.
THEN AGAIN, THERE ISN'T MUCH OF A CAREER TO HURT, IS THERE?
YOU BASTARD.
13

HI, CAPTAIN.

HELLO, BURNSIDE.

YOU ARE LOOKING FIT, CAPTAIN. ARE YOU ABLE TO DISCUSS THE BEARCLAW INCIDENT FOR A MOMENT?

I'M NOT SURE WHAT THERE IS TO DISCUSS, MR. SPOCK.

THERE IS MR. BEARCLAW'S PSYCHIATRIC PROFILE, FOR EXAMPLE.

IF YOU'VE STUDIED IT, MR. SPOCK, THEN YOU KNOW HOW HOT-TEMPERED HE IS.

TRUE, CAPTAIN. WHICH IS WHY SUCH A CARE-FULLY PLANNED MURDER IS CURIOUS FOR ONE WHO USUALLY ACTS ONLY ON THE SPUR OF THE MOMENT.

BRIDGE TO CAPTAIN.

I KNOW WHAT I SAW, MR. SPOCK.

UHM... WOULD YOU MIND, SPOCK? REACH SEEMS TO BE A PROBLEM.

LET US, CAPTAIN.

STEADY, GUYS.

REMIND ME TO HAVE THE INTERCOMS LOWERED.

14

146

KIRK HERE.

CAPTAIN, WE HAVE AN INCOMING *SHUTTLECRAFT*. THE PASSENGERS HAVE REQUESTED THAT IF YOU ARE *ABLE*, YOU MEET THEM AT THE HANGAR BAY ENTRANCE.

ON MY WAY, UHURA. KIRK OUT.

NOW WHO THE DEVIL'S SHOWING UP IN A *SHUTTLECRAFT*?

I CAN ANSWER THAT, SIR.

I HAD EVERY *FAITH* IN YOU, SPOCK.

IF A SENIOR OFFICER IS ATTACKED, THEN, AS PER THE STARFLEET *REGULATION* CREATED TEN YEARS AGO, THE SECURITY HEAD IS REQUIRED TO ALERT THE INTERNAL INVESTIGATIONS UNIT. I ASKED MR. CHEKOV TO DO SO.

WUH-UH-OH!

INTERNAL INVESTI--

YOU MEAN THE FEDERATION SECURITY LEGION?!

NOT *THOSE* LUNATICS! THEY SEE SECURITY BREACHES EVERYWHERE, ENEMIES IN EVERY CORNER.

WAP

THD THDTHD

WE KNOW WHO DID IT. WHY DO WE HAVE TO INVOLVE THEM?

REGU--

--LATIONS, YES.

147

CAPTAIN'S LOG, STAR DATE. 9001.3. IN FULL COMPLIANCE WITH STARFLEET REGULATIONS, WE ARE AWAITING THE ARRIVAL OF THE FEDERATION SECURITY LEGION. WE HAVE CONFIDENCE THAT THEY WILL BE ABLE TO PUT THIS UNFORTUNATE INCIDENT TO REST.

PERSONAL LOG, STAR DATE 9001.3. IT IS WITH A SENSE OF DREAD THAT WE AWAIT THE IMPENDING FEDERATION SECURITY LEGION INQUISITION. I'D SOONER FACE A KNIFE-WIELDING BEARCLAW AGAIN.

IS MY BREATH APPROPRIATELY BATED, MR. SPOCK?

MOST EFFECTIVELY, CAPTAIN.

SIT STILL, CAPTAIN. WHEN YOU DROP DEAD FROM OVEREXERTION, I'LL BE RUSHED TO PERFORM AN AUTOPSY. SO I THOUGHT I WOULD START NOW.

SUBTLETY WAS NEVER YOUR STRONG SUIT, BONES.

HAN

AH. IT APPEARS OUR GUESTS HAVE ARRIVED.

COMMANDER SEAN FINNEGAN AND ASSOCIATE REQUESTING PERMISSION TO COME ABOARD, SIR.

FINNEGAN?

YES, CAPTAIN. COMMANDER FINNEGAN, FEDERATION SECURITY LEGION. AND THIS IS HEATHER VAN HORNE, MY ASSOCIATE. I ASSUMED YOU WERE EXPECTING US.

I'VE HEARD MANY GOOD THINGS ABOUT YOU. IT'S A PLEASURE TO BE MEETING YOU, ALTHOUGH THE CIRCUMSTANCES ARE REGRETTABLE.

SPOCK... IS THIS THE SAME FINNEGAN WHO--?

SO IT WOULD APPEAR.

CAPTAIN, YOU'RE POSITIVELY ASHEN. ARE YOU--?

FINNEGAN...

DON'T YOU REMEMBER ME?

I'M SORRY, SHOULD I? HAVE WE MET?

WE WENT TO THE ACADEMY TOGETHER!

DID WE? FORGIVE MY MEMORY, CAPTAIN... IT WAS THIRTY YEARS AGO.

OF COURSE, I'M HONORED TO HAVE ATTENDED AT THE SAME TIME AS THE LEGENDARY CAPTAIN KIRK, BUT... I CAN'T SAY I'M REMEMBERING YOU.

MAY I SAY, COMMANDER, THAT THE CAPTAIN MOST ASSUREDLY REMEMBERS YOU.

IS THAT A FACT?

OH, YES. VERY VIVIDLY, IN FACT.

FINNEGAN, I WAS A PLEBE. YOU WERE AN UPPER-CLASSMAN. AND YOU MADE MY LIFE ABSOLUTE HELL!

MOI?

VOUS.

BUCKETS OF WATER PROPPED IN THE DOOR, I BELIEVE JIM ONCE SAID.

CAPTAIN, I ADMIT I WAS A BIT OF A PRANKSTER IN MY YOUTH... BUT NO MORE SO THAN OTHER UPPER-CLASSMEN. WE RAZZED A LOT OF PLEBES, CAPTAIN, BUT...

I'M AFRAID I CAN'T PLACE YOU IN SPECIFIC.

YOU CALLED ME "GRIM JIM"! HOW CAN YOU NOT REMEMBER?!

18

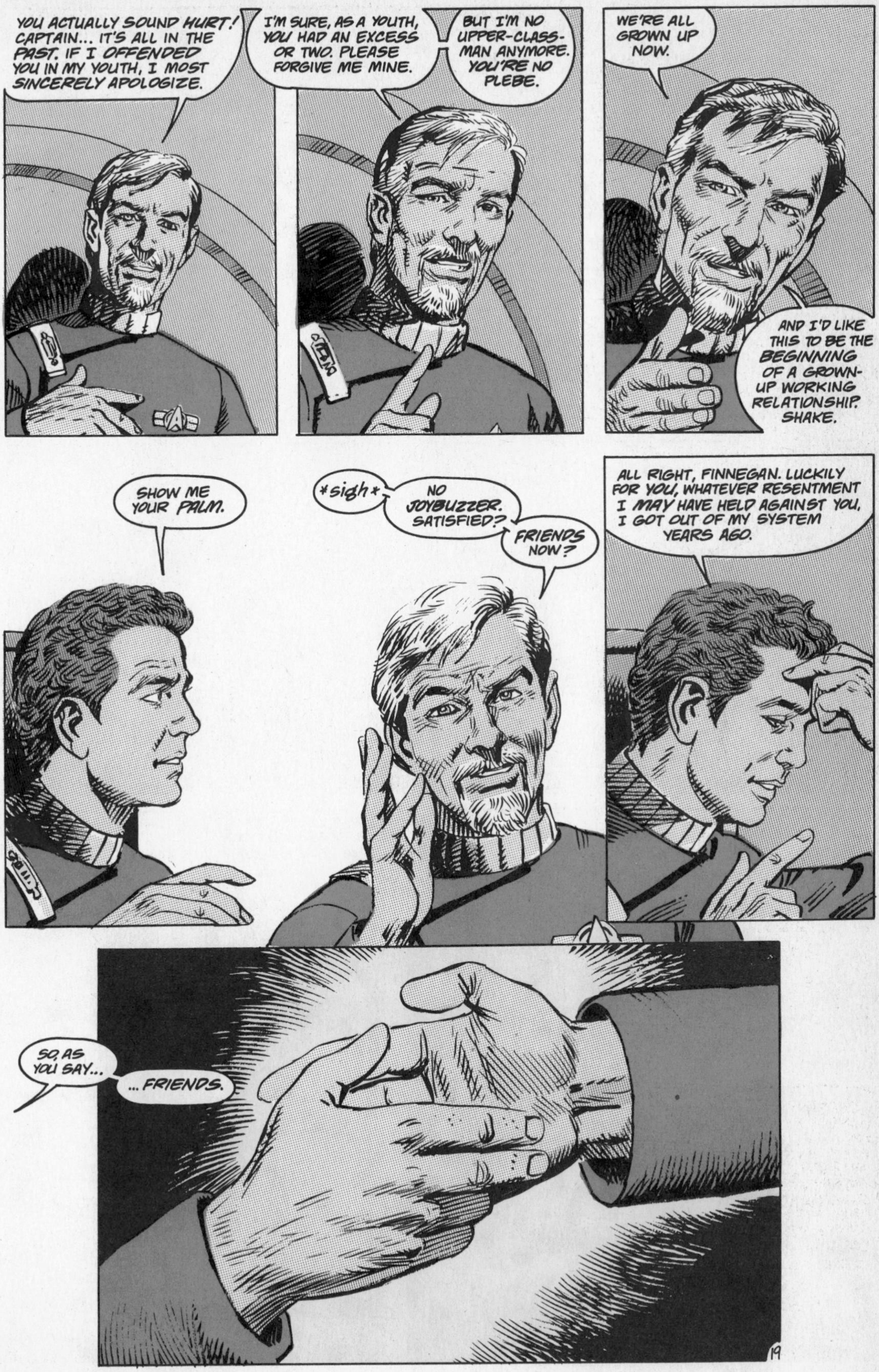
YOU ACTUALLY SOUND HURT! CAPTAIN... IT'S ALL IN THE PAST. IF I OFFENDED YOU IN MY YOUTH, I MOST SINCERELY APOLOGIZE.
I'M SURE, AS A YOUTH, YOU HAD AN EXCESS OR TWO. PLEASE FORGIVE ME MINE.
BUT I'M NO UPPER-CLASS-MAN ANYMORE. YOU'RE NO PLEBE.
WE'RE ALL GROWN UP NOW.
AND I'D LIKE THIS TO BE THE BEGINNING OF A GROWN-UP WORKING RELATIONSHIP. SHAKE.
SHOW ME YOUR PALM.
sigh
NO JOYBUZZER. SATISFIED?
FRIENDS NOW?
ALL RIGHT, FINNEGAN. LUCKILY FOR YOU, WHATEVER RESENTMENT I MAY HAVE HELD AGAINST YOU, I GOT OUT OF MY SYSTEM YEARS AGO.
SO, AS YOU SAY...
...FRIENDS.
19

AAARRHHH!

AHHH HEE HE HE HEE HEE HAW HAW!

AW, SEAN...

AMAZING WHAT THEY'RE DOING WITH PROSTHETICS THESE DAYS, ISN'T IT, JIMMY?

ELEVATES THE PRACTICAL JOKE TO AN ENTIRELY NEW LEVEL.

20

HERE YE GO, JIMMY. A GIFT... JUST TO SHOW YOU I STILL KEEP A *HAND* IN EVERY NOW AND THEN.

OH ENSIGN! WOULD YE MIND BRINGING ME TO YOUR SECURITY CHIEF. I'D LIKE TO CHAT WITH HIM BEFORE MEETING THE *SUSPECT*...

IF THAT'S *ALL RIGHT* WITH *YOU*, CAPTAIN.

FINE.

LEAD THE *WAY*, ENSIGN...

BLOEMKER.

THANK YOU. HAVE WE *MET*, BLOEMKER?

NOT THAT I *RECALL.*

SEAN! WHY DID YOU SLIP HIM THAT STUPID FAKE HAND?

OWTCH! TAKE IT *EASY*, HEATHER. JIMMY'D HAVE BEEN DISAPPOINTED IF I HADN'T DONE *SOMETHING!*

DID YE SEE HIS *FACE* WHEN HE THOUGHT I FORGOT HIM. *HEE HEE HEE...*

I'LL *GET* HIM FOR THIS.

MR. PAUL... WANT TO HEAR SOMETHING *WEIRD?*

WE JUST GOT AN I.D. COMPUTER MATCH ON THIS BODY. ALL THE OTHERS WERE COLONISTS...

OR CREWMEMBERS FROM THE SHIP THAT BECAME THE *RENEGADE.*

BUT THIS ONE... SHE WAS A CREWMEMBER ON THE *ENTERPRISE.* HER NAME'S *BLOEMKER.*

SO? THE *ENTERPRISE* WAS HERE, AND THERE WAS A *FIGHT.* SO THEY LOST ONE OF THEIR PEOPLE. SO *WHAT,* MADDY?

"SO WHAT" IS THAT THEY DIDN'T FILE A DC2051, A DECEASED CREWMAN REPORT, FOR A CREWMAN BLOEMKER.

OH, BIG DEAL. THEY'RE ALWAYS BEHIND ON THEIR *PAPERWORK.*

MADDY, WHETHER THEY GET AROUND TO PUTTING IT IN WRITING OR NOT, ONE THING'S CERTAIN...

"DEAD IS DEAD."

154

CAPTAIN'S LOG, STARDATE 9002.8. IN ACCORDANCE WITH REGULATIONS, THE FEDERATION SECURITY LEGION IS ABOARD THE ENTER-PRISE, INVESTIGATING MR. BEARCLAW'S HOMICIDAL ATTACK ON ME.

AND I HAVE LEARNED THAT THE INVESTIGATION WILL BE HEADED BY MY OLD NEMESIS, SEAN FINNEGAN.

I'M MUCH OBLIGED FOR YOUR TAKING US YOURSELF TO SEE THIS BEARCLAW LAD, MR. CHEKOV.

SO TELL ME, WHAT DO YOU YOURSELF KNOW OF ALL THIS? WE'RE AWAY FROM YOUR CAPTAIN. YOU CAN SPEAK FREELY.

I HAD NOTHING TO HIDE, COMMANDER. NOR DO I FEEL THERE EES MUCH TO DISCUSS. EET'S OPEN AND SHUT.

WELL, COMMANDER CHEKOV, THAT'S WHY STARFLEET CREATED THE F.S.L. ... TO IN-VESTIGATE SITUATIONS LIKE THIS, SINCE LITTLE IN LIFE IS OPEN AND SHUT.

AND IN A CASE AS SERIOUS AS THIS, WE NEED ALL THE FACTS TO ENSURE A FAIR HEARING.

OH, HE'LL GET A FAIR HEARING, ALL RIGHT.

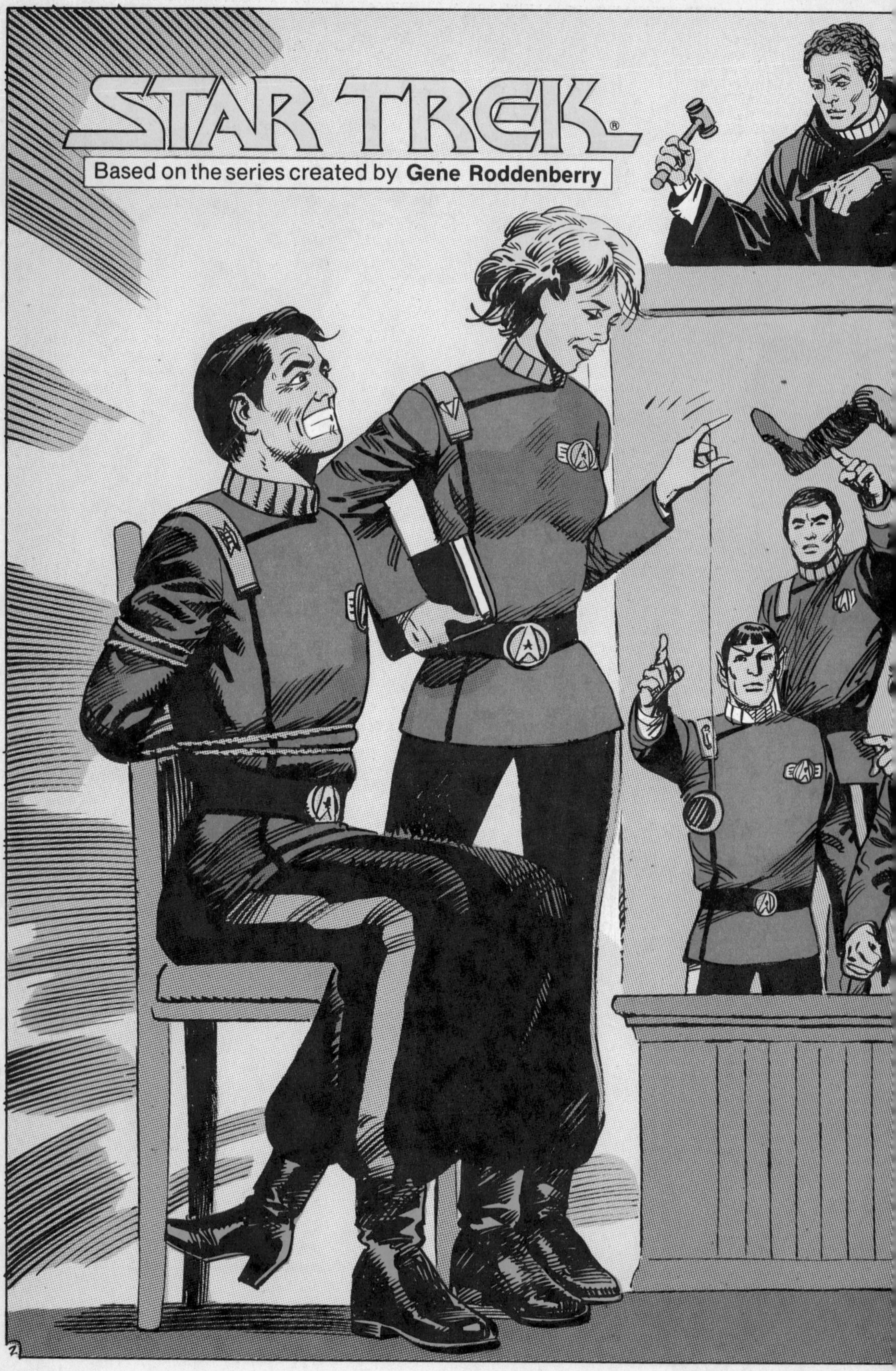
STAR TREK
Based on the series created by Gene Roddenberry

FINNEGAN'S WAKE!

PETER DAVID
LATE WRITER • TOM SUTTON + RICARDO VILLAGRÁN
TIRED ARTISTS • TIM HARKINS
SLICK LETTERER

MICHELE WOLFMAN
VETERAN COLORIST • ROBERT GREENBERGER
WARPED-OUT EDITOR

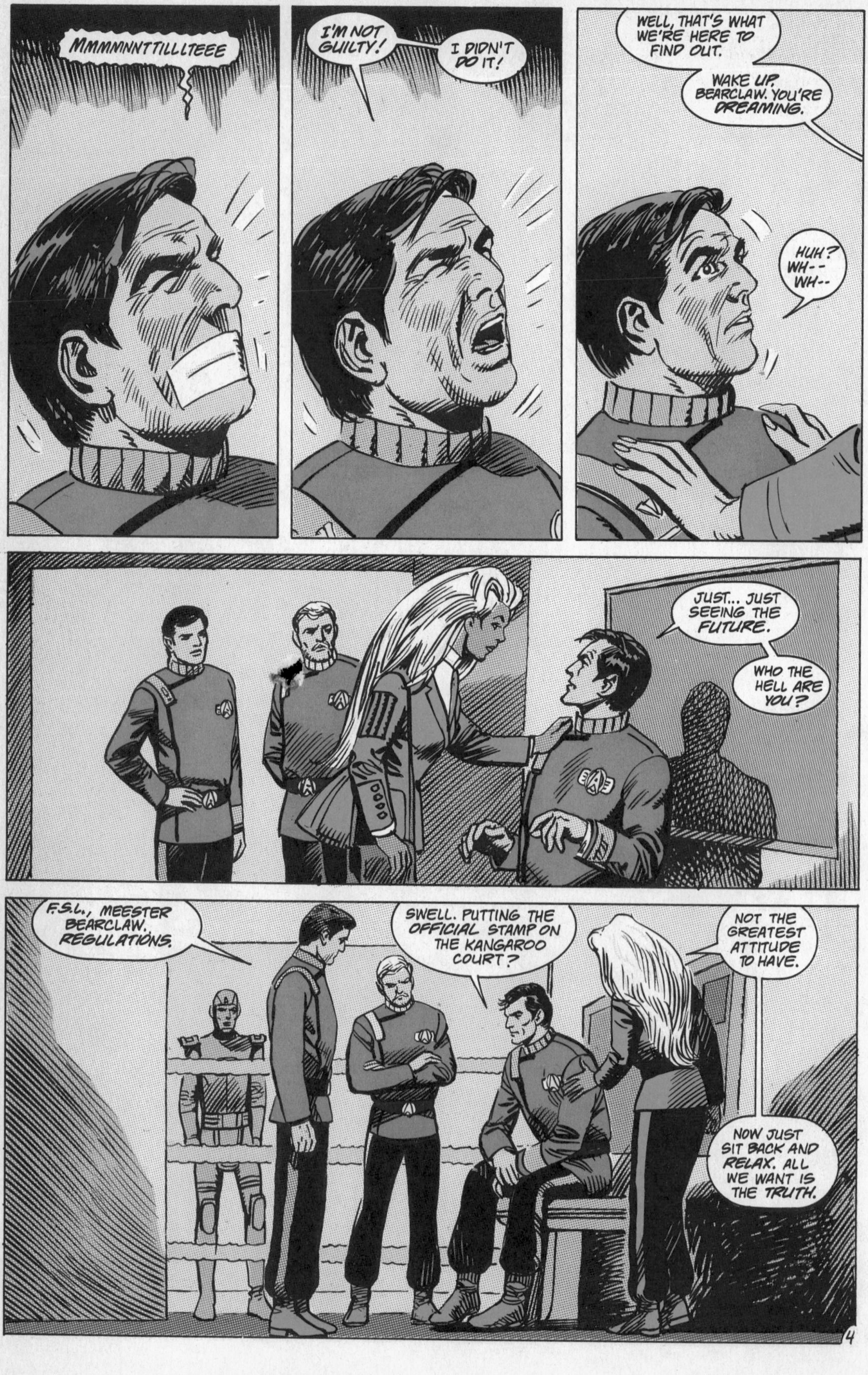
MMMMNNTTILLLTEEE
I'M NOT GUILTY!
I DIDN'T DO IT!
WELL, THAT'S WHAT WE'RE HERE TO FIND OUT.
WAKE UP, BEARCLAW. YOU'RE DREAMING.
HUH? WH-- WH--
JUST... JUST SEEING THE FUTURE.
WHO THE HELL ARE YOU?
F.S.L., MEESTER BEARCLAW. REGULATIONS.
SWELL. PUTTING THE OFFICIAL STAMP ON THE KANGAROO COURT?
NOT THE GREATEST ATTITUDE TO HAVE.
NOW JUST SIT BACK AND RELAX. ALL WE WANT IS THE TRUTH.
4

MR. CHEKOV, IF YOU WOULDN'T MIND GIVING US SOME *PRIVACY.* HEATHER WORKS BEST WITH A *MINIMUM* OF ANGRY THOUGHTS IN THE ROOM.

FINE. I'LL BE OUT HERE EEF YOU NEED ME.

OR EEF YOU *DON'T.*

WHAT'S THE STORY, MR. CHEKOV? HOW LONG HAVE THEY BEEN IN THERE?

HALF AN HOUR.

HALF AN HOUR WITH THAT *COSSACK.*

EET'S NICE THEY'RE GIVING HEEM SO MANY *CHANCES,* CONSIDERING WHAT HE GAVE THE *KEPTAIN.*

YEAH. I MET THEM WHEN THEY FIRST *GOT* HERE, REMEMBER. BLASTED BUREAUCRATS AND PAPER-PUSHERS.

WE'RE DONE, LADS.

ABOUT TIME.

WHAT'S THE WERDICT?

THE VERDICT'S STILL *OUT,* BUT ONE THING'S FOR *SURE...*

HE'S CERTAIN HE DIDN'T DO IT.

NOW WHY DOES THAT CREWMAN *BLOEMKER* LOOK SO BLOODY *FAMILIAR?*

AH, WELL, IT'LL COME TO ME.

UNBELIEVABLE. THEY ACTUALLY SEEM TO *BELIEVE* BEARCLAW.

SOME INWESTIGATORS, RIGHT, BLOEMKER?

YEAH. RIGHT.

UNBELIEVABLE.

I DON'T *BELIEVE* YOU, JIM!

IF YOU CAUGHT ONE OF YOUR JUNIOR OFFICERS PULLING STUFF LIKE *THIS*-- AT THE RISK OF HIS *HEALTH*, NO LESS-- YOU'D SHOOT HIM OUT A PHOTON TORPEDO TUBE.

CAPTAIN'S PRIVILEGE.

YOU'RE ACTING LIKE A *CADET*.

NO, WHEN I WAS A CADET, I WOULDN'T HAVE HAD THE *NERVE*.

FIRST YOU COMPLAIN WHEN I'M FEELING *OLD*, NOW YOU COMPLAIN WHEN I'M FEELING *YOUNG*. MAKE UP YOUR *MIND*, DOCTOR.

THERE'S *YOUNG* AND THERE'S *INFANTILE*.

SOUR GRAPES, BONES. WHAT IT *AMOUNTS* TO IS THAT THE MOMENT THAT DOOR CLOSES, THE TRAP IS SET...

AND I'LL FINALLY GET *BACK* AT FINNEGAN.

KLICK!

6

YOU'RE LOOKING THOUGHTFUL, NANCY.

I JUST CAN'T GET POOR LIZ OUT OF MY MIND. I DON'T KNOW WHAT TO SAY TO HER.

IMPROVISE. FAST.

OH, LIZ. HI. UHHH...

LOOK, I-- I'M SORRY ABOUT--

DON'T BOTHER, NANCY. FRANKLY, I'VE STARTED TO THINK YOU WERE RIGHT ABOUT BILL.

I TALKED TO HIM AND HE NEARLY BIT MY HEAD OFF. AND WOULDN'T EVEN DENY HE DID IT.

I... I GUESS HE REALLY DID DO IT.

YOU KNOW... I'M ALMOST SORRY YOU FEEL THAT WAY.

NOW BEARCLAW DOESN'T HAVE A FRIEND ON THIS SHIP.

BERNIE, I'M GOING ON DUTY NOW. WHY DON'T YOU--?

KLIK

DING

HMMM?

OH, WELL. BERNIE'S AN ADULT, ALBEIT A SMALL ONE.

I'M SURE HE CAN TAKE CARE OF HIMSELF.

7

MR. SPOCK? I NEED TO SPEAK WITH YOU A MOMENT.

WE-- FINNEGAN AND I -- BELIEVE MR. BEARCLAW IS INNOCENT.

MOST IMPRESSIVE, MISS VAN HORNE. I HAVE NEVER SEEN A ROOM EMPTIED QUITE SO QUICKLY.

YOU ARE AWARE, OF COURSE, THAT YOUR ASSERTION FLIES IN THE FACE OF LOGIC. IS THERE A LOGICAL ALTERNATIVE TO THE CAPTAIN'S TESTIMONY?

FINNEGAN'S WORKING ON THAT PART.

I AGREE, IT'S NOT LOGICAL. BUT BEING A LOWER-LEVEL TELEPATH, THE IMPRESSIONS I RECEIVED FROM BEARCLAW ARE OVERWHELMING.

I WISH I HAD SOME WAY OF PUTTING ACROSS TO YOU MY GUT FEELING ON THIS.

YOUR MOST TACTFUL PHRASING IS APPRECIATED.

AS WE ARE BOTH AWARE, THAT CAN EASILY BE ARRANGED.

8

THINK OF BEARCLAW.

Hmph.

VULCANS NEVER KNOW JUST HOW TO SAY "HELLO" AND LEAVE IT AT THAT.

GOOD. I'LL TELL COMMANDER FINNEGAN.

MOST INTRIGUING. I WILL... SPEAK WITH CAPTAIN KIRK.

IF I MAY... WHY MERELY A "COMMANDER"?

INSTEAD OF A HIGHER RANK? BECAUSE SEAN IS VERY IRREVERENT, AS YOU KNOW, AND HE'S OFFENDED TOO MANY OF THE WRONG PEOPLE.

CERTAIN PEOPLE HAVE SQUELCHED HIS ADVANCEMENT, HOPING HE'D RESIGN. BUT SEAN HAS NO INTEREST IN RANK. WHAT HE DOES HAVE IS... EMBARRASSING... INFORMATION ON HIS SUPERIORS, WHICH HE'LL...

...MAKE PUBLIC IF HE'S FORCED OUT.

A GENTLEMEN'S AGREEMENT.

EXACTLY. THEY LEAVE HIM ALONE, HE LEAVES THEM ALONE.

I REALLY THINK BEARCLAW WANTS TO BE LEFT ALONE, LITTLE FELLA.

BUT BEARCLAW NEEDS BERNIE.

Y'KNOW, JERRY... BEARCLAW REALLY HATES KLINGONS. I BET HE'D BE REALLY HONKED OFF IF WE LET BERNIE HERE VISIT.

9

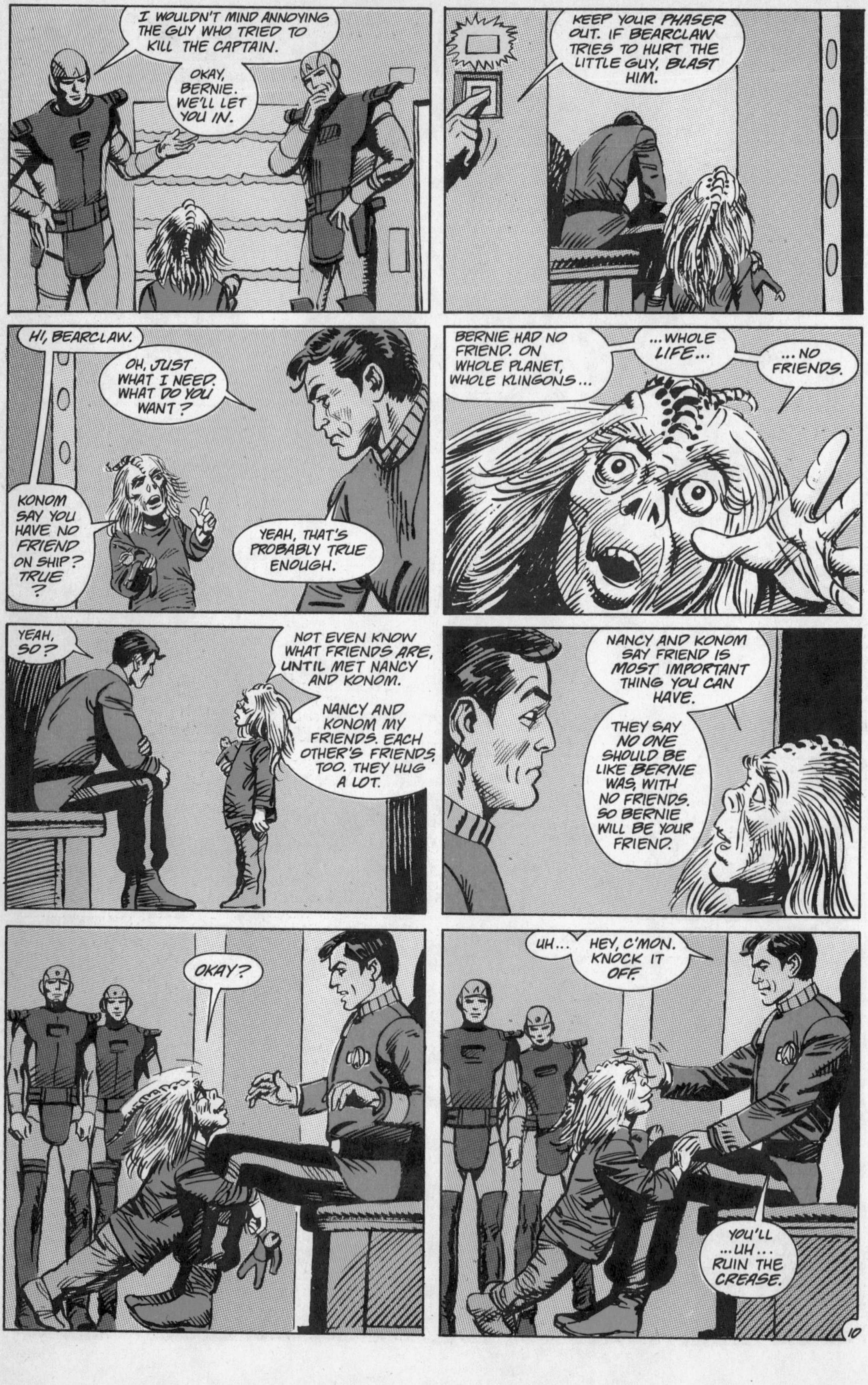
I WOULDN'T MIND ANNOYING THE GUY WHO TRIED TO KILL THE CAPTAIN.
OKAY, BERNIE. WE'LL LET YOU IN.
KEEP YOUR PHASER OUT. IF BEARCLAW TRIES TO HURT THE LITTLE GUY, BLAST HIM.
HI, BEARCLAW.
OH, JUST WHAT I NEED. WHAT DO YOU WANT?
KONOM SAY YOU HAVE NO FRIEND ON SHIP? TRUE ?
YEAH, THAT'S PROBABLY TRUE ENOUGH.
BERNIE HAD NO FRIEND. ON WHOLE PLANET, WHOLE KLINGONS...
...WHOLE LIFE...
...NO FRIENDS.
YEAH, SO?
NOT EVEN KNOW WHAT FRIENDS ARE, UNTIL MET NANCY AND KONOM.
NANCY AND KONOM MY FRIENDS. EACH OTHER'S FRIENDS, TOO. THEY HUG A LOT.
NANCY AND KONOM SAY FRIEND IS MOST IMPORTANT THING YOU CAN HAVE.
THEY SAY NO ONE SHOULD BE LIKE BERNIE WAS, WITH NO FRIENDS. SO BERNIE WILL BE YOUR FRIEND.
OKAY?
UH...
HEY, C'MON. KNOCK IT OFF.
YOU'LL ...UH... RUIN THE CREASE.
10

WHO PUT YOU UP TO THIS, ANYWAY?

NOT UNDERSTAND "PUT UP." JUST LEARNED TO UNDERSTAND "FRIEND."

BERNIE BE BEARCLAW'S FRIEND?

ALL QUIET HERE, BOYAJIAN?

CAPTAIN, I'M GLAD YOU'RE HERE. YOU WOULDN'T BELIEVE THIS IF YOU DIDN'T SEE IT.

YEAH, SURE FRIENDS.

WHY NOT? THE TWO OUTCASTS. MAKES SENSE.

ABSURD. HE DID THAT FOR MY BENEFIT. DIDN'T HE? FOOD FOR THOUGHT.

THINK, FINNEGAN. DON'T JUST SIT HERE STARING AT LISTS OF PEOPLE WHO MIGHT WANT TO KILL JIMMY.

IT COULDN'T HAVE BEEN JUST ANYBODY. IN ADDITION TO A GRUDGE, HE'D HAVE TO BE SOMEONE CAPABLE OF FLAWLESSLY IMPERSONATING BEARCLAW. HAS TO--

WAAIIIT A MINUTE. COULD IT BE... HIM? HE DISAPPEARED A YEAR AGO, SO IT'S MORE THAN POSSIBLE.

BUT HOW'D HE GET ON THE SHIP? MAYBE DISGUISED AS SOMEBODY EL...

OF COURSE!! FINNEGAN, YE BLOODY IDIOT! I OUGHT TO BE SHOT!

11

COMPUTER GAVE ME THE LOCATION OF "HER" QUARTERS.

WHERE COULD MY MIND HAVE BEEN? I MUST BE GETTING SENILE.

BLOEMKER

I SHOULD HAVE RECOGNIZED "HER" IMMEDIATELY.

IT'S ALL OVER, MISTER. I WAS ON OMICRON CETI IV. I SAW THE REAL BLOEMKER'S BODY.

YOU'RE UNDER ARREST.

ZAK

THUD

ZWAM

A VERY GOOD TRY. NOW TO SET THIS TO DISINTEGRATE...

AND I'LL HAVE LOTS OF FUN AT FINNEGAN'S WAKE.

NO, WAIT. I HAVE A MORE INTERESTING IDEA.

BLOEMKER'S PHASER RAN OUT OF POWER--FIGHTING THOSE ANDROIDS ON OMICRON CETI IV--OTHERWISE I COULD HAVE DISINTEGRATED THE BODY --LEAVING NO CLUES FOR FINNEGAN!

STILL... I CAN MAKE THIS WORK TO MY ADVANTAGE.

12

LEAVING FINNEGAN ALIVE TO TRY AND EXPLAIN WHY HE KILLED CAPTAIN KIRK SHOULD DESTROY HIS CLAIMS OF BEARCLAW'S INNOCENCE VERY NICELY.

VERY NICELY, INDEED.

SPOCK, IF I DIDN'T KNOW BETTER, I'D SAY YOU WERE JOKING.

HOW FORTUNATE FOR BOTH OF US, SIR, THAT YOU DO KNOW BETTER.

SPOCK, IT DOESN'T REALLY MATTER WHAT SORT OF "PSYCHIC IMPRESSION" EVIDENCE FINNEGAN'S PEOPLE HAVE FOUND.

I KNOW THE EVIDENCE OF MY OWN EYES. I KNOW WHAT I SAW.

OFTENTIMES, CAPTAIN, THE EVIDENCE OF OUR OWN EYES IS INSUFFICIENT. LIEUTENANT NARAHT THERE BRINGS OUR FIRST MEETING WITH THE HORTA TO MIND.

FOR THAT MATTER, YOU YOURSELF MIGHT HAVE ENDED YOUR DAYS IN THE BODY OF JANICE LESTER, HAD SOME CREW-MEMBERS BEEN UNWILLING TO SEE BEYOND SURFACE EVIDENCE.

SPOCK, ARE YOU, OF ALL PEOPLE, SAYING THAT WE SHOULD IGNORE THE LOGIC OF THE SITUATION?

I AM SAYING... JIM... THAT I BELIEVE BEARCLAW MAY BE INNOCENT. IT IS MY HOPE THAT YOU WILL TAKE OUR PAST EXPERIENCES, AND YOUR PAST RELIANCE ON MY ADVICE... INTO CONSIDERATION ON THIS MATTER.

13

CONSIDER IT... UNDER ADVISEMENT.

AS YOU WISH, SIR.

CAPTAIN! I'VE BEEN LOOKING ALL OVER THE SHIP FOR YOU. WE'RE ABOUT READY TO LEAVE...

WOULD YOU CARE TO COME TO MY QUARTERS TO DISCUSS THE EVIDENCE?

YES. I THINK THAT MIGHT BE A GOOD IDEA.

AT THIS POINT I'M CONVINCED BEARCLAW IS YOUR MAN.

HAD A CHANGE OF HEART, FINNEGAN? I MUST ADMIT... I WAS STARTING TO THINK THAT THERE WAS SOME MERIT TO CLAIMS OF INNOCENCE.

I SUPPOSE IT'S NOT SURPRISING YOU AND I WOULD NEVER AGREE AT THE SAME TIME.

HOLD ON. I WANT TO GET SOME WALKING IN, WHILE BONES DOESN'T SEE ME.

TAKE YOUR TIME, CAPTAIN. ALL THE TIME IN THE WORLD.

AFTER YOU.

SPRONG

OH, NO! I FORGOT!

14

FINNEGAN! DUCK!!

WOMPF

I'M SORRY, FINNEGAN! I WANTED TO GET BACK AT YOU, BUT NOW IS HARDLY THE--

WHAT THE HELL?

CAN'T... CONCENTRATE... HOLD FORM...

NOT AS YOUNG AS I USED TO BE.

DOESN'T MATTER, THOUGH. YOU'RE ENTITLED... TO KNOW WHO KILLED YOU.

GARTH! GARTH OF IZAR!

15

YES, CAPTAIN. A FEW MORE WRINKLES, A BIT LESS HAIR... BUT GARTH OF IZAR.

GARTH... HOW IS IT POSSIBLE? WHERE'S FINNEGAN?

UNCONSCIOUS IN MY QUARTERS... ENSIGN BLOEMKER'S QUARTERS.

USING MY MY POWER OF CELLULAR METAMORPHOSIS I IMPERSONATED HER WHEN MY PHIL BURROUGHS DISGUISE WAS NO LONGER... OOOOF!

WAK

THEN WHEN I CAME TO KILL YOU, I WORE A FOOLPROOF BODY JUST IN CASE SOMEONE SAW ME. YOU RUINED EVERYTHING BY LIVING.

STOP STRUGGLING! YOU COULDN'T BEAT ME ON YOUR BEST DAY.

RUTCH

AND TODAY IS YOUR LAST DAY!

NYARRGGH!

I HAD A FEW MORE SALIENT POINTS I WISHED TO MAKE, CAPTAIN...

BUT IT APPEARS "LORD GARTH" MADE THEM FOR ME.

16

THE POINT BEING, JIMMY, THAT GARTH WAS INDEED *CURED* OF THE MADNESS THAT EXILED HIM TO ELBA II.

THE PROBLEM WAS WHAT TO DO WITH HIM *AFTER* THAT. IN THE EYES OF STARFLEET, CURED OR NOT, HE WAS STILL VIEWED AS *"DAMAGED GOODS,"* IF YOU WILL.

NO ONE WAS GOING TO BE RESPONSIBLE FOR GIVING A FORMER HOMICIDAL *MADMAN* COMMAND OF ANYTHING MORE DEMANDING THAN A *RUBBER DUCK.*

SO THEY GAVE HIM HARMLESS, UNDEMANDING TASKS IN RECORDS AND SUCH, WITH AN EYE TOWARD POSSIBLY A TEACHING ASSIGNMENT.

SUPPLY PROCUREMENT

RECORDS DIV.

BUT HE CONSIDERED ALL SUCH WORK *MENIAL.* BENEATH HIM.

HIS LAST RECORDED PSYCH PROFILE INDICATED AN INCREDIBLY *EMBITTERED* MAN, PINNING ALL HIS PROBLEMS ON STARFLEET IN GENERAL AND *YOU* IN PARTICULAR.

THEN, ABOUT A YEAR AGO, HE *DISAPPEARED.* NO ONE KNEW WHERE, EXCEPT POSSIBLY INTO *DEEP SPACE.*

17

171

THE LOGICAL SURMISE WOULD BE THAT HE MADE HIS WAY TO OMICRON CETI IV.

WHEN THE ZEPHYR APPEARED ON A ROUTINE MISSION, GARTH KILLED CAPTAIN BURROUGHS, TOOK HIS PLACE, BEAMED UP, ORDERED THE REST OF CREW PLANETSIDE AND KILLED THEM ALL.

HE CHANGED HIS NAME TO CAPTAIN ZAIR-- AN ANAGRAM OF IZAR-- OBTAINED A CREW OF OUTLAWS AND SET OUT TO WREAK HAVOC.

BUT WHERE DID HE OBTAIN THAT UNKNOWN TECHNOLOGY? WHERE WAS HE ALL THAT MISSING YEAR?

WE'LL TRY TO FIND OUT. I PROMISE YOU THIS, CAPTAIN... IT'S NOT OVER YET.

IT IS FOR ONE PERSON.

MISTER BEARCLAW.

IT'S OVER. YOU'RE CLEARED.

I... I AM? HOW?

YOU CAN READ MY FULL REPORT. I'M MAKING IT AVAILABLE TO ANY CREWMEMBER WHO WISHES TO REVIEW IT.

SIR? ARE YOU SAYING THAT I CAN-- CONSIDER MYSELF REINSTATED AS A CREWMAN? DESPITE THE TROUBLES I'VE...

TROUBLES, MR. BEARCLAW? ODD. WITH ALL MY RECENT TRAUMAS, I CAN'T SEEM TO RECALL ANY TROUBLES.

SELECTIVE AMNESIA, I IMAGINE. YOU WOULDN'T WANT TO DO ANYTHING IN THE FUTURE TO JOG MY MEMORY, WOULD YOU?

NO, SIR.

I THOUGHT NOT. NOW, IF YOU'LL EXCUSE ME...

I HAVE ONE MORE BIT OF UNFINISHED BUSINESS.

NOW THAT WE'VE FINISHED WITH THIS BUSINESS, SPOCK, MAYBE YOUR RENOWNED VULCAN LOGIC CAN GET JIM TO REST. GOD KNOWS HE NEVER LISTENS TO ME.

DO NOT TAKE IT PERSONALLY, DOCTOR McCOY. NONE OF US LISTENS TO YOU.

ODD. I SEEM TO HEAR SOME SORT OF... CHANTING... FROM THE RECREATION ROOM.

YOU GOT HIM ON THE ROPES, CAPTAIN!

JUST HANG ON! HE CAN'T TAKE IT!

HE'S SWEATING LIKE A STUCK PIG!

FIVE TO ONE ON THE CAPTAIN.

SIX TO ONE!

THIS IS SO CHILDISH. BUT BOYS WILL BE BOYS... EVEN CAPTAINS.

YOU'RE *unh* CRACKING, JIMMY. I CAN SEE IT FROM *unh* HERE.

NOT FROM...

unh HERE.

ARRHHH!

19

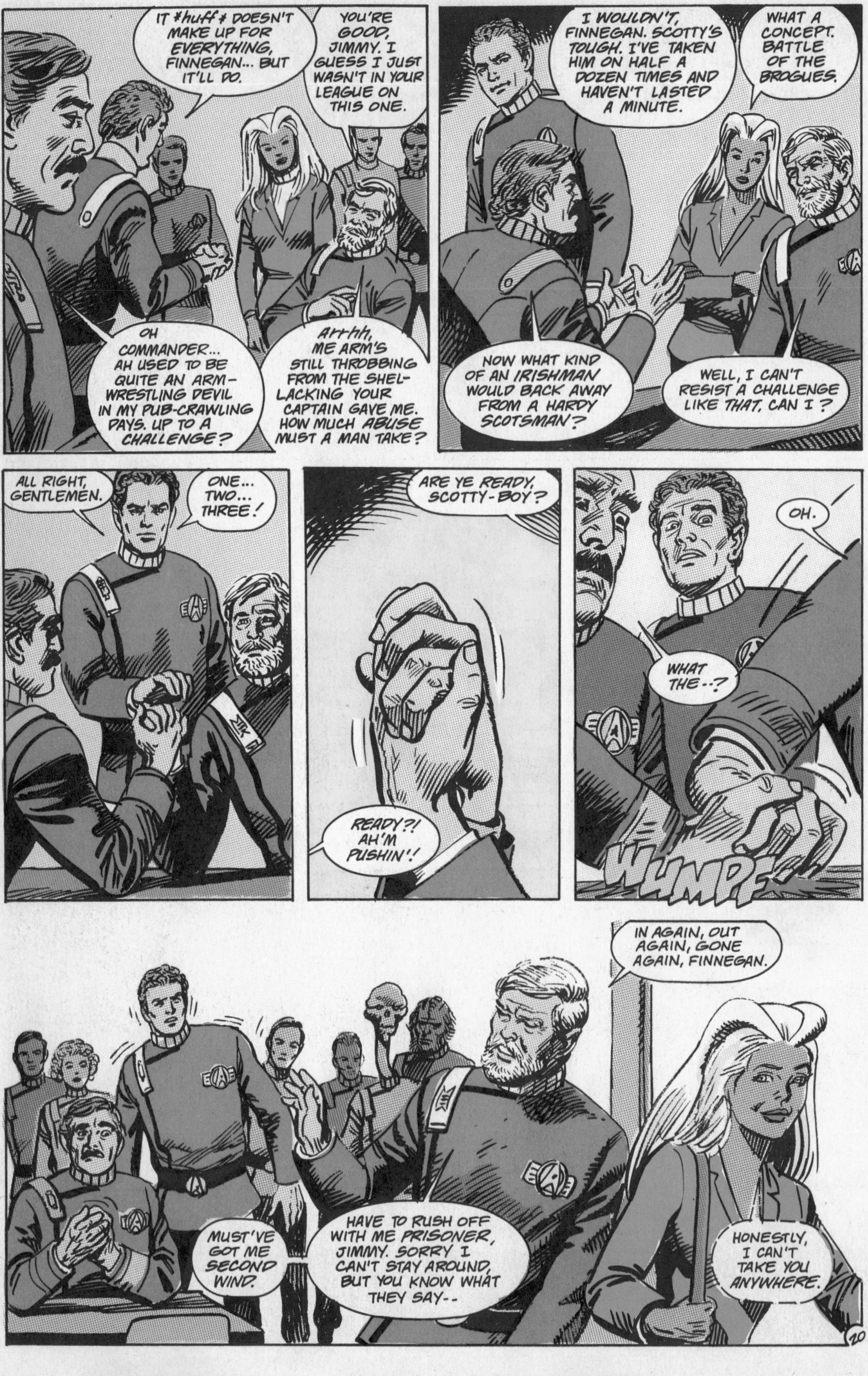
IT *huff* DOESN'T MAKE UP FOR EVERYTHING, FINNEGAN... BUT IT'LL DO.
YOU'RE GOOD, JIMMY. I GUESS I JUST WASN'T IN YOUR LEAGUE ON THIS ONE.
OH COMMANDER... AH USED TO BE QUITE AN ARM-WRESTLING DEVIL IN MY PUB-CRAWLING DAYS. UP TO A CHALLENGE?
Arrhh, ME ARM'S STILL THROBBING FROM THE SHEL-LACKING YOUR CAPTAIN GAVE ME. HOW MUCH ABUSE MUST A MAN TAKE?
I WOULDN'T, FINNEGAN. SCOTTY'S TOUGH. I'VE TAKEN HIM ON HALF A DOZEN TIMES AND HAVEN'T LASTED A MINUTE.
WHAT A CONCEPT. BATTLE OF THE BROGUES.
NOW WHAT KIND OF AN IRISHMAN WOULD BACK AWAY FROM A HARDY SCOTSMAN?
WELL, I CAN'T RESIST A CHALLENGE LIKE THAT, CAN I?
ALL RIGHT, GENTLEMEN.
ONE... TWO... THREE!
ARE YE READY, SCOTTY-BOY?
READY?! AH'M PUSHIN'!
OH.
WHAT THE--?
WUMPF
IN AGAIN, OUT AGAIN, GONE AGAIN, FINNEGAN.
MUST'VE GOT ME SECOND WIND.
HAVE TO RUSH OFF WITH ME PRISONER, JIMMY. SORRY I CAN'T STAY AROUND, BUT YOU KNOW WHAT THEY SAY--
HONESTLY, I CAN'T TAKE YOU ANYWHERE.
20

HE DID IT *AGAIN*, THAT DENEBIAN SLIME DEVIL.

JIM! GO TO SICKBAY AND STAY THERE! THAT'S AN ORDER FROM YOUR CHIEF MEDICAL OFFICER!

WHATEVER YOU SAY, DOCTOR.

AND THE REST OF YOU! GET TO YOUR POSTS!

FOR GOD'S SAKE, IF WE'RE ALL DOWN HERE, WHO'S RUNNING THE DAMNED SHIP?!

WELL...

WHAT DO YOU KNOW ABOUT THAT?

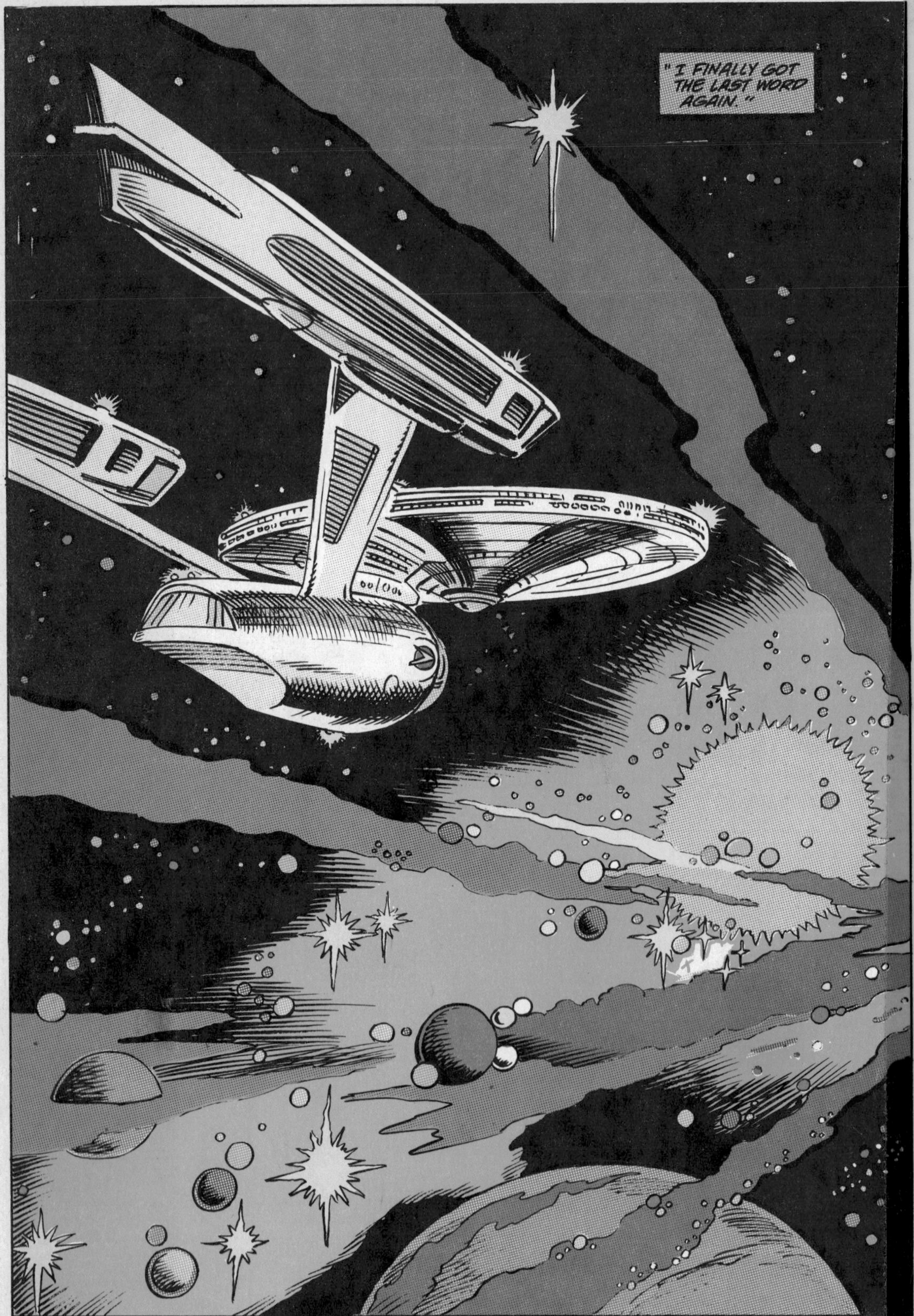
"I FINALLY GOT THE LAST WORD AGAIN."